SOMERSET GROVE

DIONNE PEART

CLARENDON BOOKS
WASHINGTON D.C.

SOMERSET GROVE

This is a work of fiction. Any names, characters, places or incidents are either used fictitiously or are the product of the author's imagination and their resemblance to any person living or dead, events, or locale is entirely coincidental.

Somerset Grove, a novel
Copyright © 2012 by Dionne Peart

All rights reserved. No portion of this book may be reproduced or transmitted by any means, electronic or mechanical, including photocopying, recording, or by any electronic storage and retrieval system without the prior express written consent of the author.

ISBN: 978-0-9884222-9-2

Library of Congress Control Number: 2012954022

Clarendon Books
Washington D.C.

Printed in the United States of America
First Edition December 2012

Cover Design: Shaila Abdullah, House of Design
Interior Layout: Nakia R. Laushaul, A Reader's Perspective
Editing by: Michelle Chester, EBM Professional Services
      Shonell Bacon, CLG Entertainment

For my mom and dad and my brother, Lawrence. I love you all. This is also dedicated to all those Jamaicans and other Caribbean descendants who had the courage to leave home and start a new life. You are inspiring...

a note from Dionne...

Taking this writing journey was not a solitary one. I couldn't have done it without the support, advice, and encouragement of so many, it would be impossible to name them all.

My parents, Monica and Victor, who always told me I could do anything I put my mind to. My brother, Lawrence "aka" DJ Fresh, whom I've always admired for his creative spirit and dedication to his passion for music. My cousin, Andrea Peart-Flores for always supporting me.

My friends, including Marie Davy, Alva Waller, and Eugene Radcliff, who read those initial drafts of stories and encouraged me to continue writing, even when I doubted myself.

My BWRC family, who not only encouraged and prodded, but in some instances threatened me to finish this book. Thank you especially to Nakia R. Laushaul, Jackie Rogers, and Michelle Chester. Your support and feedback was invaluable.

Somerset Grove

1

Angelique

Winter, 1967

The thought crossed her mind to run. She could be at the station before sunset and catch that last train into Kingston. From there, catch another train to the other side of the island. By the time they figured out where to look for her, she would be on a plane halfway to New York City.

Angelique stood at the window of the small dormitory room looking down on the street below. She rested her head against her right hand that held onto the window frame. She moved her left hand away from her hip where it had been resting and slipped it into the pocket of her navy blue tunic uniform. The coins and pound note she'd found were still there. "Found" wasn't exactly the right word. But they were hers now anyway. She gripped them tightly for a second, and then quickly released them as the stinging sensation rippled across her palm. Her hand was still sore from her earlier encounter with the headmistress that day. She removed her hand from her pocket and absentmindedly ran it over her stomach as she contemplated her next move.

"Angelique! You coming?" Faye's booming voice jarred Angelique out of her thoughts. She turned to look at her schoolmate standing in the doorway, her ample figure filling the frame. Faye raked her index finger up and down the back of her head to relieve some itch that always appeared to be plaguing her scalp. Or just out of habit. She smoothed the curly red afro pulled back into the high ponytail she wore and stared at Angelique expectantly. "Wake up, nuh. If we don' leave now we're going to miss the bus home, and I don't intend to spend one more minute of my vocation in this God forsaken place."

Angelique drew in a deep breath and sighed. *"Vocation" she pronounced it. Not "vacation." This girl is so country.* "Yes, I'm coming," Angelique said. She walked over to the single bed assigned to her and picked up the bag of clothes she had packed earlier that afternoon. She hesitated, and then walked over to the wardrobe standing between the two other single beds on the other side of the room. She pulled out her other tunic and the rest of her blouses and folded them neatly before placing them in the bag next to the barely knee-length skirts and the blouses she wore on the weekends when they weren't required to wear their uniforms. As she walked toward the door, she caught a glimpse of her reflection in the mirror. With a multiracial mix of a Scottish, Black, and Panamanian Indian mother and a father of Afro-Jamaican heritage, Angelique had a cinnamon brown complexion that changed to a beautiful reddish bronze during the summer. Her hair fell in dark long waves from the ponytail she customarily wore to school, and her hazel eyes sparkled beneath her long dark lashes. She examined her figure, which had gone from slim and girlish to that of a shapely woman, making her look more mature than her 16 years. The change was noticeable even under her school uniform. She picked up her bag and followed Faye out the door. Outside the dormitory Angelique suddenly stopped. "I forgot something. Walk ahead, I'll catch up with you."

"What? What you forget? You cyan leave it and come back for it another time? I don't want to miss this bus, you know."

"I said to walk ahead. Don't wait for me. I can find my own way home."

"Alright, well, you betta hurry or else you going to end up spending the night in here." Faye marched off in the direction of the buses.

Angelique watched Faye until she disappeared, and then headed in the opposite direction towards the train station. She made her way to the ticket window where a portly man stood hunched over the counter reading a newspaper. She waited a few seconds for him to acknowledge her before finally clearing her throat to get his attention. The man looked up at Angelique and smiled. "Good evelin', miss. What can I do for you?"

Angelique looked at the man with his bulbous nose, overgrown mustache, and pock marked skin. His big head strained against the band of his cap while his neck looked like it was trying to squeeze itself out of the white shirt he wore. Without the uniform, someone might have mistaken him for a boar. "Good *evening*," she emphasized. "How much for a ticket to Kingston?"

His eyes narrowed as he looked at the snotty private schoolgirl who dared correct his English. He sucked his teeth and nodded towards the makeshift sign with the ticket prices neatly printed on it.

Angelique pulled out her coin purse and carefully counted out her money. Even with today's bounty, she didn't have enough. She pulled her shoulders back and put on her sweetest smile for the boar. "It seems I'm a little short."

It was too late for charm; the boar had already been insulted. "Well it seems you won't be getting on this train, then." He went back to his newspaper.

Angelique pursed her lips and looked around, hoping to find someone whom she could approach to borrow some money, but the platform was empty. The train didn't leave for another hour, so most travelers had not yet arrived. She turned back to the boar and tried again. "Excuse me, please. My father is Byron Wright. He owns the furniture store by the far side of Somerset Grove. I'm sure you've heard of him. If you would give me the ticket now, I will ask him to come pay the rest of the balance immediately."

The boar was not moved. "Well, my dear, perhaps you should go and find him and come back when you have the money."

Angelique could feel the heat rising up her neck. She wasn't going to beg *this man* for any favors. She put the coin purse back in her pocket and walked away from the platform.

"Have a good *evelin,*" the boar said, smiling.

Angelique stepped off the bus at her usual stop and walked up Main Street. She inhaled the familiar aroma of Mrs. Davy's patties as she walked past the bakery towards the road leading to the house where she lived. Normally the smell of those patties made her mouth water. Today they made her sick. She continued on past the bakery and was about to turn the corner when she saw him. He was leaning against the exterior of the barbershop, one thumb hooked through one of the belt loops of his pants, and the other casually resting on his angled knee, his foot perched against the wall. Angelique's stomach jumped a little when she saw him. He was tall, lean, and athletic, and he wore his jet black hair closely cropped. His dark eyes sparkled with mischief underneath lashes wasted on a man. Clifton smiled at her, revealing even white teeth framed by full lips and a neatly trimmed mustache. The sight of him made her nervous; it always did, but she didn't let him know it. She did, however, glance around the street to see who might be watching. Two other women were also walking in Angelique's direction; one was Miss Brown, the nurse who worked for the parish doctor. Used to dealing with patients' personal maladies, Miss Brown never betrayed confidences and had a disdain for gossip. Not so, for the other woman. Mrs. Jarvis, though friendly and well meaning, had a weakness for carrying news. As fearless as Angelique was, she could not afford to have any stories getting back to her parents about her socializing with some boy. Certainly not now. Angelique slowed her pace to make eye contact with Clifton long enough to silently invite him to follow behind. He did. He kept his distance though, lagging several yards behind.

"Angelique, you're growing up so fast! It was only yesterday you was running around here wit' your two braids chasing after the man that makes the snow cones. Now look at you. You is a big woman now." Mrs. Jarvis bellowed with laughter as she caught up to Angelique.

Angelique was annoyed by the intrusion and eyed Mrs. Jarvis' voluminous skirt and field hat with disdain. She was tempted to ignore the woman, but decided against it. It was better to distract her. "Good evening, Mrs. Jarvis," Angelique replied in her perfect Queen's English. "You're looking..." Angelique paused, "well."

"Thank you, my dear. I do what I can to keep mi self together."

Angelique took in the woman's heavy frame. Mrs. Jarvis's breath labored as she walked and beads of perspiration had formed on her top lip and around her forehead, making the carefully pressed edges of her hairline revert back to their naturally textured state. Two matching dark circles appeared to grow underneath her arms and her entire body weight seemed to shift from one leg to the other as if she was trying to give each side a short break from carrying the tremendous load. Angelique noticed the woman's feet pointed in two directions when she walked—one northeast, the other northwest. She wondered when Mrs. Jarvis actually last saw her feet. "Well, you know, we all do what we can."

Angelique exchanged polite conversation with Mrs. Jarvis as they walked up the road. Her hips swayed slightly with every step and she could feel Clifton's eyes on her. Eventually they had reached a turnoff on the road, and Mrs. Jarvis headed down the path towards her house. "Tell your mother I said hello and to stop by tomorrow. I'm making coconut drops and I know how she loves those," Mrs. Jarvis called out.

Angelique's mother never liked to take food from Mrs. Jarvis; the woman perspired too much for her to be comfortable with anything that came out of her kitchen. Angelique knew Ruby Wright would not be stopping by to visit Mrs. Jarvis tomorrow and if somehow the offending coconut drops were forced upon her by way of an unexpected visitor, they would promptly end up in the rubbish bin or the hogs' pen. "Thank you, Mrs. Jarvis, I will tell her. Good night."

Clifton had hung back during the exchange talking to a neighbor who was riding a bike and heading in the opposite direction. As soon as Angelique had passed Mrs. Jarvis' turn off, he quickly ended his conversation with the biker and jogged to catch up to Angelique. "Gyal, you walk too fast! Where are you rushing to?" Clifton teased as he fell in step with Angelique.

"I'm not rushing anywhere. You need to move faster if you're going to catch me."

"I thought I already did."

Angelique blushed.

"So when are you going to make some more time for me?"

Angelique raised her chin and looked up at him. "Clifton, I am not just anybody, you know. If a man wants to spend time with me, he must court me like a proper lady," she admonished him.

"Is that right?" Clifton looked at her in mock disbelief. "And where was this 'proper' lady two months ago, because I know she wasn't the one that was with me in Spanish Town," he teased.

Angelique could feel the heat rising up her neck again and spreading across her copper-colored cheeks as she recalled the night she and two other girls had snuck out of the dormitory to meet Clifton and his friends. They had all gone down to Rio Cobre River together. Angelique had been feeling rebellious, grown up, and a little jealous of the attention that Clifton had also been giving to Gale, a tall girl with skin the color of dark cocoa and almond-shaped eyes. Gale was known for beguiling more than one of the boys in town to sample what she was more than willing to offer. When Angelique sensed that something might happen between the two, she began to exude her own charms to lure Clifton away. It had worked, but maybe too well. Clifton had led her away from the group near the bridge. She remembered the heat from his fingers burning as he pulled her close and covered her mouth with his. She remembered the feeling of that heat as it traveled down her body with every movement of his hands. She remembered pulling down her skirt and brushing the leaves out of her hair as the sound of the voices from the rest of their group rose as they approached. He'd had her, and she could say nothing. She lowered her eyes but still kept her head up. She gripped her travel bag and said to him in her most poised tone, "You could have at least offered to carry my bag for me."

"I could have done that, but what would your mother and father say when they saw some good looking boy carrying your bag up the street?" He laughed.

She watched him snicker and resisted the urge to slap him. Instead, she smoothed her hair back, picked up her pace and said, "I have to go."

Angelique stood at the front gate of the house where she lived. The heavy wrought iron gate hung from the freshly painted concrete wall that surrounded her family's property, and the well-manicured lawn was spotted with sorrel trees. The bright cream colored walls of the house contrasted with the white trim and columns that framed the verandah and would give any stranger the impression that the house was warm and inviting. The large three-bedroom house stood out among the small modest homes in the district. Her mother had wanted it that way. There was to be no question of their status in the community.

Angelique wrapped her hand around one of the iron rungs and hesitated. It was still not too late. There was still time to leave. She could handle her mother's hypercritical ways most days, but not today. Today was different.

She unlatched the gate and walked slowly up the path to the front of the house. She looked around the front room or "the parlor" as her mother referred to it. The heavy old-fashioned furniture crowded the room. It seemed as though every inch of the space was filled with wooden carvings, statues, plants, doilies, and other decorations her mother felt would give any visitor the impression that the Wrights were well-to-do. Angelique wrinkled her nose in annoyance. The room was gaudy. She would never invite any of her schoolmates that lived in Kingston to visit. Angelique was sure that those daughters of politicians and doctors would take one look at the house and see the glaring lack of sophistication that her mother so desperately tried to hide.

Voices drifted in from the back of the house. Ruby Wright was most likely admonishing one of the helpers. Angelique detoured away from the noise and headed down the hall to her room to drop off her bag before heading back out to the verandah where she could be alone. She sat on the half wall and leaned back, her left arm circling one of the white column supports of the house as she tried to catch the rays of the warm Jamaican sun on her face. A slight breeze ruffled the collar of the white blouse she wore underneath the blue tunic as she again contemplated what to do. It seemed only moments passed before the sound of her mother's voice jarred her back to reality.

"Angelique! Is that you? Come in from outside and stop burning up yourself in the sun." Her mother's voice carried through the house and sliced through her thoughts with the precision of a razor sharp knife.

God in heaven, can't I have a minute to myself? Angelique slid off the wall and reluctantly walked inside the front door again. Even though it was December, the air inside the house was still thick with the warm heat. She slowly made her way to the back of the house where her mother was talking to Miss Mavis the cook, a heavy set, brown-skinned woman who wore her hair wrapped in a colorful scarf. Miss Mavis seemed annoyed with Ruby who, as usual, was critiquing the meal.

"Not so much pepper this time, please. You nearly killed me last night," Ruby said. Although a mere 5'4", Ruby had an imposing presence with her hand perched on her curvy hips, her long wavy hair pulled tightly in a bun, and her piercing hazel eyes looking straight through the slightly taller Miss Mavis.

The cook barely responded before turning toward the stove. "Mmm hmm, sorry, ma'am." Angelique smiled to herself. She had seen that response before and knew what it meant—Miss Mavis would cook her food the way she wanted to. Maybe with a little more pepper tonight.

Ruby turned toward her daughter. "Tell me, why are you home so late?"

"I'm not late, I was in the front."

Ruby eyed her daughter suspiciously. "What is wrong with you? You sick are something?"

"I'm fine. Just a little hot."

Ruby looked Angelique up and down and then stretched forward to lay her hand on her daughter's forehead. Angelique stepped just out of her mother's reach. Ruby sucked her teeth. "Probably because you're always out burning yourself up in the sun every chance you get. Stay inside and keep yourself quiet." She gave her daughter one last look before turning her back to address Miss Mavis once again. Angelique crossed her arms in front of her, holding on to her forearms as if trying to comfort herself as she stared at her mother's back. Now was not the time. She turned away and walked towards her bedroom.

Angelique went to the wardrobe on the far side of the bedroom, pulling out a simple tan dress to put on. She took off the uniform, dropped it on a chair, and slipped the dress over her head. The dress didn't fit as loosely as it used to. Her curves were definitely becoming more noticeable. She turned back to the chair and reached inside the pocket of her tunic to pull out the money she acquired earlier that day. She walked over to the mahogany dresser to retrieve a small wooden box from the back of the top drawer and emptied out the contents. She counted the coins and pound notes and frowned. *It's not enough.* Standing alone in her room, Angelique rubbed her temples as the realization set in that her options were dwindling. New York City was out of the question for now and if she was going to leave, she would have to do it soon. Angelique put the money in the box and returned it to the drawer before walking out of the room.

Back in the large kitchen, the fragrant smell of Miss Mavis' rice and peas filled the air and mixed with the stewed chicken she had prepared. Angelique went over to the china cabinet and pulled the dishes and utensils out to set the table as she did every night she was home. Just as she finished arranging the last place setting, her father, Byron Wright, walked in. He wore brown trousers, a long sleeve shirt, and his favorite fedora hat. The dust on his shoes and forearms revealed that he had been down at his cabinet-making shop all day. He spent most of the week at the shop, creating richly crafted pieces of furniture that he sold all over the island. Occasionally he would leave the shop early to oversee the work that was being done on the family farm. Byron had purchased the 10 acres of fertile land some 18 years earlier. The location had been ideal; with a river running through the property, it was easy to take care of the livestock and produce a variety of fruits that could be sold at market including oranges, mangoes, and ackee. Combined with the cabinet-making business, Byron provided more than a comfortable living for his family; he was one of the richest men in the district.

"Angelique, I hardly recognized you. You been stealing extra helpings of cornmeal porridge at that school or what?" Byron teased, his lilting accent filling the room.

"Daddy, no!" Angelique pretended to pout.

"Don't get vexed, Angelique, you're getting sensitive in your old age," Byron said and laughed.

Angelique smiled. Her father could always lift her mood and put a smile on her face. Though stern in his discipline, Byron had a friendly manner and warm sense of humor that endeared him to most in the district. Ruby, on the other hand, always seemed so serious and concerned about maintaining respect for the family.

"Where is your brother?" Byron asked.

"I'm right here." Marlon appeared in the doorway stifling a yawn.

"Don't tell me you was asleep in the middle of the day." Byron playfully chastised his son.

"No, no, I just finished reading a book," Marlon responded.

Byron raised an eyebrow. "Then how come your face is all creased up like that?" he asked, gesturing at the sheet marks on Marlon's face.

Marlon grinned sheepishly. "Well, I was lying down when I was reading. Maybe I fell asleep."

"Oh, so the truth comes out now? Tomorrow you can come with me down to the shop and stain some furniture. The smell should keep you awake for the afternoon." Byron laughed again.

Marlon twisted his mouth in mock disappointment as he slid into his chair at the table. Truthfully, he enjoyed spending time with his father in town. He loved to sit around and hear the men in the shop joking with each other. It also afforded plenty of opportunity to observe the schoolgirls who were in town shopping with their mothers.

At that moment, Ruby walked in the room and shooed her husband and son out of the kitchen to wash up for dinner. Angelique finished helping Miss Mavis bring the rest of the food to the table as her mother looked on silently. Angelique avoided making eye contact with her mother and continued with her chores. It seemed that Ruby had such a quick temper lately and everything Angelique did seemed to set her off. It was as if she were waiting for an opportunity to criticize her daughter.

As the family sat down for dinner, Ruby began her litany of woes—she complained about the help, the cook's food was too spicy, the woman who did the laundry didn't bring the clothes back on time, and the man that helped with the farm wouldn't do anything the way she told him. Byron listened to his wife complain with an amused look on his face. Finally, he told her what a rough life she had with mock sympathy. Ruby did not find it funny and turned a scornful eye in her daughter's direction when she heard her stifle a laugh.

"And that one," her mother gestured towards Angelique, "I have to watch her. She's getting too big."

Byron brushed off the comment. "Woman, you are too paranoid."

"Never mind, Byron. You keep spoiling these children and you watch what happens." Ruby stabbed at a piece of chicken on her plate.

Byron sighed and shoveled a forkful of rice and peas into his mouth. The children followed their father's lead and began to eat in silence, passing looks between each other. Ruby gathered up her plate and utensils and rose from the table.

"I can't even say anything in my own house without everybody looking at me like I'm crazy. I don't even know why I bother," Ruby said.

Byron placed a hand on Ruby's arm, but she snatched it away and walked out. Angelique and Marlon looked at their father who waved his hand dismissively as he scooped up another forkful of food. "It's alright. Finish your dinner," he commanded. A few minutes later he got up and went outside to talk with his wife. Angelique watched from the table as Byron attempted to put his arms around Ruby's shoulders as she leaned against the same column that Angelique had been holding onto earlier when she was deciding whether to run away. Ruby tried to pull away, but Byron's hold was firm, though gentle. Eventually Ruby's body relaxed as Byron whispered something that only she could hear. He then circled his wife into a full embrace and she rested her head on her husband's chest.

Angelique marveled at how her father seemed to be the only one who could alter her mother's moods, both for the better and for the worse.

After dinner, Angelique washed the dishes while her parents relaxed in the front room. Marlon, as usual, was out visiting friends. When she had finished up in the kitchen, Angelique returned to her room, lit the oil lamp near the bed, and then walked over to the little wooden table beneath the window and poured water from the pitcher into the porcelain wash basin set to freshen up before bed. She cupped her hands in the basin and brought the tepid water up to her face. She held her hands there momentarily and enjoyed the sensation of the water running down her arms as she washed away the day. The air inside the house was stifling and Angelique couldn't tell if it was the heat or the constant tension that seemed to permeate their home. The older Angelique got, the more control Ruby wanted to exercise over her daughter. Everyone was a bad influence as far as she was concerned, and while the Wrights weren't as well off as some of the families in Kingston's suburbs, they did have enough status that Ruby felt elevated them above most of the other families in the district and as such, they should not "mix with everybody." Although they were twins, Marlon seemed to get away with ignoring those artificial rules, Angelique could not.

Angelique changed into her nightclothes, lay across her bed, and closed her eyes, inhaling the scent of the night as it surrounded her. She listened to the sounds of laughter in the distance and imagined she was in Kingston, and the joyous celebration was coming from her, carefree and celebrating the end of a hard week along with her cosmopolitan neighbors. Just then, the bedroom door swung open. Startled, Angelique rolled over quickly to see who had intruded upon her daydreaming. Ruby stood in the doorway, one hand on her hip and her eyebrow raised as she looked down at her daughter.

"You sleeping already?" Ruby inquired.

"No, I was just lying here. Just thinking."

Ruby closed the door behind her and sat on the edge of the bed. "Angelique, I want to talk to you," she began. "I know you think I'm hard on you, but that is because you're growing up and you have to be careful." She hesitated. "I heard about that Clifton boy. I don't want him hanging around here, and I don't want you to end up in any trouble. You hear me?"

Angelique sat up on the bed and looked at her mother. "What is wrong with Clifton?" she asked.

"I don't want to hear it, Angelique. Your father and I worked hard for this family, and I don't want you throwing away everything we've built. Just do as I tell you and please, don't bring any shame on me."

Angelique remained silent, trying to hide the annoyance she felt. Ruby detected it anyway, but ignored it. "I'm not joking with you," she said and with that, she rose from the bed and walked out of the room, shutting the door behind her.

2

Ruby

SPRING, 1949

The early morning light filtered in through the yellow lace curtains. Ruby lay in bed still wearing the dress that she'd had on from three days ago. It was thoroughly wrinkled now, showing no signs of the crisp starchiness that she had carefully pressed into it when she had first put it on. The other dresses she owned had been neatly packed into the worn suitcase her mother had borrowed from her friend, Lily.

Lily had been more than happy to part with her only luggage so that her goddaughter could pack all of her things to join her new husband in England though she couldn't figure out for the life of her why the girl's husband never sent money so that his bride could buy a trunk of her own.

Four days earlier, Ruby had said her goodbyes to one of her two best friends. Anne had come over before Ruby was to depart on the ship in two days. Though she was sad that she may never see her friends again, Ruby enjoyed seeing what she thought was envy flickering in her friend's eyes as she told her about her anticipated journey to join Winston. Her friend had listened with a half-hearted smile on her face as Ruby reminisced about how Winston had swept her off her feet, promising to take her away from the little two-room house with the outhouse in back that she shared with her mother. Their new home in England, Winston told her, had running water and a beautiful indoor kitchen, so she wouldn't have to prepare their meals in a cook shed anymore. And with the money he would save working as a mechanic, there would be enough to send her to school to become a nurse or teacher if she wanted. Ruby was disappointed that Anne's sister, Cynthia, hadn't come to see her off, but didn't think anything of it when Anne told her that Cynthia had gone to visit family. She was sure Cynthia would stop by before she left, maybe even ride with her to the ship's dock.

After losing her father to an unexplained illness five years ago, and then losing their family home when they couldn't pay her father's debts, it felt like life was turning around for 18-year-old Ruby.

Ruby's mother, Ingrid, came into the bedroom the two women had shared since they moved into the house and told the girls it was time for Anne to leave. Ruby missed the grave look on Ingrid's face as she was hugging Anne goodbye before turning back to finish her packing.

"There wasn't anything at the post office for you," Ingrid said to Ruby's back.

Ruby stopped packing, but didn't turn around. "It's fine. The mail must be delayed, that's all."

"You don't even know where you're supposed to be going when you get there. Did he tell you when he was picking you up from the port? Did he even tell you the address where you're supposed to be living?" Ingrid fired off questions as she watched Ruby moving about the room looking for things to pack and avoiding eye contact.

Ingrid leaned against the doorframe and let out a sigh as she began to unravel her long braid of black and gray hair that hung almost to the middle of her back. She was once what people described as exotic, with her dark satiny skin and wavy jet black hair. Her prominent cheekbones portrayed her mixed Panamanian heritage. She had moved to Jamaica with her Scottish-born husband, Samuel, who had plans of developing a large sugar estate on the island's rich soil. Those plans had perished soon after Samuel returned home one day with a raging fever. All of Ingrid's island remedies did nothing for her husband who took to his bed that evening and never rose from it. Thirteen-year-old Ruby had stood by her mother at her father's graveside with only four other people from the tiny town who showed up to pay their respects.

Ingrid aged almost overnight after Samuel died, trying to recover from the loss of her husband and their home. Her hair developed silver streaks and lines began to show in her barely 35-year-old face. She found work as a seamstress and moved herself and Ruby into a tiny house just outside the estate they once owned.

Ruby's teen years were marked with isolation. The girls looked on her dark bronze skin and flowing locks with a mixture of fascination and scorn, especially when Ruby started receiving attention from boys.

Only two girls, Anne and Cynthia Jones, befriended Ruby during her school years. Anne and Cynthia were twins who were also born of mixed heritage; their father was an Englishman who taught at their school and their mother was a petite Jamaican woman with a nut brown skin tone. The twin girls were tall and slim, and had complexions that reminded Ruby of her morning tea after the cream had been added. The three girls bonded over their differences and were as close as if they were sisters born of the same blood.

The girls attended the same school as Winston though he was two years older than them. Winston was the color of rich dark cocoa, with piercing dark eyes to match and he was regarded as one of the nicest looking boys in town. It was unclear, at first, who Winston was interested in, drawn in by their exotic looks, as he flirted equally with all three girls and all three girls flirted back. Ruby eventually became the front-runner for Winston's attention as their path home always took Ruby and Winston three-quarters of a mile past the twins' front gate. Anne shrugged off the loss since her attention was soon turned towards one of her older brother's friends. Cynthia, on the other hand, chose to address Winston's slight by saying she was never really interested in him anyway. "He seems very sneaky to me," she would say. "I wouldn't trust him."

Ruby ignored Cynthia's remarks, and the closer she and Winston became, the more distance grew between her and Cynthia, though her friendship with Anne remained strong. Ruby would gush about her blossoming relationship and Anne would always smile and listen without interrupting. The day that Ruby announced her engagement to Winston, all three girls were sitting in the twins' bedroom on the double bed they shared. It was a bright spring morning following a crisp rain. Ruby could hardly wait for the early morning storm to stop so that she could deliver her news. She undid the braided ponytail she customarily wore and styled her hair in a more sophisticated up-do. She had examined herself in the tiny mirror in the bedroom and decided to keep the style, even if it did look too formal for a Saturday morning.

Cynthia had looked at Ruby's new hairstyle with amusement when Ruby appeared unexpectedly at their gate, but she didn't say anything. The amused look quickly faded when Ruby bounced up and down on the girls' bed while she shared her future plans.

"We're getting married in two months, just before Winston

goes to England. Of course I'll be following him as soon as I send the marriage certificate and he gets all the paperwork processed and everything set up." Ruby concluded by asking Anne to be her maid of honor.

"But I want you to be my bridesmaid," Ruby said as she turned to Cynthia. "I know you don't like him."

Cynthia pulled her lips into a thin, tight smile. "I'll be there."

The day of the wedding Anne arrived promptly and stood by Ruby's side. Cynthia was nowhere to be found. She finally arrived minutes before they were about to walk down the aisle in front of the tiny crowd of 20 or so guests. A look of relief passed over Ruby's face when she saw Cynthia walk casually towards them, patting her hair into place.

"Sorry I'm late. I had a little problem with my dress."

Normally Ruby would have had some words for Cynthia, but she let it go that day. "I'm just glad you're here," Ruby said.

"You look pretty," Cynthia commented.

Ruby smiled. "I'm so nervous, and I haven't been able to keep anything down all morning."

They lined up ready to walk down the aisle—Cynthia first, Anne second, and Ruby third. Just as they were about to begin the procession, Ruby leaned forward and whispered loud enough for both sisters to hear. "I'm pregnant."

Anne looked back, not bothering to hide the look of shock on her face. Cynthia stiffened and turned her head slightly to look over her shoulder, but didn't say anything.

"I can't believe what you're telling me. When? I mean, you're not married *yet*," Anne said.

"After we were engaged," Ruby said. "And as of today, it doesn't matter. I'll be in England when the baby is born. No one will know if I'm off a month or so."

"I guess not," Anne said and looked at her sister.

Cynthia faced forward. "You ready?" she called over her shoulder.

"Yes," Ruby said.

Three days ago, Ruby received news about her husband, but it was not what she had anticipated. When Winston hadn't sent the money to pay for her fare, Ruby walked to her godmother's house to see if she could borrow the money from her and her husband. They reluctantly parted with their little savings with the assurance that Ruby would send it all back just as soon as she received it from Winston. When she reached home, she informed her mother that there was no need to worry about the fare now.

"I'm just waiting for the sponsorship papers. If you can take me to pay for my fare now, I should have everything together by the time I'm ready to leave," Ruby said.

It broke Ingrid's heart to tell her daughter what she had learned that day. Ingrid had been at the post office when the twins' neighbor had come in complaining about Jamaica's rough roads as he picked up his mail. He grumbled on about the cost to repair his car's axle, which was damaged during the drive to Palisadoes airport to drop off one of the twins who was going to England.

Ruby watched her mother's lips moving, but couldn't comprehend the words coming out of her mouth. "Cynthia…England…Winston." It was not until Anne showed up at their doorstep again, shame-faced and guilt-ridden, did Ruby understand that she would not be going to England after all, that Winston had sent sponsorship papers, but not for his new wife; they had been for Cynthia.

"I'm sorry," Anne said, before quickly leaving.

"I can't understand…how can he sponsor another woman?" Ruby asked her mother. "We're married. We have a marriage certificate," she said.

"Where is it?" Ingrid asked.

"I sent it to him."

"Then he probably burned it," Ingrid said flatly.

Ruby lay down on the bed and began to cry. "But I don't understand why," she said between gasps.

Ingrid looked down at her daughter, a mixture of sadness and anger in her eyes. "Maybe you weren't light enough," she said and closed the door behind her.

3

Angelique

Winter, 1967

The bells of St. Anthony's church promptly rung at 7:00 a.m., waking Angelique from a deep slumber. She rolled over on to her stomach and slowly opened her eyes to see the first rays of sunlight streaming through the window. She stretched her long limbs, sliding one foot from under the sheet and reaching for the spot where the sun touched the floor. She smiled as the smell of ackee and saltfish, and fried dumplings filled the air. A morning at church meant a chance to be out of this stifling house to see the friends her mother didn't want her to socialize with.

Angelique put on her housecoat and slippers and headed towards the kitchen. Marlon was already at the table drinking chocolate tea and stuffing fried dumplings in his mouth when she arrived. He barely nodded at his sister as he reached for another dumpling. "Are you going to church?" she asked.

"Have to." Marlon laughed. "After all the trouble I raised this weekend, I have some serious repenting to do!"

Angelique shook her head, but despite the envy she felt for the free and easy life her brother was able to lead, she still enjoyed hearing about whatever trouble he managed to get involved in. "Can you go with me in to town today? I want to get out of this house and you know *she* won't let me go anywhere by myself." Angelique pointed her lips in the direction of her parents' bedroom.

"It's because she knows you're no good," Marlon said and laughed again. "We can go, but when I'm ready to go, don't give me no trouble or else I will just leave you and *you* can explain it to your mother when you get home," he warned.

Angelique rolled her eyes and smiled.

Ruby walked into the kitchen and poured herself a cup of chocolate tea. The uncomfortable silence was broken only by the sound of Ruby loudly grating nutmeg into her cup. Angelique focused her attention on the plantains on her plate. Marlon, oblivious to the tension between his mother and sister, contentedly ate his breakfast.

Byron announced his arrival in the kitchen by singing one of his favorite hymns. Angelique smiled at her father. No matter what was going on, he could always lighten the mood. Byron sat down across from his wife who passed her untouched cup of tea to him and poured herself a new one. The Sunday morning tradition was always the same—breakfast with the family, followed by the long walk to the church, visiting a select few neighbors, and then a huge family dinner. No matter what tension had developed during the week, it would all seem to dissipate with the renewal that Sundays always seemed to bring.

Marlon announced that he and Angelique would be spending the day in town visiting friends after church. Ruby was not pleased, but relented when her husband nodded in approval.

"Just be careful and mind yourselves," Byron admonished with a smile.

"And be home before supper," Ruby added. "Angelique, I need your help today since Miss Mavis is off."

"Yes," Angelique responded, grateful that her mother didn't attempt to force her to return home immediately after the service. "I'll be home on time." She mouthed a silent "thank you" to her brother. Marlon nodded back at his sister as he brushed the crumbs off his pants. Spirited, Angelique got up and cleared away the breakfast dishes before running back to her room to get ready for church.

Standing in front of her wardrobe, Angelique looked thoughtfully at the dresses hanging inside before finally making her choice. She took her time getting dressed, applying her favorite body talc before slipping on her selection. She admired herself in the long oval mirror next to the wardrobe. The pale blue dress she wore with matching white gloves and hat were a gift from her godmother. Now 16 years old, the dress accentuated her newly developed figure enough to attract attention, but not enough to draw a disapproving look from her mother. She smoothed the seams around her hips and turned in both directions to see her full appearance. Angelique smiled slightly at her reflection. It still fit. Satisfied, she headed out of her room to join her family for the walk into town.

The morning sun peeked through the fruit trees lining the road. Ruby and Byron walked slightly ahead of Angelique and Marlon. Byron greeted his fellow parishioners with boisterous good mornings while Ruby clutched her Bible and nodded to her neighbors, careful to avoid making too much eye contact. Angelique held her purse on her forearm and swayed her hips slightly as she walked. She enjoyed the attention she received from the young men and some of the older ones, too. She discreetly scrutinized the other girls her age as they made their way to church. Angelique was particularly happy that she chose the dress with the fitted waistline. The other girls wore dresses that either made them look like young school girls, or older and matronly. She concluded that she was far more sophisticated than her rural counterparts.

Inside the church, the family selected a pew towards the middle. Angelique sat between her mother and her brother, who took the last seat closest to the center aisle. She glanced nonchalantly around as the people began to fill up the little church. She smiled and waved at two of her girlfriends sitting a few rows back. Marlon rubbed his chin and smiled at a group of girls sitting across the aisle. Angelique nudged her brother and stifled a laugh.

Marlon had become very popular over the last year. His copper-colored complexion, short wavy black hair, and muscular athletic build drew a lot of interest from the girls in the district. Marlon fully enjoyed the attention he received, feeling no need to commit to anyone in particular, and spending time with as many of the most attractive girls as he could.

The elderly pastor welcomed the congregation and nodded to his wife, who began to lead the group in the praise and worship portion of the service. As they sang hymns, Angelique discreetly looked around the church until she spotted the one she was looking for. Clifton was across the aisle a few pews ahead, standing beside his aunt and uncle. Just then, he turned and glanced in Angelique's direction. She drew in her breath and fanned herself casually, feeling the heat rising up her neck, but she didn't let her excitement show. She coolly nodded slightly in his direction and pretended to be engrossed in the words in the hymnal though she knew them by heart. Clifton nodded back with a little smile and turned his attention back towards the front of the church. Angelique continued to watch him out of the corner of her eye. A twinge of jealousy arose in her as she observed him nodding towards some of the other girls in the church who giggled unabashedly when they caught his attention. She pretended not to notice, standing straighter and concentrating intently on the pastor's wife as she waved her hands in time with the music.

At the end of the song, the pastor gestured for the congregation to sit down as he began his sermon. Angelique found it hard to concentrate on the pastor's words. Her thoughts continuously drifted, and she couldn't wait to get out of the stifling heat in the church. She used her white hand fan to cool herself and examined the tips of her white gloves. *Why is it so hot, and when is he going to stop talking?* Angelique shifted uncomfortably in her seat and patted her throat with the handkerchief she kept in her purse. Just when she thought she couldn't take it anymore, the pastor closed the sermon. *AMEN, finally!* Angelique bolted up from her seat almost too quickly and maneuvered her way out of the building as fast as she could. Once out in the fresh air, she found a tree that sheltered her from the sun. She leaned up against the smooth bark and readjusted her hat. She closed her eyes and fanned herself until she began to feel some relief.

"Angelique, wake up!" The sound of her cousin and best friend Hazel's voice snapped her back into reality. "What are you dreaming about?" Hazel teased.

Angelique smiled. "Nothing. I need to talk to you."

Hazel leaned in close to Angelique and smiled mischievously, anxious to hear some news. "Tell me," she demanded, conspiratorially.

Angelique looked around quickly before grabbing Hazel by the arm and dragging her to a cluster of trees further away from the crowd of churchgoers growing in the front of the church. "You must swear to me you won't tell anybody."

"What? What?" Hazel could barely contain herself.

Angelique took in a deep breath and released it. "Hazel, I think I'm pregnant."

"You is what? Lawdamercy! Angelique, a lie you a tell!"

"I wish I was lying."

"When? Who do it?"

Angelique sighed. "It was Clifton. The night we sneaked out of the dormitory and went with him and his friends down to the river."

"Clifton? Wow! What are you going to do, Angelique? You know your mother goin' kill you dead," Hazel exclaimed. Angelique observed Hazel's animated behavior. The girl looked too excited to learn this piece of news. Angelique sensed she had made a mistake in confiding in her cousin, but she had to tell someone.

"Hazel, you can't say a word. I don't know what I'm going to do, but I'll figure it out."

"Mi nah go tell nobody," Hazel assured her. "But I guess you won't be going anywhere anytime soon," she added, referring to Angelique's repeated pronouncements about moving to England or New York City.

Angelique frowned in response.

Ruby walked over and stopped a few feet away from the girls, clutching her Bible. Her long, pleated skirt hung just above her ankles in a light shade of peach. Her matching blouse was the same shade as her skirt. She peered out at the girls below the brim of her Sunday hat. "Angelique, come," she said, ignoring the girl standing next to her daughter.

"Hi Auntie," Hazel said.

Ruby looked Hazel up and down, taking in the blouse cut a little too low and revealing all the talcum powder she had apparently rubbed all over her chest and neck before coming to church. "Hazel." She nodded slightly at the girl. "How is your mother doing?" Without waiting for a response, she turned back to Angelique, "I said, Angelique come," she commanded. Angelique reluctantly followed her mother as they walked towards Byron and Marlon who were standing by the roadside waiting to make the long walk home.

Angelique felt a burning sensation radiate through her cheek where Ruby had slapped her. She reached up to protect the side of her face that had just been hit and felt the trickle of blood running down her hand from her nose. Before she could gain her balance, the same hand came back in the other direction. This time, the back of Ruby's hand glanced Angelique's right cheek, knocking her to the ground.

"Nasty, dutty gyal! You think you is a big woman? We send you to school to learn something and instead you go an' wrap up wit' some dutty bwoy!" Ruby raged on, pacing back and forth in Angelique's small bedroom. The Queen's English she reserved for outsiders was gone, replaced by the heavy patois that only arose during one of Ruby's angry fits.

Angelique drew her knees up to torso and raised her hands around her head to protect herself as she sat on the ground, still reeling from the shock of being woken up in the middle of the night and being confronted by an angry Ruby.

"Lawd Jesus, have mercy upon my soul! I'm so disgusted. How am I going to hold my head up in the street? Eh? Pregnant? What am I going to do?" Ruby began picking up items and throwing them at Angelique—a shoe, books, the dress she had worn the night before that had been draped across the chair, anything within reach.

Angelique did nothing. Any word, explanation, or even looking her mother in the eye would just draw more fury. Better to just shield herself and wait for it to be over. Ruby eventually stopped, her chest rising and falling sharply as she tried to catch her breath. Angry tears streamed down her face. "You know what? I finish with you. I try to do everything for you—clean clothes, a nice house, I send you to boarding school so you can come back here and be a teacher or a nurse or something where you can hold up your head and walk with pride because you have education and the rest of these people here don't. And look what you do. You dash it all away." Ruby threw her hands in the air. "Pay all that money for you to go to a good, good school and instead of you reading your book and go learn something, you off a wrap up wit' man." The angrier Ruby became, the stronger her patois became. "I don't know what you a go do, but I tell you one thing, you are not going back to that school. In fact, you sit down in this house and don't let me catch you outside, you hear?" Ruby stormed out of the room, slamming the door behind her.

She lay on the floor tracing the centers of pain across her body and assessing the damage before she slowly arose from the floor and walked over to the dresser. She filled the wash basin with tepid water from the pitcher and used the white cloth to wash away the blood from her nose.

Thoughts swirled around her head as she tried to figure out how her mother had found out. She sat down on the bed looking at the pile of clothing and items that Ruby had hurled at her just moments earlier. Her eyes passed over the Sunday dress she wore yesterday, and then she froze. Hazel. How else could her mother have known? Anger and feelings of betrayal replaced the shock and embarrassment of Ruby's attack that had been radiating through her body. Her mind began to race as she thought about what to do next. Then, out of nowhere, it came to her. Angelique rose from the bed and walked over to the wardrobe. She picked out her best dress—a pale yellow frock with capped sleeves, a white collar, and matching hat and gloves, and laid them on the bed, then selected a few more items and laid them out next to the dress. Finally, she retrieved the money from the wooden box on her dresser drawer and added it to the money in her coin purse. She sat back down on the bed and waited for hours, listening for any sounds in the house. Just before dawn, she packed her things and got dressed before leaving the bedroom. She waited in the darkened hallway, alert for any sounds of stirring. After a few moments, she made her way down the hallway and slipped out the front door.

As she walked down the road, she could hear the money jingling in her purse, and her mind drifted back to how she obtained the last of it a few days earlier. Angelique had been sitting in the headmistress' office receiving a stern lecture from the woman in charge of the boarding school when she'd stepped outside momentarily to speak to one of her staff, leaving Angelique alone in the office. Bored and feeling rebellious, Angelique had taken the opportunity to rummage through the headmistress' desk. She'd found the coins in the top desk drawer while searching to see what notes had been made in her school file. Buoyed by the unexpected find, she had listened for the sound of the headmistress' footsteps as she continued her search through the drawer hoping there was a pound note or two hidden somewhere. At the heavy sound of the headmistress' shoes moving towards the room, she'd quickly closed the drawer and slipped back into her seat to await her punishment. The headmistress had eyed Angelique curiously for a moment as she walked in before taking her seat and resuming her admonishment of the teenager.

"I don't know what is wrong with you, but I'm getting tired of seeing you in this office."

Angelique had said nothing, but glared defiantly at the woman. The headmistress had furrowed her brow in response as her jawline tightened with anger. She'd reached for the handle of the drawer that Angelique had been searching through just moments earlier and yanked it sharply towards her. Angelique inhaled slightly and her expression had quickly gone from defiance to panic as the woman's hand disappeared in the drawer and began moving things around in the desk. The headmistress caught the change in Angelique's demeanor and a slight look of satisfaction had spread across her face when she discovered what she had been looking for. As she'd pulled her hand out of the drawer, Angelique had watched in anticipation. Just as quickly, a sigh of relief escaped from the anxious student's lips and she sat back in her chair. Puzzled by the schoolgirl's response, the headmistress' expression had grown hard again. She glared at Angelique, gripping the treasure she had finally located in the drawer.

"Give me your—" The headmistress's voice trailed off and her mouth had hung slightly open as she'd looked down in front of her. Angelique had already slid her left hand across the desk, facing upward and waited expectantly. She'd stared directly into the headmistress' eyes as the woman had hesitated only for a second before bringing the ruler crashing down on her naked palm. She never flinched as the punishment had continued. She hadn't felt it at all. All she had felt was the warmth of those coins she clutched in her right hand. It had been worth it. Today, things would be different.

She arrived at the train station just as the ticket window opened. Standing at the counter was the same boar-like clerk that she had seen the day she was coming home from school. His eyes flickered with recognition and he looked down arrogantly at Angelique. "Full price," he said in greeting. Angelique had no smile for him today. She didn't need anything from him.

"One ticket to Kingston," she said and dropped the money on the counter.

He narrowed his eyes and carefully counted the money before finally handing her the ticket. Angelique cut her eyes at him before snatching the ticket out of his hand. "Good morning," she said before walking off down the platform.

4

Angelique stood at the front door of the large estate. She looked around at the expansive verandah that wrapped around the house, tastefully furnished with two large chairs and an elegant table. The well-manicured lawn seemed to stretch out for at least a quarter of a mile. Two shiny black cars were parked one behind the other in the long driveway leading up to the house and white lion statutes flanked either side of the staircase she had just climbed. Underneath her feet lay the marble that ran the full length of the verandah and the stairs. She slipped one foot out of her shoe and quickly ran her toes against its smooth surface before slipping her shoe back on. It felt nothing like the rough cement covered flooring of her verandah back home. She looked at the front door made of heavy solid wood and reached out to touch the freshly polished doorknocker in front of her, running her fingers across its gleaming surface.

Angelique straightened her skirt and adjusted the hat on her head. She quickly rummaged through her purse and retrieved the compact to apply more powder to her face. Her nose was a little swollen, but the makeup covered most of her bruised cheek. She pulled the brim of her hat lower and to one side, to hide beneath its shadow. Satisfied, she returned the compact to her purse, pulled her shoulders back, and grabbed the doorknocker, rapping the door with three quick knocks. A few seconds later the door swung open. A maid dressed in a uniform and white apron stood in front of her. The woman discreetly looked Angelique over before asking, "May I help you, miss?"

Angelique raised her chin. "Yes, I would like to speak with Mr. Clifton Chambers, please." The maid stepped to the side and opened the door wider so that Angelique could enter. She led the girl into the parlor room and disappeared down a hallway. Angelique placed her suitcase on the floor and began to explore the room. There was a settee against the far wall with two wing back chairs facing it. The room was tastefully decorated with a few ornaments, books, and a mini palm plant placed beside the settee. The room was large, with dark wooden beams running throughout, contrasted by the bright white walls. Angelique walked over to the large window that took up most of one wall and let in streams of light through the crisp white sheers hanging over it.

"Angelique! What are you doing here?" Clifton looked at her, the shock at seeing her standing in his family's parlor, over 30 miles away from her home in Somerset Grove was clearly written on his face. His mouth hung open slightly and he blinked his eyes slowly and deliberately, as if something in them was causing him to see something that wasn't there.

She spun around and looked at Clifton. A small feeling of excitement began to stir in her stomach at the sight of him, but she dared not let him know. "Hello, Clifton," she said, more calmly than she felt. "I need to speak with you." She shifted her gaze slightly to the maid who stood behind Clifton, obviously curious as to the purpose of this mystery visit from a young girl trying to pass herself off as a sophisticated woman. Clifton looked down at the suitcase at Angelique's feet, then followed her gaze to the maid and sensed that whatever she came to say, it should not be discussed in front of just anyone.

"Thank you, Miss Rita," he said, dismissing the maid.

Miss Rita did not move. "Would you like me to bring something for your guest? Some tea or ice water or something?"

Clifton looked over at Angelique, hoping she would decline the offer.

"I will take some tea, please. Thank you." Angelique nodded slightly at the woman who scurried off quickly to make the tea so that she would not miss whatever news was to be shared.

"So, what are you doing all the way in Kingston? And how did you know where I lived?" Clifton inquired.

"It's not very hard to find a Cabinet official's home. Some people kindly pointed me in the direction of the house."

Clifton crossed his arms in front of him and cocked his head to one side as he drank in her appearance. The short-sleeved dress she wore fell just below her knees. The slim fit accentuated her figure just enough to show off her still-developing curves. The pale yellow complemented her skin. Her hair, typically worn in a ponytail, was cascaded over her shoulders in loose curls beneath the hat she wore.

"So, you came all this way to see me?" he said, grinning.

Angelique had thought long and hard on the train ride into Kingston about how she would handle this situation. Clifton was young and a playboy, but she also knew the importance a prominent family such as his would put on appearance. She stepped towards him and looked him steadily in the eye. "I'm pregnant."

The smile faded from his face and his eyes grew large as the full weight of her words hit him. He reevaluated her appearance and felt a tightness in his stomach as he realized the curves he had been admiring weren't merely those of a girl developing into a woman. They were the curves of a woman who was pregnant. Still, he stared at her in disbelief.

Angelique watched the shock registering in his eyes. At the same time, she felt her courage growing. "You deceived me, Clifton. You told me everything would be all right and look what happened." Seeing his reaction, she pressed on. "If I had known you would do this to me, I would never have gone off with you that night."

"What? Well what do you expect me to do?" Gone was the confident young man who charmed many with his smile and easy nature, replaced by a worried and nervous 19-year-old, wishing he was anywhere but standing in his family's parlor, staring at this woman who had just shattered his world.

"Look. I come from a very respectable family. If you think I am going to go back to Somerset Grove and have this child alone, you made a sad mistake. If my father finds out that you are the one who did this to me, there's going to be one hell to pay. I am not going to be holding my head in shame." She placed one hand on her hip and waved the other around the room. "And I know your family would not want any rumors floating around that would bring disgrace on all of this." She gazed at him steadily. "I am not bearing your illegitimate child, Clifton."

Clifton shifted his weight between both feet and rubbed his hand over his head as he stood in front of his parents. His mother rubbed her temples with her fingertips, trying to massage away the throbbing pain that was beginning to form. His father stood with his arms folded across his chest, his jawline pulsing as his eyes shifted between his son and the young girl seated quietly in the wing back chair located out of the sunlight. Her hands were folded neatly in her lap as she looked back at Clifton's father. The look of calmness on the girl's face threw Tony Chambers off. He couldn't quite figure out why a 16-year-old pregnant girl would have such an air of composure in such a situation. *She seems almost confident*, he thought. He reminded her of someone else and of a time some 20 years ago when he'd seen a woman with a similar look on her face. He looked over at his wife who was still rubbing her temples in an overly dramatic manner, and then back at his son. He let out a sigh. "When is she going to have this baby?" he pointed his lips in Angelique's direction.

"Your grandchild will be born in seven months," Angelique said.

He felt as though he should have been offended by the girl's bold nature. He wasn't talking to her, but she was clearly not going to be excluded from the conversation. Surprisingly though, he was actually smiling to himself. His son had spent the last year and a half aimlessly running up and down around the island partying like he had no sense. Tony Chambers couldn't get him to focus on a profession. He'd had his son successfully placed in prominent training positions in a bank, a doctor's office, and several other businesses. Each position would only last a few months before Clifton would be discreetly asked to leave. Now, Clifton would have no choice but to settle down and act like a grown man. And this girl, who had boldly turned up at his doorstep to tell him his son had seduced her, seemed just the person who could straighten his man-child out. "Well, I guess yuh spread yuh bed, now yuh mus' lay down in it," Mr. Chambers said, slipping into patois.

Mrs. Chambers let out a soft gasp and began to softly dab at the tears forming in the corner of her eyes.

"It's no use you crying now," Mr. Chambers said, turning to his wife. "It was you who spoiled him you know," he added, "and whatever you sow, you shall reap."

Mrs. Chambers glared at her husband in response.

"Clifton and, what is your name again, Miss?" Mr. Chambers looked over at the girl.

"Angelique," she replied. She knew that was meant to be a subtle insult for her. It was meant to make her feel like she was some fast girl, showing up out of nowhere demanding that his son make her child legitimate. She looked around the elegant room, admiring the décor and smiled to herself. She would take his small insult. Besides, once he met her family, he and his wife would know that she came from a proper family, too.

The maid announced her presence. "Excuse me, ma'am," she said, looking over at Mrs. Chambers, "yuh want me fi set an extra place fi suppa tonight?"

Mrs. Chambers looked Angelique up and down for a moment and then nodded towards the maid. "And fix up the guest room, too."

5

The wedding happened quickly. Barely a month had passed since Angelique had shown up on the Chambers' doorstep demanding that Clifton take responsibility for his actions and now, she was married. The small ceremony wasn't the wedding that most girls would dream of. Especially given the status of the families involved, but it was a wedding nonetheless. It had still been elegant. Her family had attended; her brother Marlon was the only one that seemed to be happy for her. Furrowed lines of worry crisscrossed the planes of Byron's typically cheerful countenance. The carefree little girl he once knew was gone, replaced by a young woman he did not recognize.

Ruby had stood stone-faced throughout the ceremony. She did not cry the tears of a joyful mother on her daughter's wedding day. The only flicker of emotion she displayed came near the end of the formal reception. Angelique had watched as Clifton's mother had drawn Ruby to the side in what appeared to be the act of one mother trying to build a rapport with another, as two families melded. The women had spoken for a few minutes in a seeming exchange of pleasantries. At one point, Mrs. Chambers even laughed while patting Ruby's arm. Ruby, however, had not joined her in the laughter. Mrs. Chambers had leaned in, as if to share a secret. Almost immediately, Ruby walked away from her to stand by her husband who, sensing something was wrong, placed a protective arm around his wife. She remained by his side for the rest of the afternoon.

Despite the forced nature of the event, Angelique basked in her new position as the wife of a man belonging to one of the most respected families in Kingston. Her anger at being betrayed by Hazel had even dissipated, especially since the girl had gushed over the manor that Angelique now called home. "Gyal, dis is really high class!" Hazel had twirled around Angelique's room, her hands outstretched as if trying to touch the walls. Angelique had acted as though she had been living that lifestyle all her life.

"Yes, it is quite suitable," Angelique had said as she'd straightened her wedding dress in the standing mirror.

"An' wit dat dress, yuh cyan't even see the belly. No one would know you had to get married." Hazel fussed over Angelique's veil.

Angelique had bristled at the comment, but Hazel had not noticed.

"It would have eventually happened anyway. I'm not just anybody you know. Enough high class men out there would've loved to have me for a wife," Angelique had said.

"Mmmhmm," Hazel said. "Well, you sound like you were born in Kingston. You don't sound like you're from Somerset anymore." Hazel had burst out laughing and Angelique eventually joined in. Hazel was right. She had been consciously trying to blend in and develop a regional accent. Whether it was to move to Kingston or New York City or Canada, Angelique wanted to make sure she didn't sound like she was from a small town. Now, Angelique stood to one side of the large room looking at all of the important people that had come to her wedding. She watched as Mrs. Chambers floated around the room attending to most of her guests dressed in their black suits or formal spring frocks. Mr. Chambers was off to one side with another slightly older gentleman, likely discussing some business venture. Clifton as usual was entertaining everyone around him making jokes and toasting with white rum at every opportunity.

Angelique was a little perturbed that her new husband hadn't paid her as much attention as she would have liked during the reception, but she dismissed the doubting thoughts almost as soon as they entered her head. He was simply being a good host, carousing with some of his friends for what would likely be the last time. She was still a little bothered by the attention Clifton seemed to be getting from some of the young women at the party, but brushed this off too. She was Mrs. Clifton Chambers now. He was her husband and this was *her* home. Opulence, cars, fine fabrics, and trips to other countries were a part of her world now and the small country existence in Somerset Grove was behind her.

Ruby appeared and touched her daughter on her forearm, jarring her out of her daydreaming. "Angelique, we're leaving now," Ruby said.

"Thank you for coming, Mum," she smiled, "and don't worry about me, I'm in good hands."

Ruby took Angelique's hands in hers and shook them for emphasis as she spoke. "You are my daughter. No matter what happens, you are always welcome to come home. And no matter what anybody says, you hold your head up, you hear?" Ruby looked into her daughter's eyes to make sure she was listening.

Angelique looked at her mother in confusion. Ruby was not prone to making overtures of affection. It felt strange for her mother to be holding her hands and the sadness in her voice made it almost unrecognizable. She squeezed her mother's hands and smiled. "I will." Angelique walked her family to the door and watched them get into the car, her father closing her mother's door for her. She watched the car as her father slowly maneuvered it down the long driveway and disappeared out of sight.

6

Ruby

Spring, 1949

Ruby eventually got up, but not on her own. After several attempts to coax her out of bed, Ingrid finally grew tired of her daughter pining away over that worthless husband.

"I said to get up!" Ingrid unceremoniously ripped off the bedspread that Ruby had buried herself under and yanked her daughter into a sitting position.

Ruby sat listlessly on the edge of the mattress looking down at her feet. She had lain in bed so long she had lost track of the days. She pinched her face, signaling she was getting ready to cry.

"Stop it." Ingrid planted herself in front of Ruby and shook her finger in front of her daughter's face. "Enough with the moping and crying. You think he's fretting over you or that baby?" Ingrid pointed at Ruby's stomach. "It's time you get yourself together and figure out what you're going to do. I don't care what it is, but you're not going to be lying around crying over some bloody man." Ingrid pulled Ruby into a standing position, then removed the bedding from the bed before marching out the room, mumbling, "Not in MY house."

Ruby decided to do something. She bathed, dressed, and walked deep into the bush behind their home until she came across the old gray-haired man that mothers always warned their children to stay away from.

The obeah man eyed Ruby's blossoming form and her red, puffy eyes and told her he knew why she had come. She stood looking at him, not saying a word, but letting her eyes tell everything. His eyes responded, *"Are you sure?"* She nodded slowly. He moved about his little hut, examining herbs and pulling together a small satchel for her. A little of this herb, a little of that one, until he had the right blend. Finally, he handed the mixture to her and gave her instructions on how to make the tea and when to drink it. She paid him the money and retraced her steps back down the hill and through the bush.

When she came through the last thicket of trees into the yard, Ingrid was there laying white clothing on the rocks to bleach out in the sun. She stopped working and looked at Ruby suspiciously.

"Where have you been?"

"I went for a walk," Ruby said, avoiding her mother's eyes.

"Where?"

Ruby shifted her stance. "Nowhere in particular. Just around. I'm going inside the house." Ruby walked hurriedly through the back door as Ingrid's eyes followed her. Once inside, Ruby looked around for a safe place to hide the satchel of herbs. She went into the bedroom and retrieved one of her shoes from underneath the dresser, carefully tucking the satchel in the toe before replacing it beside its mate. She then went into the front room and made herself busy folding the laundry that Ingrid had started ironing.

Ingrid came in and announced she would be leaving for work soon and instructed Ruby to turn over the sheets she had laid out in a couple of hours so that the other side could also bleach. Ruby nodded and quickly answered yes. Ingrid packed her lunch and headed out the door, mumbling that she was already late. Ruby watched her mother disappear up the road and then waited for awhile until she was sure her mother would have arrived at work and would not be permitted to leave.

Ruby put a pot of water on to boil and retrieved the satchel. She steeped the herbs in a cup then sat down at the tiny kitchen table with the brew waiting for it to cool. The inky black liquid filled her nose with an unpleasant aroma and she sat mesmerized, wondering if she could bring herself to swallow it.

She didn't have a chance to find out. Ingrid seemed to have appeared out of nowhere, snatching up the cup and tossing its contents out of the window. She turned and glared at Ruby who was staring at the red blotch growing on her mother's hand where the liquid had splashed her when she grabbed the cup.

Ingrid didn't flinch as she watched the look on Ruby's face turn from shock to understanding as to why her mother was standing before her instead of at work. Ruby had been in such a stupor for so long, she had forgotten what day it was. It was Saturday—Ingrid's day off. When Ingrid told Ruby she was going to work, it was because she knew something was not quite right; only the obeah man lived up in the hills. No good could've come out of the walk that Ruby had taken behind the house earlier that day. When Ruby thought Ingrid had left for work, Ingrid had only gone up the road and waited a while before doubling back to see what Ruby was up to.

Ingrid grabbed the half-empty pouch that still sat on the table and shook it in front of Ruby's face. "I can't believe you. What in God's name were you thinking?" Ingrid said, in a tone that made it clear she wasn't looking for an answer.

Ruby stared at her mother with a look of hopelessness in her eyes and Ingrid softened.

"Life is rough sometimes, but God only gave you one, so you better live it like you're grateful for it and every blessing he gives you," Ingrid said. She walked outside to the edge of their property and emptied out the contents of the pouch into the surrounding bushes. When she came back into the house, she put Ruby to work cleaning the place from top to bottom. "Idle hands are the devil's workshop," she told her daughter when she protested. She didn't let Ruby stop until it was time to eat dinner.

For the next several days, they repeated the routine, with Ingrid giving Ruby a list of chores she could manage so she could keep her mind off pitying herself. By the end of the week, Ruby had gotten into the rhythm of the days again and her mood had lifted with the productivity. The following Saturday Ingrid took Ruby into town to shop at the market. It was there, picking over green bananas and cassavas that Ruby ran into Byron Wright.

Byron was several years older than Ruby and she had known him for years during the time that she was in school. He was of average height and build, with cocoa-brown skin. He was not extraordinarily handsome, but he had a bright, friendly smile and easy-going manner.

Byron had never been shy about letting Ruby know he was interested in her, but she had politely brushed him off in favor of the much younger Winston.

"Ruby," Byron called to her from the next stand. Ruby turned to look in his direction. He waved at her smiling brightly as he accepted his change back from a vendor. He walked over and stood in front of her. "I haven't seen you in a long time. You look nice," he said, still beaming.

Ruby smiled for the first time in days and self-consciously smoothed her hand over the front of her dress.

"I thought I heard you had moved to England or something."

Ruby's smile faltered a bit. "Well, I was supposed to go…" She licked her lips and looked around anxiously for Ingrid who was several stalls away inspecting some spices. Ruby turned back to Byron who instinctively reached out and gently touched her arm.

"Well, England's loss is Jamaica's gain," he said, and flashed another smile.

Ruby relaxed and smiled gratefully.

"Since I know you're still here, maybe I'll stop by your home and say hello."

"I suppose that would be alright," Ruby replied, trying not to sound too inviting.

"I'll take an 'I suppose.'" He grinned. "See you soon," he said and walked off before Ruby could respond.

Ingrid suddenly appeared next to Ruby. "Who was that?"

"Just someone I used to know when I was in school."

"He's a little older than you, isn't he?" Ingrid said, looking in the direction that Byron had walked. "Anyway, his father is a carpenter or something, right?"

"I don't know, Mum. I think so. Let me carry that for you." Ruby took one of the bags from her mother. "I'm tired. Are we ready to go?"

Byron appeared the next week, stopping by to say hello as he promised. Over the next month, he came by two to three times a week, usually offering to help with some handyman projects. Ruby began to look forward to his visits and found herself disappointed if more than a couple of days passed before she saw him again. Ingrid didn't mind the extra help, but cautioned Ruby.

"Remember, you are still married and pregnant. Have you told him anything?" Ingrid had asked Ruby one day after Byron had stopped by. He had brought his tools to fix the back steps that had threatened to come loose. He had declined Ingrid's invitation to stay for dinner though he assured her that the stewed chicken she was preparing smelled really nice.

"Maybe I can convince Ruby to come out with me later, though. I need to go home and bathe first," he said as he brushed the dust from his clothes. Ruby had smiled despite herself, but politely declined, thinking about her mother's words.

The next time Byron came around, he and Ruby went outside on the verandah. Ruby sat in a chair leafing through a book while Byron painted the door trim.

"Thank you for doing all this work around here, Byron."

"It's no problem, no problem at all. I like taking care of you," he said as he stirred the paint.

Ruby blushed and laid the book over her growing stomach. At four months, she was beginning to show and while she was not over Winston, she found Byron's caring ways making a tiny dent in her heart.

"You don't have to be ashamed." Byron gestured at the tiny bump Ruby was trying to hide. "That man is a fool," he said, referring to Winston.

It was the first time Ruby had heard any trace of anger in Byron's voice. It made her want to cry again, but this time in a way that made her smile.

Later that week Byron came back, this time to speak with Ingrid. He told her that he had spoken with a lawyer and that Ruby's marriage could be annulled on the grounds of fraud. He also told Ingrid that he would take care of Ruby and her child. Ingrid believed him. To Ruby, he promised a beautiful house on the other side of Somerset Grove with a view of the mountains. "It's not England, but I'll make sure you will never miss it," he told her.

By the end of the week the three of them were in town visiting the lawyer that the Wright family always used to draw up their wills and handle their business matters. Ruby had almost backed out before Byron arrived to pick them up, but Ingrid convinced her it was her only real option. "No sense in looking back."

A week later, Byron delivered the order that effectively told Ruby she had never been married. Feeling numb, she accepted Byron's official proposal, and they were married by the time Ruby entered her fifth month of pregnancy.

Byron began building the house as he promised. His father took workers off other projects to be sure that it was completed before Ruby gave birth. Byron took Ruby to the site several times, carefully leading her around to show her where all the rooms would be and how far their property extended. Ruby slowly became excited about her new home as it took shape and would share the progress reports with her mother, the only person she trusted besides Byron.

The week they moved in, Byron drove to the country to bring Ingrid for a visit. Ruby proudly waddled through the house showing Ingrid each of the rooms and smiling as her mother nodded in approval. Byron followed and remained quiet for the most part, except when he pointed out the crib that he had personally crafted from mahogany wood. Ingrid smiled, pleased more by Byron's clear intent to embrace this child than his craftsmanship.

At dinner, Ingrid made two announcements—first, she would be staying with them for a while to help Ruby through the first few weeks after the baby's arrival. The second was that when she left there, she planned to return to Panama for a while.

"For how long?" Ruby asked, the corners of her mouth pulling down as she spoke.

"I don't know, Ruby," she said. "I haven't been home in so long. I don't even know if my own mother would recognize me." Ingrid let out a little laugh.

Ruby pondered her mother's words. For so long it had been just the two of them and her father before he passed away. Her first thoughts had been about how much she would miss her mother. It never occurred to her before that moment that Ingrid might be missing her mother, too.

Ingrid seemed to read Ruby's thoughts. "I do miss my mother. I haven't gone back all these years because I wanted to make sure you were ready to leave home. Now that I know you have someone to look out for you." she reached over and took Byron's hand, "I can finally go back."

Byron laid his hand on top of Ingrid's. "You don't need to worry about a thing. I'm going to take good care of my family."

Ruby smiled at Byron, but the worry lines still crept across her forehead. Ingrid reached across the table with her other hand and rubbed Ruby's forearm.

"Don't worry yourself right now. That's weeks away and we have lots to do before then, right?"

"Right," Ruby said, blinking away her tears.

7

Angelique

Spring, 1968

The sun streamed through the dark plantation shutters, warming the floor, and illuminated the large bedroom. Angelique opened her eyes and stretched as she looked about the room. Various books were neatly stacked on one side of the dresser and a cream-colored vase blooming with Birds of Paradise perched on the other side. The cream-upholstered settee made of the same carved wood as the dresser stood a few feet away from the window. The rich red painted walls contrasted warmly off the dark wood floors with wainscoting that framed the whole room.

Angelique slid her left arm across the sheets to the other side of the bed. They were cool. Again. She turned over and looked at the empty space beside her. Had it not been for the indentation in the feather pillow next to her own, she would not have even been sure that her husband had lain there at all last night. At least he had been there, even if for only a brief time. Over the last several weeks Clifton had grown distant. The position in his father's office as an aide seemed to engulf all of his time. Most mornings he was gone before Angelique awoke and wouldn't return until after she had gone to bed. On those mornings when he did stay around long enough for Angelique to see him, he was sullen. His lack of enthusiasm for the job that forced him to give up his boyish ways was apparent in every action. From the painstakingly slow way he would get dressed to his sunken shoulders and the heavy sound of his footsteps as he walked out of the door as if going off to his death.

Angelique moved her hand across her swollen belly and a slight smile formed across her lips. The joy she experienced at her impending motherhood surprised no one more than her. She had successfully turned something bad into something good.

She pushed herself up and off the bed, massaging her lower back as she looked down on the floor. No question that Clifton had been there. The once crisp white shirt and gray trousers he wore the day before lay in a rumpled pile on the floor beside the far corner post of the bed. She walked over and picked up the clothing. She paused and closed her eyes as she fought to keep the bile down that threatened to erupt from her throat. The peculiar odor emanating from his clothing combined with the heat of the room made her suddenly feel weak. She steadied herself against one of the bed's four posters. After a minute she reached down for the offending garments and held them at arm's length as she walked towards the dressing area and stuffed the items into the clothes basket for the maid to pick up later. She washed up and gathered herself together before heading downstairs.

Dew drops gently kissed her bare feet as Angelique stood outside in the fresh morning air. The fragrant scent of ripened fruit warming under the sun filled her lungs. The solitude of these mornings was liberating. No white gloves, no tailored frocks, no smart looking hat pinned to her neatly coiffed hair. Only the thin cotton layer of her nightgown separated Angelique from nature. She smiled to herself. Her mother would have screamed to high heaven if Angelique had ever stepped outside of the house in her bed clothes. It was improper and a sign of bad breeding. Now that she was the lady of her own house she could do as she pleased. Especially here. The house, situated in the same hills as Clifton's parents' home, was a slightly smaller replica of the Chambers' estate. Mahogany and marble accents could be found throughout the house. A full-time maid ensured that Angelique never had to lift a finger. Her status in the community was immediately recognized and, as Angelique quickly learned, coveted by many of the young women in the city. This was all hers and if she wanted to dance barefoot through it all, she would do it.

The waves of nausea she felt earlier on in her pregnancy had passed for the most part, replaced with the familiar craving for her favorite fruit, and she had no patience to wait for anyone else to pick it. Angelique went around to the mango tree at the side of the house in search of its offerings. The branches hung heavy with the golden red fruit. With a little effort, she managed to knock down one of the treasurers with a stick she found lying in the yard. The warm juice of the mango ran down her lips and hands and stained her white cotton gown. She laughed to herself as she devoured the mango, licking the sweetness from her fingers. Normally, she consumed them in the dining room, neatly sliced and pealed for her along with a variety of other fruit. But nothing compared to the sensation of this morning ritual. Her feet moist from the night dew and her face sticky from the nectar, she looked like a little girl, but she didn't care.

Hearing voices near the back of the house, she quickly finished up the mango and threw the seed on the ground before running inside to get dressed. This private morning ritual was hers alone. It would not do for anyone, even the help, to see her running around outside in her nightgown and devouring fruit like she had no home training. Like she didn't belong here.

Angelique stood inside the post office with Mrs. Chambers as she claimed her packages from the clerk. It had been one of those infrequent invitations to accompany her mother-in-law in to town to run errands, since Jennifer Chambers usually sent someone to take care of these tasks for her. Occasionally she would take care of business herself, more for the purpose of being seen than the need to attend to things personally. Angelique was glad for these rare trips with her mother-in-law. She not only had the opportunity to "be seen" by the people in town too, she also hoped to somehow strengthen the tenuous relationship she had with the woman. Angelique hadn't come into this family in the most ideal fashion, but under different circumstances, she believed her mother-in-law would have immediately loved her up.

Angelique was standing slightly behind Mrs. Chambers as she examined her packages when they were approached by two women.

"Hello, hi, mi dear!" the elder of the two women addressed Mrs. Chambers who rolled her eyes before turning to look at the source of the noise. Mrs. Weston stood beaming at her expectantly. Mrs. Chambers was sure Mrs. Weston was anxious to catch up on the latest gossip. She had a distinct dislike for the woman standing before her with her gossiper-in-training at her side. Whenever there was a story unfolding, Mrs. Weston was first on the scene, ready to download the facts and spread the news as far and as fast as she could. Ironically, the most long running news in the city involved her own son, Roland, who she had touted as the most eligible bachelor in town. Roland had graduated at the top of his class at one of Jamaica's most prestigious schools for boys and went on to a career practicing law.

Throughout his life Mrs. Weston had always doted on her son. Mr. Weston often quarreled with his wife about making his boy "too soft" but she ignored him. Roland was described as nice, both in his looks and his mannerisms, and had had his pick of any number of young women. It came as a total shock to everyone when Roland decided against one of the many women in town, choosing instead to run off with his firm's mailroom clerk, a 20-year-old boy, whose effeminate mannerisms had long since led others to conclude that he was "funny." After that scandal, Mr. Weston refused to acknowledge that he'd ever had a son. Many speculated that Mr. Weston's sudden absence from society was due to the time he spent locked away in his now separate bedroom, drinking white rum until he passed out every night.

For her part, Mrs. Weston turned her attention to her daughter, Millicent, an awkward and furtive girl who chewed her lip incessantly and had the unfortunate circumstance of looking like her older brother, and for that, drew the undeserved scorn of her drunken father. Millicent was secretly happy for the turn of events involving her brother, which resulted in her finally getting some consideration from her mother.

The effect of the incident with her son was noticeable in Mrs. Weston's appearance. She wore her hair in short pressed curls and her makeup was too heavy, Angelique thought as she glanced at the foundation that was a little too light for this woman's complexion and the lipstick that was a little too bold for daytime hours. Almost like she was trying to hide behind it. Still, the woman had a pleasant expression on her face. Her eyes crinkled behind her glasses as she smiled. Angelique looked at Millicent who appeared to be a younger replica of Mrs. Weston, only slimmer and without glasses. *A little too slim*, Angelique thought as she sized up the girl whose frock hung awkwardly on her body and barely covered the knocked knees hidden underneath. Millicent was about Angelique's age, but had that wide-eyed innocent look like she had never experienced the world from more than a few feet away from her mother's watchful eye.

"Hello, Mrs. Weston. Good to see you, you are looking well," Mrs. Chambers responded. It was clear from the closed-lip smile that Mrs. Chambers gave and the way she tried to look everywhere else but in the woman's face that she was trying to make this unpleasant encounter as brief as possible.

Mrs. Weston appeared not to notice. "Thank you, my dear. Do you remember my daughter, Millicent?" Millicent smiled on cue, eager to please. Although she was a little plain, her brilliant smile lit up her face.

"Yes, yes, Millicent. You've grown into a nice young lady." Mrs. Chambers pretended to gush, making Millicent smile even wider.

Mrs. Weston looked at Angelique who stood waiting expectantly. Mrs. Chambers continued to smile, but remained silent. Mrs. Weston looked on a little confused, but smiled again. "Um, how is your husband and your son? A long time mi nuh see that boy. He must be a big man now," she said and laughed.

"Oh, everybody is fine. Mr. Chambers is busy with work as always and now Clifton is working in his office as well."

Mrs. Weston was barely listening as she continued to look at Angelique's prominent belly with interest; a sparkle gleamed in her eye. "And who might you be, my dear?"

Before Angelique could speak, Mrs. Chambers jumped in. "Oh, Clifton got married a few months ago, you know." She gestured towards Angelique without looking at her. "This is my daughter-in-law."

"What? I never know Clifton was engaged and I saw you must be four months ago and you never said anything, Jennifer, and you never invite me!" Mrs. Weston playfully admonished the woman. "What is your name, dear?"

"Angelique."

"Oh, what a beautiful name. So how long you been married now?"

Angelique answered before Mrs. Chambers could jump in again. "Almost three months."

"Three months, eh?" Mrs. Weston looked again at Angelique's stomach as she surmised the situation. She gave Mrs. Chambers a self-satisfied smile, but it was short-lived.

Jennifer Chambers looked that woman square in the eye and asked, in a slow and deliberate voice, "Speaking of which, why haven't I heard anything about *your* son getting married?"

The smile on Mrs. Weston's face lost its joy. Her mind struggled as she tried to put together a reasonable answer. Although everyone suspected that her son preferred the company of young men, nobody ever talked about it to her face. She'd never had to deal directly with any questions about where her son was after he left the city. She would sometimes volunteer that he was off in England receiving more professional training with a prestigious firm. Most times, people would politely smile and then just talk behind her back. Not today though. Today, she baited the wrong woman. Mrs. Weston began to stutter as little beads of perspiration formed around her hairline. She looked over at Millicent who was busy chewing her bottom lip, and then back to Mrs. Chambers who returned her look with one eyebrow raised.

"Well, we have to get going. Good day to you, Mrs. Weston." Mrs. Chambers grabbed Angelique by the elbow and led her down the street before Mrs. Weston could recover enough to respond. Angelique looked back at the two women standing in front of the post office as she walked beside Mrs. Chambers. She almost felt pity for Mrs. Weston who was dabbing her moist forehead with a handkerchief. Although they were walking away quickly, Angelique could swear she could make out the smirk on Millicent's face.

By the time they returned to the Chambers' home it was late afternoon. After their run in with Mrs. Weston, they had continued on with their errands, stopping in various shops to pick up items, mostly for Mrs. Chambers—perfume, clothing from the seamstress, and of course, they had to stop at the bakery for patties, hard dough bread, and rum cake. Angelique's mother-in-law had been in a better mood since their afternoon run-in with Mrs. Weston, even joking with Angelique about the incident. "You see how her face almost dropped on the ground? Good! Next time she won't be so quick to fasten in *my* business."

Angelique had laughed even though she still felt slighted by Mrs. Chambers' apparent discomfort at having to introduce her. The woman had acted like Angelique was some ashy-kneed rusty girl from the street that someone had mistaken for her child. Any of those women back home would have been proud to say that were related to the Wright family. Things were different here though, and Angelique felt the constant urge to prove her pedigree.

Mrs. Chambers handed the bags of groceries to the maid then set about cutting the strings and removing the brown wrapping from the packages she had picked up at the post office. The first package contained mostly accessories—several pairs of cotton gloves in a variety of pastel shades, silk scarves, and two satin clutches. The second package contained more clothing items—crisp white shirts and trousers made of gabardine, several blouses, petticoats, and nightgowns. She inspected each of the items carefully, running her fingers over seams and feeling the quality of fabric. "We get most of our things from England," she remarked. "Here," she handed Angelique one of the nightgowns and two of the petticoats. "Now you can say you have something nice from England. Those are from Marks and Spencer, you know," Mrs. Chambers said proudly.

"You ever hear of it?"

The condescending way in which Mrs. Chambers spoke to Angelique like she wasn't used to nice things made her want to throw the nightgown back in her face. Instead, she smiled. "Of course. My mother used to order from Marks and Spencer all the time." Angelique barely managed to hide the annoyance in her voice. She glanced over at one of the blouses Mrs. Chambers had so lovingly admired a few moments ago. "You'll look very nice in that one." She pointed with her finger. "My mother bought the same one last year."

Jennifer Chambers' mood immediately soured. If she had been a few shades lighter, her cheeks would have shown the flushed red of embarrassment. "They must have sent me that one by accident," she said. "You can send it to your mother if you like."

"Well, that is very kind of you. But, perhaps I wasn't so clear. My mother purchased that one last year as a Christmas gift for our maid. You should keep it. You seemed to like it a few minutes ago." Angelique smiled. She could see Mrs. Chambers' façade cracking. *Good!*

8

There it was again. That now familiar stale scent that made her stomach churn. It was so strong and yet it seemed as if nobody else noticed it. Or maybe they noticed it and didn't care. It wasn't always there; some days she did not detect it. Other days, the odor assaulted her senses and she would be forced to leave the room. No explanation was ever given for its source or why it was there. Everyone else around moved about as if everything was normal. But it was not. This odor spoke more than words ever could. Its presence was approved of, even welcomed in this home, maybe more than she was. It took up residence in the house. It found its favorite chair in the study and marked it. It showed up for dinner with the family in the evening and intruded on her dreams at night. Occasionally, it had shown up at church, but not too often and not for a while now; that was probably the one place where it felt uncomfortable, where others would wrinkle their noses in displeasure and furrow their brows at it as if to say, "not here, not today." It should go back to the house and wait if it must, or better yet, it should just go away, at least until tomorrow. Today was for the Lord, for appearing righteous in the house of God and in front of others, for heads to be held high and for families to appear united.

On these righteous days, a warm hand would slip around Angelique's waist as Clifton introduced her as his wife. On these Sundays, a hand would reach out and grab her forearm, pulling her this way and that as she was presented to different church members as "my lovely daughter-in-law." On these Sundays, visitors who came by for dinner would see a loving hand placed on her shoulder whenever someone mentioned her or the baby boy everyone hoped she was carrying. But when the scent was there, when Sundays were over, things changed. Angelique would become almost invisible, or a reminder that things were not as they should be.

This time the stale scent permeated the air in the living room. It had moved from its favorite chair over to the sofa where Angelique liked to take her morning tea as she would lay back in the cushions to relieve her back which seemed to ache more and more these days. The smell was too powerful to ignore and she could not get comfortable among the pillows.

"Miss Bailey?" Angelique wrinkled up her nose as she pushed herself off the sofa.

A woman about her mother's age appeared in the doorway wiping her hands on a towel, her hair pulled back in a bun from her pleasant face. "Yes, Miss Angelique?"

"Everything in here smells bad. I can't stay in here one more minute. Please, do something. I can't take it anymore." Angelique's hands rose and fell at her sides in exasperation. Miss Bailey threw the towel on to her shoulder and looked at Angelique as a mother looks upon a child who has just asked her to do the impossible.

"I'll take the cushions and put them outside to air out and open up the windows so we can catch a likkle breeze," she said as she began putting pillows underneath her arms. "But you know it will keep coming back." She looked at Angelique and communicated with unspoken words. Miss Bailey had seen this scenario many times with her other employers. Each one handled it in their own way; some raged against it while others acquiesced. Some pretended it didn't exist while some appeared to be frozen, uncertain of what to do. Angelique appeared to be in the latter category, but Miss Bailey could not be sure. She watched as the girl stood looking around the room frowning, as if trying to figure out how to deal with the situation while she rubbed her swollen belly. "Maybe you should go sit outside for a while. Get some fresh air for you and the likkle one," she said, gesturing towards Angelique's stomach.

Angelique looked up as if she just realized where she was. "Yes, perhaps I will go for a walk or something." She smiled faintly. Miss Bailey had been working at the house since the time that Angelique had arrived. Initially Angelique had kept her distance from the woman as she had seen her mother and Mrs. Chambers do with the help. But as time passed, Angelique found herself looking for reasons to spend more and more time around Miss Bailey, asking for things she did not need or for advice on things that did not really require her input: "*Miss Bailey, it look like rain to you? Should we postpone our trip to the market?*" Or, "*Miss Bailey, you think I should bring a cardigan? You think I might catch a cold in this?*" Miss Bailey never looked annoyed or refused to answer and never pretended that Angelique wasn't there.

Forging a relationship with her mother-in-law was more difficult than Angelique had anticipated. She was carrying the woman's grandchild, yet Jennifer Chambers had still remained cool toward Angelique—polite, but cool. Miss Bailey, on the other hand, had taken on somewhat of a maternal role to Angelique—bringing her a cup of mint tea when her stomach was upset or baking her a rum cake on her day off. Sometimes she just listened to Angelique whenever she complained or went on about anything, contributing only a "mmm" or "mmhmm" to indicate her agreement or dissatisfaction with whatever was being reported. She was careful though, to never engage in any gossip or criticism of anyone, particularly in the family. Miss Bailey had long known the duty of loyalty and her role as a confidante in her employ.

Today Miss Bailey bit her tongue as she went about cleaning and airing out the living room. It was not her place to comment on what she had seen or heard going on in that house. As much as she would have like to have said something, would have liked to expose the Chambers for who they were, she said nothing. But words weren't the only way to communicate a message. The decision to change her cleaning routine so that the living room was the last area attended to was not a random one. Nor was the decision to move the setting up of the morning tea and fried dumplings into the living room from the dining room. "For your back, mi dear. I thought you would be more comfortable in here with the pillows and everything." Angelique appreciated the gesture at first; it was a peaceful and serene place to begin the day. Lately though, Angelique's thoughts had not been so peaceful in that room. A fire was beginning to stir inside her.

"Miss Bailey, I am going to surprise my husband and go visit him for lunch. What do you think?"

Miss Bailey kept moving cushions to the floor as she spoke. "I think that would be a wonderful idea, mi dear. Wear one of your nice frocks and mek all them know seh you are the wife."

Angelique looked at the woman and smiled before she headed out of the room.

9

The building where Clifton worked stood out amongst the others in the area with its ivory-colored walls and well-manicured lawn. The building seemed a flurry of activity. Men in tailored suits walked in and out of its doors carrying on intense conversations with each other. Inside, a few women dressed in their smart-looking skirt suits bustled about with papers carried in the crook of their arms dipping in and out of offices with their deliveries. Angelique walked down the hall until she found the office she was looking for and went inside. The room was starkly furnished with a few chairs and a table with copies of *The Jamaican Gleaner* neatly folded on top. An elderly woman sat at the receptionist desk to the left. Her gray hair was neatly styled into soft roller set curls that framed her face. She wore her reading glasses down at the end of her nose as she typed up her shorthand notes into a letter. She peered over the glasses at Angelique. "Can I help you?"

"Yes, I am Mrs. Chambers, and I am here to see my husband, Clifton, please."

The receptionist looked up and down at the young woman standing before her in a powder blue frock with matching hat. Her hair was brushed and pinned up neatly at the sides, with soft waves cascading just past her shoulders. She was polished. Almost too much so. Like she was trying too hard. "Have a seat over there so." The receptionist gestured towards one of the empty chairs on the other side of the room as she spoke. "He was working in the back the last I saw him. Let me just go and see." Angelique settled herself in one of the chairs as the receptionist pulled herself up, sighing with the effort, and disappeared through the door, but not before Angelique heard her mumble, "Married? Humph."

Angelique could feel the heat rising up her neck as she waited. She clenched her jaw slightly and pursed her lips wondering if she'd really heard what she thought she did. Before she had enough time to think about it, the door swung open and the receptionist walked through followed by Clifton. She pointed at Angelique and looked up at Clifton as if to say, "That's the one there," like it was necessary for her to be pointed out. Clifton walked past the woman and over to the seating area where his wife waited. Angelique looked up at him without moving.

"You came all this way and now you act like you're not even happy to see me." Clifton flashed one of his charming smiles as he took Angelique's hands and gently pulled her from her seat.

"Well, I…"

"Come nuh! I want to introduce you to Mrs. Morgan. She runs everything out front here, including her mouth." Clifton teased the elderly woman who swatted at him with a writing pad.

"Clifton, don't say such things about me. It's very disrespectful." Mrs. Morgan tried to look at him sternly over her glasses while stifling a smile.

"Sorry, sorry." Clifton feigned remorse. "Mrs. Morgan, this is my wife, Angelique."

Mrs. Morgan looked at Angelique again, as if seeing her with new eyes. "Clifton, you never tell me you was married," she said.

"What? Of course I did."

"No, suh!"

"Mrs. Morgan, you're beginning to forget some things. I worry about you, you know."

"Is nothing wrong with me," she protested. "Anyway, the way you carry on—"

"Come Angelique." Clifton took his wife's arm and quickly ushered her towards the door. "Should we leave and find a nice restaurant or something? You hungry?" Clifton was talking a mile a minute as they hurried outside the building.

"Clifton, why are you rushing me so? Don't you see I'm pregnant? Cha, man!" Angelique wrestled her arm from Clifton's grasp and smoothed her hands over her dress. She looked at him suspiciously. "What are you up to, Clifton? And don't tell me nothing because I know something is wrong. Why you trying to get out of here so fast?" Angelique crossed her arms in front of her chest and waited expectantly.

Clifton knitted his eyebrows together and started shaking his head, as if denying unspoken accusations. Angelique narrowed her eyes at him, then looked around the courtyard at the faces that had begun to watch them with curiosity and amusement. This was not the place. She would deal with him later. She stuck her hand out in front of his chest. "Give me some money. I need to buy a few things while I'm in town," she demanded.

Glad for the temporary reprieve, Clifton pulled out his money clip and peeled off a few bills to hand to Angelique. He was not getting off that easy. "Is that all? What do you expect me to do with this?" She raised her voice a little louder.

He reluctantly peeled more bills from the fold and placed them in her hand. She snapped her fingers shut on the wad and looked up into his eyes. "I'm not finished with you, you know." She cut her eyes at him before turning and making her way down the sidewalk towards the street, leaving Clifton to stare after her as she disappeared out of sight.

The clock ticked incessantly, piercing the silence in the house. The only other noise was the faint sounds of the neighborhood dogs greeting each other as they prepared for their evening of prowling and mischief. Angelique rubbed her eyes as she tried to stay awake. She wanted to talk to Clifton, but there was no sign of him. She had eaten dinner alone, walked around the property, and watched the sunset from the verandah, waiting for Clifton to appear and explain himself, but she was getting tired. The pregnancy was sapping her energy and, with few people stopping by to visit and no school classes to attend, boredom was the only thing that kept her company. She had taken to napping to pass the time away. Napping, however, led to more tiredness and waking up at odd hours. Yesterday she woke up at 3 a.m. and couldn't get back to sleep. Clifton had actually been in bed at that time, but he slept like a single man—face down like a starfish with his head nearly hanging off the bed. He did not hold her at night. He did not lay on his side with his arms wrapped around her and his head buried in her neck. He did not lay on his back so that she could lay her head on his chest. He was as disconnected to her at night as he was during the day, except for those times when he wanted to be intimate and even then, she felt it wasn't that he wanted to be close as much as it was about satisfying himself.

She got up and moved towards the window to stare down the long driveway. There was no movement; at least out in the yard. Inside her belly was another matter. This little one inside of her had started kicking and dancing, making sure his or her presence was known. She ran her hands over her stomach caressing and soothing the restless spirit who seemed so anxious to make an appearance in the world, so anxious to escape. Angelique went to her bedroom and lay down on the bed. She continued to caress her stomach as she fought to stay awake. Slowly, the baby's kicks started to fade, lulled to sleep by the soothing touch. The heavy humidity of the late night summer weighed over Angelique like a heavy blanket. She finally gave way and slipped into a deep slumber.

Morning arrived as it always did. The sun streaked across the floor as it always did. Angelique instinctively reached across the bed in search of Clifton's form as she always did. His side of the bed was cold as it usually was. She exhaled loudly in frustration. She would need to have the sheets changed. It was unusually hot and she felt soaked from head to toe, even between her legs. Disgusted, she raised herself up on her elbows and immediately dropped back as a lightning bolt of pain ripped through her body. She lay frozen on the bed trying to comprehend what was going on. As the pain continued to shoot through her a scream rose out of her as loud and as powerful as any hurricane she'd ever lived through. She screamed not only in pain, but in fear of being alone.

Where is everybody? Oh God, why am I all alone? She screamed so loud she did not hear the sound of footsteps pounding across the floor.

10

He watched as the small form swaddled in the little white blanket that lay in the bassinet writhed, stretched, and then went back to being still. The little mouth yawned wide as the eyes squinted then opened and focused on his bleary form. He reached down and delicately touched all the fingers on the little hand that stretched out to him, and then locked his finger in a tight grip. He bent down and slowly picked up the baby who intermittently let out little peeps between sucking noises. He studied the baby's features—a head of curly hair, a little bow mouth, and skin the color of pale wheat. He gently touched the round little nose that was distinctively familiar. "You've got at least one thing from me." The baby cooed in response.

He began to hum an old Jamaican lullaby as he quietly walked around the room, careful not to wake Angelique who had been sleeping on and off most of the day, waking up just long enough to feed the baby before slipping back into a light slumber. The labor and delivery had been long and hard. Clifton had arrived late in the morning to find Miss Bailey, his mother, and two of his aunts walking briskly in and out of his bedroom as Angelique shrieked at the top of her lungs. He had tried to take a peek inside the room and had the door unceremoniously slammed in his face, but not before his mother had cut her eyes at him. His father had been sitting in the kitchen reading a newspaper, staying as far away from the bedroom as he could get. He did not look up as Clifton entered the room looking for something to eat.

"Is now you're just getting in?" His father turned a page. Clifton didn't answer.

"You mean tell me you have this girl pregnant and up in the house by herself and you up and down in the streets until all hours of the morning?" His father looked up at him expectantly.

"How was I to know she was going to have the baby today? I didn't even know it was that time already." Clifton shrugged.

"Babies come when they're ready. Not when you decide. Suppose Miss Bailey didn't stop by this morning? Eh? That girl could have been left in here alone all this time. And you running around all night like you don't have a home," his father said. "You must learn to take some responsibility. You're not a young boy anymore."

Clifton had let out a sigh. It would have been no use trying to explain anything to his father. He had no interest in what Clifton had to say.

"And is no use you sighing. This is all your doing."

Clifton nodded silently. His father turned back to his newspaper and mumbled under his breath, "All I would need is for these people around here to come talk about how you left the girl in the house for de whole night. Anyt'ing coulda happen. What an embarrassment." Clifton had known it was best to keep quiet whenever his father traded in his proper English for the familiar patois he saved for the occasions when his closest friends were around or when he was angry.

"So, you think it's a boy?" Clifton had asked, hoping to lighten the mood.

"You askin' me? I don't know anything. Ask your mother."

"She shut the door in my face."

"Good!" His father had laughed. "Lessons for the day. Stay out of women's private business and bring your backside home at a decent hour."

Clifton had smiled in spite of the anger he felt towards his father for talking to him like a child. Now, as he looked down on this new baby smelling of light baby powder, he felt a growing sense of responsibility, a need to be around this child, to provide protection and love.

Angelique stirred from her sleep, pulling herself up in the bed and looked over at Clifton.

"When did you get here?"

"I…" he stumbled, "it doesn't matter anymore. I'm here now, right?"

"It matters alright. I said I wasn't finished with you yet," Angelique snapped.

"Lawd, gyal! Don't you see I'm trying?"

"Just bring the baby come," she ordered.

He reluctantly walked over and relinquished the child. "So," he tried to lighten the mood, "I guess we need to agree on a name, right?" He smiled at Angelique.

"You're too late as usual," she told him. "Her name is Carmen."

11

The temperature hovered around 85 degrees as the sun blazed brightly in the afternoon sky. A gentle tropical breeze kept most of the people waiting on the train platform comfortable. Several of the women still waved fans in front of their chests and throats while some of the men removed their caps, fanned themselves absentmindedly, and then put them back on their heads. Restless little children jumped up and down on the wooden slats and tried to escape from the grasp of the mothers who held on to them tightly while scolding, "Stand still and keep yourself quiet before you get hurt! You want the train fe come and lick you down?"

Angelique stood amongst the crowd, shifting her weight between her feet as she balanced a chubby Carmen on her hip. The baby clung to her with one hand while looking around quietly at the figures moving about her, lips drawn tightly closed and eyes that resembled her mother's taking in everything they could. Angelique straightened the child's dress and rubbed her back as little Carmen let out a peep that sounded much like a sigh of impatience.

"You have somewhere to be?" Angelique teased. Carmen looked up at the sound of her mother's voice as if trying to comprehend what her mother was saying before finally giving up and returning to her observation of the world around her.

The sound of the train approaching brought excited noises from the crowd as people straightened up their clothes and moved further down the platform. Angelique looked anxiously about the stream of passengers until she finally saw the person she was looking for and let out her own squeal of excitement. "Hazel, over here!" Hazel looked around for the voice before spotting its source and making her way towards it.

"Gyal, a long time mi nuh see you," Hazel exclaimed as she rushed over with her suitcase in hand. She hugged her cousin briefly before reaching for the baby who studied her curiously. "Wow! Look at this baby. How come you so serious?" She held the little girl who seemed entranced by this new person. Hazel tickled Carmen's belly and underneath her chin before she finally let out a squeal of delight. "Yes, she is serious like her mother," Hazel said and laughed.

They put Hazel's bags in the car and decided to walk through downtown to catch up. Hazel stole glances at Angelique as she pointed out the sights. Her clothes were stylish and she was put together as always. But the light was gone. The perfect hair, makeup, and clothes were merely tools to mask the dullness that seemed to lie within. Angelique talked about the beautiful home they lived in, how they had the best of everything, and how influential the family name was. But when Hazel asked about how things were going with the family, Angelique was vague and quickly changed the subject. Things had not gotten any better. After Carmen's birth, Clifton had seemed like he enjoyed the idea of his new family. He stopped staying out late and had been very affectionate for a time, but after a few months he fell back into his old habits. The only thing that hadn't changed was his interest in his daughter. He played with the child constantly, singing to her and doing anything to make her laugh. It seemed that every time they were in the same room he would take the baby from Angelique, only returning her when she needed to be changed or fed. Angelique began to feel more like a nurse maid than a mother. Loneliness was her constant companion and along with it, a sense of unfulfilled restlessness.

They walked through the marketplace, looking at the various wares of the many vendors. They inhaled the scents of the tropical fruits mixing together—mangoes, star apples, and papayas all beckoned to them and stirred their appetites. They settled on some patties from a nearby bakery and fresh ginger beer, and then topped it off with shaved ice cones. Hazel relayed all the latest news from Somerset Grove, like who was getting married, who left the town and under what circumstances, and who had lost their mind.

As for Angelique's family, Hazel reported that overall, everyone was well. Her father was keeping busy with his furniture business and Marlon was now working full time with their father. Ruby, as usual, kept to herself, explaining away Angelique's sudden departure as not really sudden at all, but something they had planned and just kept quiet. Hazel handed a parcel wrapped in brown paper and tied with a string. "They told me to bring this to give to you." Hazel gestured towards the box. "Just some things for the baby and things to remind you of home." Angelique examined the package.

"Open it, nuh," Hazel ordered and laughed.

Angelique untied the string and pulled the paper back. There were a few outfits and toys for the baby along with a framed picture of the family and some letters. Angelique ran her fingers across the picture frame. The sound of Hazel's voice interrupted her thoughts.

"I can't believe you're married and settled down. I always thought I would come visit you in New York or someplace,"

Hazel remarked as she finished off the last of her ginger beer.

"I have a good life here. A lot of people would love to be in my shoes."

"Yes. But you always told everybody you were leaving Jamaica."

Angelique absorbed the words for a moment. The pull of that northern Mecca where so many people she had known had gone off in search of a better life had always been great. The longing was still there for her. It had always been there. "Well it's not just me anymore, you know. I have a child and a husband now. I can't just pick up and leave." She bounced a restless Carmen on her lap who seemed to sense her mother's agitation. "We should go to the house. Carmen will start fussing out here if she don't get to sleep soon."

Hazel's eyes roamed all over the house. She wandered from room to room drinking in everything in sight. Angelique watched her cousin's movements with interest. She had worked hard to get the house in order before Hazel's arrival. She made sure the top of every doorframe was dusted, every room was swept from corner to corner, and all the white bed sheets and table linens had been laid out in the hot island sun to bleach out. She'd even broken her silence and sweetly asked Clifton for money for a new outfit to wear on the day she would be picking up Hazel.

"What for? How many dress you have in there that haven't even seen the light of day?" he had asked. Angelique had just stared at him for a moment before adding, "And a new handbag too." He'd given in without a fight and peeled off several bills from his billfold. She'd tucked the money in the pocket of her skirt and walked away. She would never let him know that she ever needed anything. The power was in not needing it, or him.

"So, only the three of you in this big house?" Hazel ran her hand along the plush fabric of the settee in the living room.

"Yes."

Hazel's eyes ran across the lines of the mahogany furniture. She wandered into the guest bedroom and drew in her breath as she took in the large, bright sunny space. Great care had been taken to set up this room in particular. New linens and a rich, golden-colored spread covered the large bed. Fresh flowers adorned every surface, and Angelique's best towels were folded and placed near the new porcelain wash basin she had just purchased. Angelique could see the longing in her cousin's face. Hazel's family was not exactly poor, but she and her two younger sisters used to share one bedroom back home. More than once when they were growing up, Hazel's mother had swallowed her pride to ask Angelique's mother for things for the children. Angelique had gotten herself in trouble for giving her cousin some of her "good" clothes. It didn't matter how much it cost or how her mother scolded her; anything she didn't consider stylish enough went home with Hazel who was happy to have anything brand new.

"Life is treating you well," Hazel said, smiling.

Angelique shrugged.

"So how is it being a member of the well-to-do Chambers family now?"

Angelique mulled the question over. Some things had gotten better, but nothing was as she thought it would be. She was married to a man that acted more like a boy. His parents were standoffish towards her and now appeared indifferent to their son's behavior. Mr. Chambers had grown tired of talking to his son about responsibility, leaving it instead to the mother who did nothing. Jennifer Chambers either gave up out of frustration, or simply ignored her son's antics as long as it did not reflect badly on her. At least she had a beautiful granddaughter she could spoil. She came by regularly to "steal my grandbaby away just to take her up the road for a bit." At first, Angelique was happy with the attention Mrs. Chambers paid to the baby. It gave Angelique time to rest and she hoped

Mrs. Chambers would warm up to her. This was not always the case. Mrs. Chambers kept a polite distance from Angelique, saving all her affection for little Carmen.

"It's fine," she said distractedly, then immediately brightened when she saw Hazel's worried face. "Hey, you bring anything dressy to wear? I know you love a good party and these people love to show off so tonight should be fun." Angelique said.

Hazel hesitated for a second before reaching for her suitcase and smiling. Well, I did bring this one dress…"

"Let me see it. If I don't like it, you can have one of mine."

Hazel pursed her lips and raised an eyebrow.

"Don't bother making up your face like that. We have to show them who we are. Besides, I've never seen you turn down an offer for a new frock yet."

"Alright, give me a dress. I'll look better in it than you anyway."

Angelique kissed her teeth and laughed. "Okay, let's hurry. I know you'll need time to work on that head of yours too," she said, reaching towards Hazel's hair.

Hazel playfully shoved her hand away and walked towards the bathroom. "I'm going to go bathe. Just have my new dress and shoes waiting for me when I get out," she called over her shoulder.

Angelique smiled to herself and headed out of the room. "Yes, Miss Hazel."

For years, the Chambers had been known for their lavish parties. The laundress and house maids would spend days washing linens, buffing the wood floors until they gleamed, and polishing the silver. The gardeners would spend hours manicuring the property so that any guest's first impression when they arrived would be a lasting one.

The Chambers' parties were attended by Kingston's elite—doctors, lawyers, government officials, and wealthy business owners. Angelique had only attended one such event soon after she'd first arrived on the Chambers' doorstep a little over a year ago. Mrs. Chambers had remained close to her future daughter-in-law that night; Angelique thought it was to make sure that she was comfortable and to share some humor about the guests, but as the night went on, she had the impression that these were more nudges to show her how to act. "That dress is too short!" or "Why she didn't take a fork *and* a knife?" or "Some people like to smile too much." Angelique had hid her annoyance at the time out of respect, but she wasn't going to let that woman treat her like she was country again.

The event planned for today would be a chance for Angelique to release some tension and to give Hazel a glance into her new world. There were more guests than usual and a greater variety of people. Not all were of the "high class" that normally attended. A few people of questionable background seemed to be milling about the property, especially some of the young women that Angelique's mother would describe as "slack," those girls who didn't enunciate their words, who slurped tea, and talked with their mouths full. Angelique snickered to herself when she saw one girl in particular. She was about 20 years old and was savoring the chicken that the Chambers' cook had prepared with such care—seasoned, cooked, and carefully arranged on a platter. Mrs. Chambers watched in horror as the girl proceeded to clean all the meat off the chicken bone with her teeth, and then expertly sucked all the marrow out of what remained while she moved about the room eavesdropping on various conversations until she got bored with the topic. There were a few others like this girl. At first glance they could blend in, but a closer look revealed the cheapness of their dresses, the shoes that didn't quite fit right, burning with each step as they tried to hide the limp. And cheap perfume. The kind of perfume that when it mixed with the warm air and clung to the body too long, it left a musty and frowzy scent. It was then that

Angelique discovered the source of the odor that had been plaguing her for almost a year.

Clifton stood amongst a small crowd of people laughing and drinking shots of dark rum. He was in the center of the crowd, as usual, telling stories and making jokes. Angelique frowned when she saw a girl she did not recognize, one of "those" girls, laughing a little too hard at whatever Clifton said. As she watched it appeared to her that the girl never strayed too far from wherever Clifton was. Angelique crossed the room and hooked her arm into Clifton's, and then turned to stare directly at the girl. The girl laughed slightly and sucked her teeth. Angelique narrowed her eyes and looked at her with disdain. "Do I know you?" she asked.

The girl stretched her face into a grin, revealing slightly crooked teeth, like she had sucked her thumb as a child. "No, you don't know me, but I know him." She nodded at Clifton.

"How do you know my husband?"

"Your husband?" She laughed and turned slightly away.

Angelique stepped forward menacingly and stopped. There it was. That musty, stale scent that had permeated her house and spoiled her sheets. That smell that assaulted her whenever she picked up Clifton's dirty clothes off the floor. It was her smell. The girl seemed to sense that Angelique had figured out who she was and smiled even broader.

"You nasty—"

"What is going on here?" Mrs. Chambers appeared out of nowhere, one hand on her hip, the other holding her drink. Angelique said nothing, but her clenched fist and pulsating jaw line told Mrs. Chambers everything she needed to know. Mrs. Chambers stepped toward the girl, leaning forward so she could whisper low enough for her to hear. "You get out of my house right now, you hear? Take your nasty dirty friends with you and don't come back."

The girl twisted her mouth to the side and looked over at Clifton who was stealthily making his way to the other side of the room and away from the growing conflict.

"Your husband," she sniffed at Angelique, "I hear you went and got pregnant. That's how you ended up with a husband."

Angelique growled. "Yes, *my* husband," she emphasized. "You don't worry about my business. You just need to make sure you don't cross me," she threatened.

The girl let out a dismissive laugh and began to turn away from Angelique. She didn't move fast enough. The large red stain grew as the red rum punch dripped from her face and seeped its way down the front of her dress. The smug look she had worn only moments earlier had quickly turned to shock after Angelique had snatched the glass from Mrs. Chambers' hand and threw the contents in the girl's face. Mrs. Chambers had stood frozen for a second before moving swiftly to redirect the crowd's attention away from the altercation. Angelique watched, satisfied as the girl hurriedly exited through the front door. The only evidence she had been in the room was the trail of droplets of red juice left on the floor. That and the fading scent of her cheap perfume.

After throwing the drink on the girl, Angelique began to hunt for her husband who had taken refuge around the corner of the verandah, watching the drama unfold as his mistress made her quick exit, wiping fruit punch from her eyes. He did find the situation funny at first, holding his lean stomach with one hand while covering his mouth with the hand holding his drink as he doubled over with laughter. That was until he saw his wife come outside looking for him. Her body was so tense with anger, and he could almost see the fire dancing in her eyes, even in the twilight of evening. When she found him, she unleashed a string of curses that prompted his horrified mother to insist that he take his wife and leave her property immediately. His father tried to calm Angelique down.

"Hush, hush," Mr. Chambers kept saying to her while he held her flailing arms down and glared at his son. "Fool, fool boy!"

Hazel had stood by, shock registering on her face as she covered her mouth with both hands. Angelique could not be soothed and proceeded to call her husband every foul name she could think of. The only way they could even get her to leave the yard was for Clifton to lead the way. She marched behind him all the way back to their house, cursing at his back while a stunned Hazel dutifully followed her cousin as passersby looked on with curiosity or amusement. Inside the house Angelique began hurling fixtures and ornaments in addition to the insults.

Clifton weakly attempted to defend himself. He hurled back insults, and then accused her of trapping him into marriage. That had been a mistake. Angelique quickly reminded him of the circumstances of that fateful night and concluded by warning him that if he ever shamed her again like he did that night it would cost him more than he could ever imagine. "And if I see that girl again, there's going to be one hell to pay, you hear?"

Clifton had strode over to Angelique and stood toe-to-toe with her. He was dumbfounded as her eyes blazed right back at him, unflinching. He had realized then, the full impact of what he had gotten himself into. Angelique was not the soft, naïve girl that he thought she was. He had declared that no woman would talk to him like that in his own house. He did this as he backed away from her. He continued to assert his manhood as he rummaged in the wardrobe for the extra sheets to make up his bed on the settee, mumbling to himself before finally falling asleep.

Hazel had hastily returned back to Somerset Grove the next day, but not before trying to convince Angelique to take her baby and go back home with her.

"I can't," had been Angelique's reply. Hazel had been puzzled, asking why in God's name she would want to live like that. Angelique recalled her last moments in Somerset Grove when her mother had attacked her after learning she was pregnant. More painful than the physical punishment was the emotional pain and embarrassment of the incident. No better than a common tramp, her mother had said. Had told her that she would never be better. Even though her mother had tried to make amends at the wedding, she could not forget those words. She would never go crawling back to that woman's house. "When you see my mother please tell her I said hello," Angelique instructed. "And make sure you don't tell anybody about that little disagreement from last night."

Hazel had nodded unconvincingly.

Angelique thought back to how she concluded that Hazel was the one who told her mother about the pregnancy and how quickly she had revealed Angelique's secret. Hazel could fold like a chicken coop in a hurricane if asked the right question. "Hazel, I *know* you. It's because of you why I had to leave home the way I did. Do *not* say anything. If I hear anything, it's going to be me and you," she had warned.

Hazel had looked around at the house. Cushions, picture frames, and broken china figurines still lay on the floor where they'd landed the night before. Evidence of what Angelique was capable of when she felt betrayed. "I won't say anything. But don't be afraid to come home."

Angelique watched as the car drove away from the house, Hazel leaning out the window waving goodbye. She sighed heavily as she sat down on the steps of the verandah, feeling the moist heat of the day rising. She closed her eyes and leaned forward as she tried to breathe deeply. Tears rolled down her face and spilled freely into her lap. The sound of a car rolling up the driveway made her look up. She wiped her eyes quickly as she saw Clifton get out of the car looking at her cautiously. He flashed one of his cocky smiles at her as he pulled a gift wrapped package from the vehicle. She held his gaze for only a moment before getting up and walking in the house, slamming the door behind her.

12

"Mummy!" Angelique finally looked up from the newspaper and smiled wearily at her three-year-old daughter. Carmen pulled her mother's skirt and bared her teeth at her in one of those smiles that said she was ready to have her picture taken. Angelique laughed at her daughter who didn't really want anything, other than her mother's attention.

Carmen resembled her mother in every way except for the eyes rimmed with long, dark lashes—those belonged to her father. The little girl had long, tight, spiral curled hair that Angelique carefully brushed into two braided pigtails and tied with ribbons that always matched her dress. Her skin was that same copper red as her mother's. The most striking resemblance was the restless spirit she carried. Angelique often bragged that as soon as Carmen was able to walk, she was off as fast as her little legs would carry her. And more than once they'd found her wandering around in the yard after figuring out how to unlatch the door and climb down the stairs. No matter how she was scolded or threatened, Carmen would laugh and run off again as soon as she was able. Most of the discipline for these escapades came from Angelique; Clifton was usually too wrapped up in his own mischief to worry about whatever wrongs his daughter was committing. While they had not had a repeat episode of that night at the Chambers' party two years ago, the memory and a vague hint of tension remained between them.

"Where are you going?" Angelique called to Clifton who was headed towards the front door.

Clifton looked back. "Just up the road," he said casually.

"Take your daughter with you."

"I'm just going up the road for a minute."

"So what's the problem then? Take your daughter with you, please. Ever since you cut back on Miss Bailey's days, I've had so much more to do, and it's hard to do it when I have to keep track of this one." She tilted her head to one side and smiled as sweetly as she could at her husband. Clifton was grateful for any moment when Angelique was not angry with him. Ever since that day almost two years ago, he had gone out of his way to be more respectful, though his nature still led him astray. He relented and scooped up his daughter before heading out the door.

"I need some money," Angelique called to him before he could step outside.

"What happened to the money I gave you three days ago?"

"How long did you expect that little bit of money to last?" Angelique said. "I need to go to the market and Carmen needs some new clothes," she added.

He sucked his teeth before putting Carmen down and pulling some bills from his pocket. "Here." He held out the money towards her. "Don't spend it all."

"Don't tell me what to do."

He smiled and leaned over to kiss her. She turned her head and the kiss landed on her cheek. She slid off the chair away from him and smiled coyly. "I have things to do. What time are you coming back?"

Clifton rubbed the back of his neck and raised an exasperated eyebrow at his wife. "I don't know. I won't be too long." He picked up Carmen again and walked out the door, leaving Angelique alone in the house.

She walked over to the window and watched them leave before heading to her bedroom. She traced her fingers along the family photo sitting on top of the dresser, then stooped down to pull the last drawer all the way out, placing it carefully on the floor. She reached her hand inside and felt around until she located the envelope and pulled it out. A familiar ritual now, she counted the bills and coins inside before adding some of the bills she'd managed to pry from Clifton. She retrieved a crinkled up note from inside the envelope and carefully unfolded it, smoothing it out once more. It was one of the letters she had received years earlier when Hazel came to visit. She re-read the words on the page:

Dear Angelique,

I hope this letter finds you well. I have sent Hazel some things for the baby. The money inside the envelope is from your father so you can use it to come home for a visit or for whatever you need. I'm hoping to see my grandchild soon. Everyone here is doing well, but not too much is going on. Mrs. Brown's daughter, the one you went to school with before you were made to leave, has gone off to New York City to become a nurse. She made her mother and father so proud. The rest of your friends from school are still living here. Anyway, tell everybody I said hello. I hope to receive a letter from you soon as I haven't heard from you since your wedding. Love to all your dear family.

Mum

Angelique thought back to the day when she'd first read the letter. She could feel the sting of her mother's words from miles away as if she'd reached through the paper and slapped Angelique in the face. She had not been thrown out of school as her mother intimated. She knew the truth. Even more hurtful than that subtle rewriting of the story was the way her mother had to tell her that Mrs. Brown's daughter had gone off to chase *her* dream. As if to say, "Look at her and look at *you*." *She* was the one that was supposed to be in New York City, not that girl. Lisa Brown had never even said anything about wanting to emigrate. Angelique had crumpled up the letter and thrown it in the rubbish, the family photo relegated to the back of the bottom drawer. But the day after the Chambers' party she had retrieved the letter, smoothing it out carefully to reread it. The photo took its place on the dresser to remind her of where she had been. From that day she had saved every bit of money she could, skimming off a pound or two or few shillings here or there from whatever money Clifton had given her for the household. Each time she managed to get more she would store it in the envelope, reading the letter over and over each time, waiting for her turn.

The familiar smell of fried dumplings and sweet plantains filled the house. The Chambers gathered around the dining table for their usual Sunday morning breakfast before church. Mrs. Chambers sat poised, absentmindedly smoothing her hands over her outfit and patting her hair every few minutes as if she were on display in front of dignitaries having tea with the queen instead of in her dining room with her immediate family. Clifton played with Carmen, making her giggle out loud. Mr. Chambers, as usual, frowned over his reading glasses at his son before returning to his task of thumbing through his Bible, looking for a scripture to read to the family before breakfast. Angelique rested her chin in the palm of her hand as she leaned over the table watching the family routine. It was both amusing and annoying to her, this Sunday ritual. Mr. Chambers never cracked that Bible open except for Sunday mornings at the table or in church, and Mrs. Chambers treated the day like it was a fashion show, saying her hallelujahs a little too loudly to gain more attention from the other parishioners than she was trying to gain from God. Not that Angelique had ever been very spiritual, even though she'd always gone to church every Sunday, but at least her family never put on a show. And Mr. Chambers playing pastor at the breakfast table every Sunday was a bit too much. Angelique rolled her eyes and twisted her mouth to the side. Mr. Chambers didn't seem to notice Angelique's expression and found what she thought was a particularly long and condemning passage to read. As he droned on, Angelique stared at her plate, wondering if the dumplings would still be warm by the time he finished. Mr. Chambers had barely spoken the last word before the sound of forks clinking against the china filled the room. The cook had laid out the remainder of the dishes—ackee and saltfish, roasted breadfruit, and tea rounded out the breakfast offerings, and it appeared none of it would be going to waste.

Midway through the meal Angelique spoke up. "I want to go to nursing school," she announced.

"You want to do what?" Mrs. Chambers raised an eyebrow.

"Nursing school," Angelique repeated. "I want to become a nurse."

"For what?" Mrs. Chambers was genuinely confused.

"I'm tired of sitting home all the time. I want to do something. I was very ambitious when I was in school, you know," Angelique said proudly. "I always planned to travel and work abroad."

"Well, looks like that plan's really not going to work now, is it?" Mr. Chambers shoveled a forkful of food in his mouth, not really interested in the answer. "Besides, you never did finish school, did you?"

Angelique was not deterred. "I can still become a nurse," she insisted.

"Really? And who is going to look after Carmen while you're off pursuing this nursing business? Because I'll tell you now, it's not going to be me." Mrs. Chambers had put down her fork and was staring at Angelique.

"I'm not asking you to do anything for me. I can take care of us myself."

Clifton sat watching the ping pong match between his mother and wife. He knew he should stick up for his wife, tell his mother that it was fine with him if Angelique wanted to go to school. It would be good for him—school would give her something she could focus her attention on besides what he was doing. She was not the carefree girl he knew before she'd gotten pregnant; she would cut him down anytime she thought he was out getting into anything. It was like being married to a razor. But, he did not want to speak up against his parents either. They already had enough reason to criticize him and this would not make it any easier for him. *Look, even that country girl you got pregnant and married have some ambition. What is wrong with you, man?* He got up and wandered off to the kitchen in search of more dumplings.

Angelique watched Clifton walking away and shook her head. *If I have to wait on that man to stand up and do anything, I'll be waiting until Jesus comes.*

"You don't need to go to school for any nursing. You already have somebody to take care of full time." Mrs. Chambers gestured towards Carmen, who, after losing her playmate, had amused herself by squeezing the plantains in her hand and dropping them in big greasy clumps on the floor. Angelique grabbed the dish away from Carmen and started wiping the child's hands with a napkin.

Mr. Chambers shook his head. "Imagine if you had two of them."

Angelique froze for a moment. What if she had two of them? She saw her future mapped out in front of her with two, three, or four children. And then walking through Kingston wondering if every child she saw in town was the half-brother or half-sister of one of her own.

"Best you forget about that nursing business and take care of this one you have here," said Mr. Chambers. He dropped his fork with a clatter and wiped his mouth with a napkin as if to signal the end of the discussion.

Angelique looked down at her plate and silently fumed. Nobody was going to stop her from doing what she wanted. Carmen looked at the faces around her for a moment before going back to playing in her food. Clifton came back into the room, empty handed but chewing on something, seemingly oblivious to the tension in the room that he so cunningly avoided a few minutes ago. He sat down and looked over at Angelique's plate. "You going to finish that?" he asked. Before she could answer, he had already snatched the last fried dumpling off her plate. She watched him chew, mentally counting the money she had hidden in the dresser.

"What is wrong with you? You sick?" Mrs. Chambers looked at Angelique from the other side of the bakery where she'd been examining rum cakes. Angelique was leaning against the window, fanning herself and dabbing at the small beads of perspiration that lined her lip and forehead. She felt lightheaded. Her stomach was unsettled; the bile rose up in her and threatened to spill out. This feeling had been plaguing her for several days now, but this had been the worst day so far. Every time it felt like she was feeling better, the next day she would wake up horribly ill, barely making it to the bathroom to empty the contents of her stomach. She had felt a little better today, and so decided to accompany Mrs. Chambers on one of her excursions around town. That was a decision she came to regret as the queasy feeling soon reappeared and all Angelique wanted to do was get away from the sickly sweet smell that filled the air in the bakery.

"I-I don't know. My stomach is hurting me," Angelique managed to say.

"Your stomach sick? For how long now?"

"I don't know. The last two or three days."

"So why you never say anything?" Mrs. Chambers walked over and felt Angelique's forehead. She welcomed the coolness of the older woman's fingers. "We should go home." She turned back to the woman behind the counter to retrieve her package and ushered Angelique out the door. "I wonder if you're pregnant?" she said more to herself than to Angelique.

Angelique laid her hand on her flat stomach as if doing so would immediately confirm or deny Mrs. Chambers' suspicions. A small feeling of panic rose up inside her at the thought. She looked up the street to avoid making eye contact with her mother-in-law. She felt a shiver go through her. "I think it's just the flu or something."

Mrs. Chambers studied her a moment longer and frowned. "I don't know where you would catch the flu from." She touched Angelique's forehead again. "You're probably right though. Look how you're shivering. It must be 90 degrees out here."

Relief spilled over Angelique. Despite her discomfort she managed a faint smile.

"What are you smiling for? You're glad to be sick?" Mrs. Chambers shook her head. "Come, let's go home. Looks like whatever you got is creeping up in your head."

When they arrived home, Mrs. Chambers immediately began firing out orders, starting with Angelique. "You, get into bed," she said, pointing at the guest room. Angelique would rather have gone back to her own house, but she was too exhausted to argue and so she dragged herself towards the bedroom. "Rita, make some soup, please. And bring her some of that cerasse tea, too." Angelique cringed at the thought of drinking that nasty bush tea. It reminded her of being back home.

"If you have regular black tea, I would prefer that."

Rita looked at both Angelique and Mrs. Chambers, unsure of what to do.

"You think this is a fancy hotel, or do you think you know better than me?" Mrs. Chambers kissed her teeth. "You'll drink the cerasse tea unless you like being sick." Angelique gave up protesting and went to lie down in the guest bedroom.

Over the next several days, Angelique battled her sickness. Mrs. Chambers handled most of her care personally. She would wipe down Angelique's face with a cool wash cloth when she was feverish or tuck her in with extra blankets when she had chills. She would bring in the spicy chicken soup prepared by Rita and stay with Angelique until it was all finished. On more than one occasion, Angelique would wake up to find Mrs. Chambers studying her, pressing her hand lightly on Angelique's cheek or forehead to check her temperature. Angelique could not remember the last time she felt the loving touch of a mother's hand. Her own mother seemed to save all of her affection for Angelique's brother once she'd turned twelve. "You're not a little girl anymore," her mother would tell her whenever she sought attention. She almost enjoyed being sick and having Mrs. Chambers personally take care of her.

Three days later, Angelique awoke with the morning sun peeking in through the curtains. She slipped her hand from underneath the blanket and placed it on her forehead. It felt neither warm nor clammy. The sinus headache that had plagued her for the last day and a half had disappeared. She slipped the hand back under the covers and then slowly stretched her limbs, which no longer ached. She kicked the covers off and slid her feet over the edge of the bed.

"You're back from the dead," Mrs. Chamber's exclaimed upon entering the room. She held a tray filled with juice, water, and the dreaded cerasse tea.

Angelique smiled faintly. "Yes, so I don't need *that* anymore." She pointed at the teacup.

"Nonsense! You want to get sick again? As a matter of fact, drink it first," her mother-in-law ordered. "You can have the juice after you take your bath." She began walking around the room, snapping open the drapes and flooding the room with light.

She pinched her face as she forced herself to swallow the bitter liquid in as few takes as possible. She shook her head and squeezed her eyes closed as she finished the last of the tea, then exhaled. "Where is Carmen?" Angelique asked.

"You must be feeling better. That's the first you've asked about that child in days."

Angelique ignored the comment. "Is she here?"

Mrs. Chambers ran her finger across the top of the dresser and frowned at the dust. "She's been here the whole time. I couldn't let her come in here, of course. You would've made that child sick."

"Well, I'm feeling better now. Make her come in, please."

"No. This room has more germs than anything."

Angelique rolled her eyes while her mother-in-law gingerly held the pillows as she tried to pull the pillow cases off with only two fingers. "I'll take them off, thank you."

Mrs. Chambers immediately dropped the pillows and absentmindedly brushed her hands together as if trying to rub dust off of them. "Well, come to the kitchen when you're ready," she said as she headed for the doorway.

"Where is Clifton?" Angelique asked.

Her mother-in-law stopped in her tracks but didn't turn back toward Angelique. "I don't know," she said before exiting the room. It was true. Clifton had disappeared the day his mother told him his wife was horribly sick, leaving his daughter with her without so much as a "soon come" to let her know when he might return. Now that it was the weekend, who knew when he would return from his week of frolicking. His father had washed his hands of him again, vowing to fire his worthless backside when he returned to work. Mrs. Chambers had been torn between wanting to defend her free-spirited son and being angry with him for leaving her to care for the wife and daughter he had apparently grown tired of and decided to dump on her. He treated Carmen like a toy that he only took out to play with on occasion. So absent was he that Carmen would call him by his first name instead of "Daddy" until her grandmother would correct her. "That is your father. You don't call him by his first name."

Carmen would just look at her grandmother, her little hands pressed against her hips and ask, "Where is Daddy Clifton?"

Her grandfather would dismiss his wife's attempts to correct their granddaughter. "Well if he acted like a father, his daughter wouldn't be calling to him like some stranger. A grown man like that carrying on like he has no sense."

Still, Angelique held out some hope that he would turn around, become attentive, and treat her like he cared for her. Not like she was one of those common girls who sucked on chicken bones in public because they weren't raised with any manners. Her patience was wearing thin, though. She thought about the dresser at home that held the folded letter and money she had hidden away before dragging herself in the direction of the washroom.

13

They stood in front of the house looking up at the walkway leading to the verandah. The house somehow seemed much smaller since the last time she had been there. Carmen stood impatiently by her mother, kicking at the red dirt. Angelique looked down to see her daughter scuffing the new white shoes she'd just purchased.

"Stop that!" Angelique scolded her daughter. She pulled a handkerchief out of her purse and wiped the dirt off the shoes, then tugged sharply on the hem of Carmen's dress to straighten it out. Carmen tried to pull away, but Angelique had a firm grasp on her as she continued fussing over her appearance. "Stand still and let me fix you up. I don't want anyone thinking I don't know how to take care of you." Carmen continued to twist in vain. Finally satisfied with her daughter's appearance, Angelique once again turned her attention to the house looming in front of her. "Come. Let's go inside." Angelique tugged Carmen towards the front steps.

"Where are we going, Mummy?" Carmen asked.

"To meet your grandmother."

It seemed like several minutes had passed after Angelique had knocked on the door. She thought about leaving several times before the front door finally swung open. The woman stood in the doorway drying her hands on a dish towel. She looked the same as she had the last time Angelique saw her, with the exception of a few stray gray hairs that escaped from the low bun she wore on the back of her head. The woman examined Angelique carefully from head to toe, taking in the crisp skirt suit, white linen gloves, and the wide brimmed hat tilted smartly to the side. A bit much for a Thursday afternoon in the country, but she said nothing. She turned her attention to the little girl who had been staring at her with an expression of curiosity, then turned back to her daughter.

"So, you're not going to hug your mother?" Ruby asked.

Angelique stepped to her mother to be embraced. She stiffened slightly at the elder woman's touch and backed away quickly, pulling her daughter in between them. "This is Carmen," she said as she pushed the little girl towards her grandmother. Carmen looked up at the woman studying her.

"She's pretty," Ruby remarked. She reached down and touched the little girl's cheek. "What are you putting on her skin? You should put cocoa butter on her. Especially since you have her burning up in the sun."

Angelique bristled at the criticism.

"Where's Daddy?" she asked, ignoring her mother's comment.

"Down at the shop as always. He soon come. Are you hungry?"

She fought the urge to tell her mother she didn't need anything from her, even though she was starving from the long drive from Kingston and she knew Carmen was probably hungry too. They had left the home in such a hurry that Angelique did not think to pack any food for the trip. The last argument with Clifton about him staying out all night with God knows what piece of trash had been the last straw. Her mother-in-law couldn't bring herself to say anything critical to her son, and his father had washed his hands of the whole business, leaving Angelique alone to handle it. Angelique had packed two suitcases with clothes, her papers, and the money from the bottom of the dresser drawer. She threw everything in the car and pulled away, almost running over Clifton when he tried to stop her from taking his car.

"Move before I run you down tonight," she had shouted at him. He'd gotten out of the way at the last second, still cursing at her as she drove down the driveway.

Carmen had shown no signs of anger, confusion, or sadness. She'd just watched as the arguing went on and dutifully climbed in the car when told to. She'd watched her father growing smaller as they drove away and waved goodbye to him while he stared at the car as it left.

Angelique looked down at Carmen who was trying to peer past her grandmother into the kitchen. "Whatever you're cooking smells nice. Maybe we'll have just a little taste."

They walked back to the kitchen. The rooms looked the same as the day Angelique left, almost four years ago. The heavy mahogany furniture in the living room was in the same place it was before and the old pictures that had looked old fashioned back then still hung on the walls in their respective spots. The place still seemed overstuffed with things and Angelique began to feel that familiar closed in feeling. Their stay here would be short, Angelique decided.

The air in the house seemed as heavy with humidity as it was with tension. Angelique couldn't wait for someone to come home or some distraction to arise. Anything to take her mother's focus off of her. She'd run out of small talk and spent so much time fussing over Carmen's appearance that the little girl became annoyed and began pushing her mother's hands away. Finally, the back door to the kitchen swung open and Angelique's father appeared in the doorway. He had grayed around his temples and his eyes crinkled more when he laughed, but otherwise he looked the same.

"Oh my goodness! My mind jus' pass on you and here you are." Byron laughed at the sight of his daughter. She ran over to hug him, inhaling the familiar scent of wood and dust on his clothes. He embraced her warmly before turning his attention to the little girl who studied him from the kitchen table. "Is that my granddaughter? What a way but she big," he exclaimed with pride as he picked Carmen up by her arms and wrapped her in a bear hug. Carmen had no reaction for a moment, but soon started giggling.

"Well, she has certainly taken to her grandfather. Just like her mother," Ruby remarked. Angelique thought she detected something in Ruby's face, but her mother quickly lowered her eyes to avoid making contact.

"So how long are you staying?" Byron asked.

"I hadn't planned any specific date to leave."

"What does that mean?" Ruby asked. "All this time you've been away and you never had time to come back. Now all of sudden you don't have any schedule for when you returning to your own house? What is going on?"

"I don't have to answer to anyone. I can come and go as I please. If you want me to leave I'll leave, don't worry yourself."

"I didn't say I wanted you to leave. You're welcome to stay. I just wanted to know what brought you here all of a sudden."

Angelique looked at her mother. She thought about telling the truth, but decided against it. "Nothing is wrong. I just came to visit."

Ruby eyed her daughter suspiciously, but decided to drop it. "Your room is still the same as when you left it. Your father can bring your bags in for you."

Even though the days floated into weeks, it seemed like time had stood still. The routine was the same—breakfast, clean up, sitting on the verandah watching the sun slip over the trees while Angelique waited for something to happen other than the random visits from curious neighbors who would stop by to see whether she was still there and more importantly, why her husband never showed up. Angelique was curious, too. She was sure Clifton would have made his way to Somerset Grove by now, if only to curse her out for leaving and tell her she must come home and stop shaming him. The long walks to the post office seemed to take even longer on the return trip when she learned there was no mail for her. He couldn't even be bothered to write.

That's what made the decision to leave so much easier.

"We're leaving."

"To where?" Ruby threw the question over her shoulder as she inspected the contents of the pot boiling on the stove.

"Toronto."

"To who?"

"Toronto. In Canada."

"I know where it is," Ruby said, annoyed. "But what do you mean, you're going to Toronto? Where did this come from all of a sudden?"

"I've been planning it for quite a while now. There are lots of good jobs out there, and I'm going to nursing school once I get the few high school credits that I need." That wasn't exactly the truth. She had really just decided on it over the last few days. New York City had been the goal, but Ruby had spent the better part of last night's dinner talking about how Mrs. Brown's daughter was doing so well in the big apple and had recently gotten married to a Trinidadian who had some sort of import business and treated his new wife like a queen.

"Imagine that," Ruby had said.

Angelique made up her mind; the further north she traveled, the better.

"So, who is going to take care of Carmen while you're in school and Clifton is at work?"

Angelique didn't answer and tried to avoid her mother's stare as Ruby turned around to look at her.

"I don't know how you think you're going to manage by yourself. No family to watch the child, working and paying for your schooling. You're better off just staying where you are. You can't be dragging that little baby to a foreign country all by yourself." Ruby replaced the lid on the pot and walked out of the room, leaving Angelique lost in thought as she watched her daughter flipping the pages of a picture book.

14

Ruby

WINTER 1949

Ruby sucked in her breath as she grabbed onto the doorknob and bedroom doorframe to steady herself. Her mind whirled around as she tried to grasp what was happening. The sudden pain caught her off guard since the baby had been less active over the last week or so. When she caught her breath, she called for her mother who lay sleeping in the next room. As soon as Ingrid assessed the situation, she quickly led Ruby back to her bed before running to the kitchen and asking Miss Mavis, the cook Byron had hired, to run for the midwife. When Miss Mavis returned, Ingrid asked her to send someone to look for Byron who had left early for work that day.

When Byron arrived Ingrid instructed him to sit down in the living room and wait. She told him everything was fine, but the slightly panicked look on her face led Byron to believe otherwise. He paced up and down, pausing only briefly whenever he heard Ruby cry out in anguish. Finally, the screams stopped and it was quiet. Too quiet. The bedroom door opened and Ingrid emerged looking tired and defeated. She didn't have to say anything for Bryon to know that her silence meant stillness.

Ruby lay in the bed staring vacantly at the wall on the other side of the room. On the right stood the midwife who had just finished wrapping the tiny form in a blanket after bathing the lifeless body. Ruby couldn't bring herself to hold him at first, but the midwife convinced her she needed to say goodbye. Later, they buried their baby in a small plot by the edge of the property. Ruby stared dry-eyed into the hole, but hung onto Byron for strength.

Ingrid left for Panama a few weeks later. Her sorrow over the loss of her grandson made getting home to see her aging mother all the more urgent. She didn't say when she planned to return and Ruby wasn't sure that she ever would.

"You don't really need me now," she told Ruby when she asked when Ingrid would be back. Ruby didn't reply, but hoped her mother would read the truth in her eyes—she would always need her.

15

She moved through the days as one would watch a movie they walked into the middle of. Detached, lost, and ready to leave if the storyline didn't improve. At first Byron tried his best to cheer her up, but then decided that Ruby just needed more time to get over the loss of her son and the departure of her mother. He did believe that she would come back to life again, and believed that another child might be the answer. It had been more than six months and Byron thought that pregnancy would pull Ruby out from under her dark cloud.

Ruby was not over the loss. She was not sure she was ready to be. The baby had been her last tie to her ex-husband, Winston. At one time the pregnancy meant that she would have to stay here. Now it meant that she could leave if she wanted to.

Ruby had heard that Winston and Cynthia were no longer together, but that was only rumor. She hadn't spoken to Anne since moving to the other side of Somerset Grove and hadn't heard that Cynthia had returned to Jamaica. Still, she could go to England and look for Winston. She didn't have a husband to send for her, but she could get enough money from Byron to afford to go visit for a few months. She could figure out how to stay once she got there.

The more she thought about it, the more convinced Ruby was that she *needed* to take this trip. Winston owed her. She wanted to see his face when she told him their child had died. She wanted to show him that she had moved on. But, she also wanted to know why he had abandoned her…and maybe to see if he could revive that spark in her again.

Ruby guessed that Byron must have sensed something. He didn't smile as much as he used to and when he spoke to her he looked into her eyes as if silently imploring her not to leave. When he wasn't talking, he would move about the house shuffling his feet, head hung low. Ruby felt a twinge of guilt, but it couldn't compete with her longing.

She didn't expect to see him there, clearing away the overgrown grasses and weeds that crept up around the tiny cross. Ruby stood several yards away watching as she clutched the small bouquet of hibiscus flowers she had planned to place at the site for the last time before she would leave. She had no idea that Byron came down there to tend to her son's grave. Even in death, Byron claimed as his own the child that Winston had abandoned. Her heart melted once again and the longing Ruby felt seemed to dissipate like the wind.

Ruby quickly turned back toward the house, her thoughts now focused on what she would make her husband for dinner when he returned home.

16

"**Mummy! Tell** him to leave me alone!"

"Stop the fighting, please," Ruby told them both. She stepped out into the yard to find Marlon with a handful of guinep in one hand and the other poised to throw one of the grape-like fruits at his twin sister. Angelique cringed, her skinny 10-year-old body turning away and hands held up defensively to avoid the pelting. Marlon let the guinep fly anyway, striking Angelique in the thigh.

"I hate you," cried Angelique, rubbing the spot where she was hit.

"You mustn't say that, Angelique," Ruby said. "It's only the two of you, you know."

Angelique stared at Ruby, her brows knitted in a frown and hands balled into fists at the sides of her body. "Why don't you say anything to him?" Angelique pointed a finger at Marlon who grinned while standing by his mother.

"Because I'm talking to you right now. I'll deal with him later. You go inside and help Miss Mavis peel the yams since the two of you can't behave."

Angelique opened her mouth to protest then decided against it. She spun on her heel and marched inside the back door, letting it slam behind her.

Ruby rolled her eyes and turned to Marlon who quickly tried to hide the grin that had spread across his face. The first time Ruby held Marlon when he was born, she marveled at how much he looked like the baby she had lost two years earlier. Marlon immediately stole her heart. Ruby hadn't known she was carrying twins until birth when Marlon had shown up after a second wave of labor pains hit minutes after Angelique was born. Ever since that day, Marlon's mischievous ways always made Ruby smile and made it hard for her to discipline him. Byron warned her about favoring one child over the other, but Ruby always brushed it off, and Marlon learned early on that he could get away with much more than his sister. Ruby was tougher on Angelique, but rationalized to herself that it was necessary. She didn't want her daughter growing up to be at anyone's mercy.

"You mustn't tease your sister like that," she told Marlon, then sent him on his way to "find something fi do." Inside, Angelique watched her brother darting off through the grove. Ruby walked in and watched Angelique hacking away at the piece of yellow yam Miss Mavis had given her to peel.

"Angelique, what are you doing? There won't be anything left to cook by the time you finish with it," Ruby said.

Angelique wiped at her eye with the back of her hand and continued butchering the yam.

"Why are you crying? I just asked you to peel one piece of yam and look how you're carrying on," Ruby said.

"Why don't you tell Marlon to peel them?" Angelique mumbled.

"Excuse me? What did you say?" Ruby approached Angelique who threw the yam and knife into the pot and flew out the back door just ahead of Ruby's grasp.

"You love him better than me." Ruby heard her daughter's accusation sail through the open door as she disappeared across the yard.

Ruby turned back and looked at Miss Mavis furiously. Miss Mavis picked up the discarded yam and began to slice it. She didn't say anything to Ruby, but her expression said it all.

"She's getting to be very rebellious," Ruby said defensively.

"She's probably just a little jealous. Maybe she wants to be your favorite," Miss Mavis suggested.

"That's nonsense. I love them equally. Angelique needs some discipline, that's all. I'm going to have a good talking with her when she comes back," Ruby said. "Call me when she comes in the house, please." Ruby disappeared out of the kitchen before she could see Miss Mavis shaking her head in response.

Ruby and Byron ate dinner alone that evening. When Byron asked where the children were, Ruby avoided his eyes and told him she didn't know. "They had some little fight over some foolishness and then they both ran off."

"How long have they been gone?"

"I don't know. A few hours, I guess. I'm just so tired of all of this. Every day they're fussing and fighting," Ruby said, exasperated.

"That's nothing. They're not any different than any other child."

"Maybe they need to be separated more. I was thinking maybe Angelique could go to one of those all-girl schools like in St. Elizabeth's. It will be better for her future anyway."

"What about Marlon? Where do you want to send him?" Byron asked as he examined his wife.

Ruby shrugged. "He can stay here. He should be spending more time with you anyway if you want him to take over the business."

"You can't send one and not the other," Byron warned. "What if Marlon decides his future is not here either? He needs to be prepared."

Ruby stared at Byron.

Byron made the decision for her. "They both go."

17

Angelique

Fall, 1971

The golden hues of the morning sun peeked through the trees as it slowly danced across the sky, bringing with it the promise of an oppressively hot day. The moisture from the night dew hung heavily in the air making the freshly pressed dress Angelique wore cling to her skin. The few curls she let escape from the twisted ponytail she wore began to frizz in the morning heat. She ignored the rumble in her belly awakened by the scent of fried plantains and fish that floated on the breeze as she passed by the last house on the road into town. She looked back up the road she had come. A few people had begun to stir outside their houses as the workday began. A cow wandered aimlessly in the road, her tail occasionally fluttering to brush away a bothersome fly. In the distance, a dog barked at some unseen intruder. "Stop that damn noise!"

rang out from the same direction. The dog let out one last defiant bark before falling silent.

Angelique quickened her step despite the rising heat. The suitcase she carried in her right hand was growing heavy, but she didn't have time to rest or risk drawing questions from curious neighbors.

Thirty minutes later, she arrived on the main street of the town. She set down the suitcase, pulled a white cotton handkerchief from her handbag, and dabbed at the perspiration on her forehead as she looked up and down the street. Finally, she waved down a lone taxi covered in dust from the road. Two other passengers peered out of the window at her. "Where are you going?" The taxi driver leaned out of the window and looked down at the suitcase at her feet.

"Montego Bay."

"*Where* in Montego Bay?" the driver responded, not bothering to mask his annoyance.

She resisted the urge to tell him off. She needed the ride and right now, his rusty shared taxi was the only option. "The airport."

"Come. I'm going that way."

Angelique hesitated and looked up and down the quiet town street before looking back in the taxi. The man in the front seat eyed her with a sly smile. The woman in the backseat turned her attention to the window on the opposite side of the taxi and didn't acknowledge her.

"Come nuh!" the taxi driver demanded impatiently.

Angelique opened the backdoor and put the suitcase between herself and the woman. She'd barely shut the door before the car sped off, leaving a trail of dust.

"Your papers, please." The man behind the counter held out his hand without looking at her.

She handed the documents to him, and then stepped back from the counter. The man reviewed the papers, occasionally peering at her over his reading glasses.

"Purpose of your trip?" he asked.

Angelique pulled her shoulders back as she spoke. "School. I'm going to be a nurse," she said matter-of-factly.

The official looked her up and down again and continued shuffling through the documents. "Are you traveling with anyone?"

She swallowed hard. "No."

He grabbed his rubber stamp and began pounding several pages of her papers with it before handing them back to her. "Welcome to Canada."

18

The first thing she noticed was the bone chilling cold. She pulled her thin coat tighter as the wind wrapped around her and held her in its icy grip. She wiped at her eyes which had begun to water and sniffed to keep her nose from running. Winter had not even hit Winnipeg yet and already the city was feeling its effect. She trudged four more blocks from the bus stop before finally reaching the Victorian-style house she'd been living in ever since she arrived from Toronto. By the time she reached home, her fingers were already tingling with numbness and she struggled to unlock the door to her second floor apartment.

"Angelique, is that you, gyal?" a voice called from upstairs.

Angelique stepped back from her doorway to look up at the woman leaning over the banister. Her neighbor Dahlia grinned down at her. Dahlia was short and curvy, with skin the color of mocha and narrow slanted eyes that nearly closed shut whenever she smiled. She was average looking, but won everyone over, men and women alike, with her playful personality. It was Dahlia who was the first to befriend Angelique at the nursing home where they both worked and who told her about this apartment when Angelique arrived from Toronto after learning that it was too expensive for her to live in that city. Dahlia was also the one who watched out for Angelique at work and chased away the aggressive men who tried to talk to Angelique whenever they went out. "Me seh fi move yourself! Nobody want you!" she would yell and slap away the hands that reached for Angelique's elbow or attempted to snake their arms around her waist. Angelique enjoyed having an older sister watch over her, though she didn't want her to push away all of the men.

"But he's cute," Angelique would sometimes protest.

"Cute mi backside! That one up to no good," Dahlia would say, and that would be the final word.

"I'm cooking some curry chicken." Dahlia held the spoon over the railing as if she needed to prove it.

"It smells good. I'm just going to take a quick bath and come up."

The smell of home wafted through the air of Angelique's tiny three-room apartment and carried her away from the dank, depressing cold that had become her reality. Her body ached from lifting and moving the elderly and infirm at the nursing home. She peeled off her clothes and threw them in the laundry pile before stepping into the tub to wash the acrid smell of death from her body. She submerged herself as far down in the bath water as she could and let loose the flood of tears she'd been holding in for the past three months. Tears streamed down her cheeks in rivers and mixed their saltiness with the bath water. The job was horrible; the old people were nasty and smelled liked they never bathed good one time in their lives. They had the nerve to treat her like they were better than her even though they had been abandoned by their families and couldn't keep from shitting on themselves.

And the little money she was making was not enough. By the time she paid for rent, bus fare, food, and her uniforms, there was hardly anything left. It certainly was not enough to allow her to take her night school classes and then go to nursing school in nine months when she would be qualified to become a landed immigrant. Angelique looked around the depressing dark little apartment with the windows she had to stuff towels in to keep the cold from blowing in through the cracks. This existence was a far cry from the luxurious house on the hill in Kingston and even the little house in Somerset Grove. The money she had brought with her was already dwindling, but they would never know the truth of her existence back home. She would continue to send home money orders for Carmen, and the letters would continue to report the successes of living in a growing metropolis, a nice home, and having a blossoming career.

"Don't worry to pretty yourself up too much. Is only the two a we tonight," Dahlia teased when she telephoned Angelique to find out what was taking so long.

"All right, I'm coming," Angelique said and laughed.

They sat at the tiny table in Dahlia's kitchen eating the curry chicken and rice she had prepared. Brightly colored fabrics adorned the windows and covered the worn furniture. The décor, combined with Dahlia's bright personality, made the room feel warmer than it was, despite the cold wind blowing outside. Angelique's eyes wandered around the place, and then settled on a small silver picture frame sitting on a side table. A small boy dressed in a khaki school uniform with sad eyes stared back at her from the photo.

"Who is that?"

Dahlia looked in the direction that Angelique was pointing. She stopped chewing and remained silent for a moment before turning her eyes away from the photo. "That's Everton. My son," she added and released a heavy sigh.

Angelique looked at Dahlia for a moment before asking the obvious. "He's not with you?"

A little nervous laughter escaped from Dahlia's lips as she smoothed the unwrinkled tablecloth and re-centered the plate in front of her. "I left him with my sister. It was only supposed to be for a little while until I got settled and made enough money to send for him." She looked at the picture quickly, and then looked away again before continuing. "But you know times is hard and the few dollars them paying me is barely enough to buy food and pay rent, so…" her voice trailed off.

"When is the last time you saw him?"

Dahlia pressed her lips together and blinked back the tears that threatened to flow before answering. "That picture was taken just before I left. That was three years ago."

Angelique's eyes widened in surprise. *Three years? How could she leave her child for three years?* When Angelique left Carmen with her mother, she assumed that the little girl would be joining her within the year. That would be nothing. Carmen would get settled quickly and it would be like they were never apart. Angelique was not concerned. "My daughter is with my mother, but I'm sending for her before the end of this year," she said between forkfuls of rice.

"You know I told myself the *same* thing?" Dahlia said. She took a sip from her glass and loudly chewed one of the ice cubes.

Angelique shrugged. Why people always wanted their bad fortune to be yours, she never understood. She pushed the food around on her plate as they sat in silence. It didn't taste so good anymore. She wanted to leave, for the phone to ring, or for someone to walk in. Anything to break up the awkward stillness that had settled over the room like a dense fog. Many of the Caribbean women they worked with at the nursing home had left family behind for the promise of opportunity and a better life, only to find out that the temporary absences could stretch out for years as they struggled with immigration and to make enough money to bring their families back together. That underlying current ran through every conversation, through every woman's face as she silently rationed out her check on payday, and every look of longing as she watched couples and their children coming in for their bi-weekly visits to the mother or father they had stored away in the nursing home so they wouldn't inconvenience their lives. Angelique didn't count herself among them. Everything was going to work out as it should. Still, the vibe in the room was depressing. She ventured a change in the subject. "So, you hear of any dances going on this week?"

Dahlia immediately brightened. "You know, I did hear about something this Friday or Saturday. I would love to get out and dance to some sweet music." Dahlia closed her eyes and swayed in her chair to some secret rhythm that only she could hear. "I'll have to check with my little friend. He knows everything what goes on in town."

Angelique laughed to herself. "The little friend" was Isaac, a mechanic that Dahlia and Angelique had met at a dance a little over a month ago. He had walked up to the two of them while they were sitting at a table and said hello. Even though he had been looking at Angelique when he said it, Dahlia had leaned over and stuck out her hand and enormous chest, blocking Angelique from his view. Isaac had sat down with them and Dahlia had dominated the entire conversation, grinning up in his face like he invented reggae. When he stood up from the table, Dahlia had shoved a piece of paper with her phone number into his hand before he had a chance to leave, staking her claim on him. Angelique had been amused by her friend and her pushy self. One of the first things she noticed about Isaac after his bright smile was the grease still caked under his nails. Angelique didn't have a car, so he couldn't do anything for her anyway. She didn't need a mechanic. Angelique just turned her attention to other couples on the floor grooving to the fast ska beat and let Dahlia have her way. If Angelique really wanted Isaac, she could have had him.

As if on cue, the phone rang. Dahlia jumped from her chair, nearly knocking over the table to answer the call. From the way her friend cooed and giggled into the phone, Angelique could tell it was Isaac on the other end. It was no coincidence that he was calling at dinner time, probably offering to stop by since he was in the neighborhood. Dahlia was always up for company, with her fast self. Angelique got up from the table and signaled she was going to leave when Dahlia waved her hand up and down and mouthed, "Not yet. Sit."

Angelique reluctantly sat down and waited for Dahlia to get off the phone.

"Isaac is coming. Help me clean up, nuh?" Dahlia begged as she quickly began shoving things in closets or in the oven. "I have to get ready, too. What should I wear?" she wondered aloud.

"It's just Isaac. You can put on any old frock."

"Hush!" Dahlia scolded her. "You know I love him like cooked food!"

Angelique sucked her teeth in response and got up to wash the dishes. Dahlia ignored her friend and ran to her bedroom to look for a dress. As Angelique finished with the last pot, the doorbell rang.

"Answer it for me, please." Dahlia stuck her head out of the bedroom. Angelique looked at her friend trying to squeeze her heavy frame into a dress that looked at least one size too small and just shook her head.

Isaac looked surprised to see Angelique at the door. His smiled broadened as he shamelessly let his eyes wander over her curves. She cut her eyes at him and pointed to the sofa. "She'll be out in a minute." Angelique turned and walked back towards the kitchen.

Isaac looked towards the closed bedroom door and bypassed the sofa. He watched as Angelique dried the pots and put them away. "So, you're working hard I see," he said.

Angelique could feel his eyes burrowing into her. She pretended she didn't hear him.

"It smells good in here. You do the cooking?"

"No, Dahlia made everything. I'm just cleaning up," she replied as she wiped the counters.

"So when are you going to cook for me?" he teased.

Angelique gave him a puzzled look. "Why would I want to do that?" she said and turned back to the counters.

He smiled and moved close enough to reach out for her arm. "Because, I—"

"Isaac?"

The sound was almost shrill, filled with a mix of shock, anger, and fear, and maybe some desperation. Isaac turned around to follow the sound of the voice and saw Dahlia standing in the doorway. The dress she finally decided on was still too tight. The buttons strained to hold the fabric together and if she breathed any harder someone in that room would surely end up blinded by one of them. Her eyes asked the question she did not have the courage to say out loud: *What are you doing?*

"Angelique was just keeping me company while I was waiting on you and boy, you look sweet! Well worth the wait," Isaac said smoothly.

"You looked like you was looking for more than just company." Dahlia looked between the two of them for an explanation. Angelique tilted her head to the side and raised her eyebrows at Dahlia as if to say, "Please!"

"Stop that foolishness, there's nothing going on here. I didn't come here to argue with you so if you want me to leave I'll just leave." Isaac moved towards the doorway and attempted to walk past Dahlia. She grabbed his arm and quickly smiled.

"No, no, I wasn't arguing. I just, never mind. You hungry? I cooked," Dahlia said excitedly.

Angelique watched Dahlia fuss over Isaac so he wouldn't leave, and watched him settle in comfortably at the kitchen table with a plate of food. He seemed amused at his ability to make Dahlia run around the kitchen for his every request, finding hot pepper sauce and beer to go with his extra helpings.

Whenever Dahlia wasn't looking, he would fix his half-hooded eyes on Angelique while sucking on a chicken bone. She looked at his greasy lips and shook her head. He laughed silently and continued to smirk. His bad boy ways were almost attractive on some level, the way he boldly flirted with his woman's friend when her back was barely turned. Angelique felt her ambivalence, almost dislike for Isaac melting away. She refused to sit down at the table with them though, and kept her distance at the far side of the kitchen, which seemed to suit Dahlia just fine.

"I'm leaving," Angelique announced, a little too loudly.

Dahlia barely waved and didn't bother to turn her head to look in Angelique's direction.

"You don't have to go anywhere. I was enjoying having the company of two beautiful women," Isaac said.

"If she has to leave, let her leave," Dahlia said a little too quickly. "Besides, I'm sure her husband back home wouldn't want her to keep you or anyone else company."

Angelique's eyes grew wide. She tried to search Dahlia's face for an explanation, but her friend would not look in her direction. Isaac, however, seemed intrigued. His eyes flashed with mischief when he looked at Angelique, like a boy who had just found his father's secret hiding place for his dirty pictures. Something forbidden was always more desirable.

Angelique tossed the dish towel in the sink and walked out of the kitchen. Dahlia jumped a little when the apartment door slammed shut.

19

The early spring morning had a chill in the air, but Dahlia couldn't tell whether it was the weather or the cold reception she received from Angelique. The two women had barely spoken since that night at Dahlia's when Isaac had shown up. Since then, Angelique had switched shifts so that they almost never worked together anymore and they never crossed paths coming in and out of the Victorian-converted apartments they both shared. That had been almost four months ago.

Today they found themselves at the same little Caribbean grocery store. Each time the door opened, the cool breeze snaked in, rustling newspapers stacked on the ground and numbing the exposed ankles of customers rushing to get their spices, dried peas, and salted meats so they could get home in time to make their Saturday pepperpot or red pea soups before the sun faded from the late afternoon sky. Dahlia had been in the back of the store getting flour and cornmeal when she noticed Angelique looking perplexed as she picked over the meager selection of imported yams, trying to figure out which piece was good.

Angelique did not look up when Dahlia called her name. Dahlia moved close enough to be sure she was in ear shot and called her again.

"I heard you the first time," Angelique said, without looking up.

"So why you never answer me?"

"So you know me today? When last I saw you, you were so busy trying to get that man's attention I could've dropped dead in front of you and you would've step right past me to make sure he wasn't traumatized by the sight of me on the ground."

"You were flirting with him," Dahlia accused her.

The storekeeper lowered the newspaper he was reading and pretended to rearrange some items on the counter so he could focus on the two women's conversation.

"Me? You must be mad. I don't want that man," Angelique shot back.

"Why? What is wrong with him?" Dahlia said defensively.

A middle-aged woman asked the storekeeper if he had any allspice. He dismissed her with a wave and a quick "back there," annoyed by the interruption. He stopped his work rearranging the candy and leaned over the counter, openly amused by the impending drama unfolding in his store.

"I didn't say anything was wrong with him. I said I don't want him. What is wrong with you?"

"Nothing is wrong with me, but you seemed *very* interested in him from what I saw." Dahlia put her hands on her hips and waited for a response.

"Perhaps you should buy some glasses because it seems like your eyes are playing tricks on you."

"So you think every man want you?"

Angelique held a piece of yam in her hand and glared at Dahlia. She looked around the store and noticed several sets of eyes discreetly looking in their direction. The storekeeper openly stared at them, equally curious about the fight, and concerned about whether he would be selling the produce or cleaning it up in the aftermath. "Look. I don't have time for this foolishness. You can think whatever you want, just don't bother me with it anymore."

Dahlia watched her friend storm out of the store. She looked up at the storekeeper who shook his head before picking up his newspaper again. She felt the heat of her anger flowing out of her replaced by the flush of her cheeks as she realized the scene she had created. Isaac hadn't even returned her call in the two weeks since he'd left her bed one morning. She had been angry with him when he'd commented that he hadn't seen Angelique around. When Dahlia accused him of flirting with her, he told her she was silly. He was merely teasing Angelique because she was one of those women that was used to being taken care of and it seemed funny to see her with a dish cloth in her hand. What kind of woman did he think Dahlia was? A maid? She and Angelique worked at the same place and did the same job. She tried to ignore the comment and let him stay the night anyway. He thanked her the next morning as he put on the clothes she had washed for him. And when he asked her to pack up the food from last night's dinner for his lunch, she did so without hesitation, even though it meant she would have to go grocery shopping again because she had planned for that meal to last her a few days. When she asked if they might go out the following weekend, she ignored the long pause he took before he told her he had to work, but would call her, then waved as he headed out the door without so much as a goodbye kiss.

Dahlia ignored the rumors when she heard he'd been out around town that very weekend with a slim, brown-skinned woman from Port Antonio. And so when she finally saw Angelique, the type of woman that men took care of, the type that was paraded around town and not the one that men like Isaac only visited when they needed their shirts washed, their bellies filled, or their beds warmed, Dahlia forgot about her friendship and confronted Angelique for being who she would never be.

Dahlia caught her reflection in the glass door as it swung shut. She looked at her too-tight skirt hugging the hips too large to be defined as "healthy," even by Caribbean standards. She turned her eyes away from the door and grabbed two loaves of hard dough bread from the shelf behind her and plunked her items on the counter. "I'm not ready yet. I need another basket," she declared to the storekeeper, before heading back to load up a second time.

He watched her walk from the bus stop towards the nursing home at the corner of the street. This would make the sixth week he had seen her. He had her schedule figured out. She would get off the bus just before 12 p.m. and head into the nursing home. If it was nice enough, he would see her again taking her dinner break outside around five, just when he was getting ready to leave the office for the day. She used to sit outside with a thickly shaped girl, but he had not seen that one with her in a few weeks.

She must've had Tuesdays and Wednesdays off, which made the middle of the week disappointing for him. He always made sure to take his lunch break around the time she arrived for her shift so that he would not be distracted by the figures he was adding up in the ledger. His boss never complained about his junior accountant's strict schedule since he began voluntarily coming in on Saturdays to do extra work without asking for extra pay.

He was disappointed when the late spring rain kept her inside, or made her run to the shelter of the building when she got off the bus. He liked it best when the days were sunny and she would venture outside to warm her copper-colored skin. He also liked it when she wore her long ponytail loose rather than in the bun, so he could imagine running his fingers through the waves in her hair. He wondered if she ever noticed him or if she would ever notice him. He was not striking by anybody's imagination, but he was pleasant to look at. He wore his hair cropped closely to his head and tried to keep the goatee and mustache he wore neatly trimmed. His clothes were not always the latest style, but they were always cleaned and pressed, and when he walked he held his head up high so he seemed taller than his 5'9", except when he saw her, then his nerves would take over and he would lose some of his confidence.

He had almost gotten up the nerve to approach her one afternoon as he headed out of the office towards his car. He was irritated that his boss had kept him in a meeting longer than planned, cutting into his observation time. She was still out there though; she had been sitting on a bench reading a book when he walked towards her. She suddenly snapped the book shut and jumped up from the bench, nearly knocking him over.

"Oh, sorry, excuse me, please," she said as she gathered up her things from the bench.

He smiled and started to speak, but she was already off and rushing towards the building, mumbling something about being late again. He watched her disappear inside the doorway before turning up the street towards his car. She had almost run him over and still barely noticed him.

He was disappointed that he did not see her on Thursday or Friday and he had no real reason to come into the office that weekend. On Monday he had been out at an appointment in the morning, but rushed back to the office just in time to see her bus pulling off from her stop. She was not there. He'd resigned himself to the possibility that maybe she had quit or lost her job for being late. This was why he was surprised two days later when she appeared out of nowhere and spoke to him.

"Excuse me, please. Do you know if the Smith Street bus passed by already? I need to register for school," Angelique asked him.

He stared at her for a moment until she raised her arm out further to show him the piece of paper with the address on it.

He shook his head, attempting to recover quickly, and started to give her driving directions to the location.

"I don't have a car. I was hoping you could tell me if the bus passed already," she said again.

"Oh! Sorry, sorry," he began. "I just assumed…" his voice trailed off as she gave him a curious look. "You know I'm not going far from there. I could give you a lift if you feel comfortable."

Angelique smiled. "I'm not worried. Everybody in there knows where you work anyway." She nodded towards a group of women leaving the home.

He kept stealing glances at her the entire car ride to the college. She didn't notice, or at least, she pretended not to. He was pleased that she asked him questions about himself and smiled when she learned he was from Mandeville, Jamaica. They talked about their families and he was impressed by her plans to put herself through school and to eventually send for her daughter. She was smart, beautiful, strong, yet soft. She laughed with confidence and when she smiled his heart melted.

When they arrived at the school he offered to wait for her and drop her home. She thanked him with a big smile before running into the school. He sat in the car and waited almost 45 minutes for her to reappear again. After that, he drove her home and offered to pick her up for work the next day once she told him that she now worked the 8 to 4 shift. She graciously consented. The drive took him out of his way, but he didn't mind. He would use the time to think about what he would write in the letter home to his mother telling her he thought he'd found his future wife.

Angelique was in a better mood than she'd been in for a long time. Being attacked by Dahlia had caught her by surprise. She now avoided her whenever possible, switching her evening for a day shift with a more senior coworker who had decided sleeping in was better than getting off work early. She felt lonely. Despite how Dahlia had treated her, she missed their friendship. There were less Caribbean people in the city than she'd expected and the cold winter months made it harder to meet the people she was most familiar with. The way white people seemed to study her when they thought she wasn't looking or openly staring at her when they didn't care, fascinated by the sight of a real black person and not entirely sure whether they were comfortable with it, made her feel even more isolated and alone. So when she noticed Dennis looking at her from across the street every day and showing up to work on the weekends when the accounting office was closed, Angelique felt a curious sense of relief. He was not her usual type, with his large eyes hidden by lashes long enough to scrape against his round spectacles and a chin people might describe as weak. He wasn't tall and he moved with a bit of awkwardness, almost as if he wasn't sure of himself as much as he tried to mask it with feigned confidence. But, he seemed to have a kind manner. He never left work early and always seemed to take only the exact amount of time allotted for his lunch. His clothes were neat, but he could use some help updating his look. His unassuming appearance made him seem trustworthy somehow, which is why Angelique was unconcerned about convincing him that he should drive her to school to make changes to her class schedule because she was tired of taking the bus there.

 Dennis drove Angelique to and from work or class during the week and would take her out to dinner and the movies on the weekends. Angelique helped him pick out new clothes from Eaton's department store and pushed him to be more assertive whenever they felt they weren't getting proper service. She persuaded him to pursue the promotion at work that he felt he deserved, and they celebrated with Angelique reluctantly agreeing to make red snapper for him, even though she disliked cooking and hated the smell left behind by the fried fish even more.

When she finally consented to go to his place one Saturday afternoon, she was pleasantly surprised to find that he lived in a fairly new, three-bedroom home. It didn't compare to the large home in Kingston she had shared with her husband, but it was much better than the single rooms or apartments that she knew most Caribbean transplants lived in when they first arrived in Canada, including her own one-bedroom apartment. Soon after her initial visit, they were down at the local department store where she picked out new linens and curtains for the rooms. Dennis initially grimaced at the amount of money Angelique had him spending on the place, but she convinced him these things were necessary. He eventually gave in and smiled as she busied herself around the home he had long decided he wanted to share with her.

Dennis loved Angelique's outgoing and strong personality. She spoke with ease when he introduced her to his boss and coworkers at an office event, charming the men with her exotic beauty and intellect. She was a little more flirtatious than he would've liked, laughing a little too hard at his boss' jokes and standing close enough for the man to know what soap she used. He confronted her about this on the car ride home. She had folded her arms across her chest and turned her attention to the scenery outside her passenger side window, refusing to look at him or respond to his accusation. He had barely brought the car to a full stop when they arrived at her apartment before she was out of the car and standing on the curb. He started to open his car door, but she told him it would not be necessary for him to walk her inside the building, thank you very much. She slammed the door shut and ran up the walk, disappearing inside the front door.

Dennis soon dropped the issue when each time he called to talk about it, she would politely but firmly tell him, "Dennis, I do not wish to speak to you until you can learn to act like you have some sense," before hanging up the phone on him. After nearly two weeks of her not speaking to him, he showed up at her apartment door with a gift wrapped ruby pendant and eyes almost as red as the stone he presented to her, from lack of sleep.

She studied the piece of jewelry for a moment before thrusting it back at him. "Look, if you're going to act jealous, I'm telling you right now that things will not work between us," she said calmly.

Dennis became defensive. "Who tell you I was insecure? It's a matter of respect, that is all."

"That had nothing to do with respect for you, but it was very embarrassing for me and if that's the way you're going to behave, then I have no interest in dealing with you." She stared at him unwaveringly and waited for his response.

Dennis opened his mouth to defend himself, and then stopped. Angelique had remained calm during this entire exchange and in the weeks following the incident, she had never yelled or gotten upset any of the times she had hung up on him. It was clear to him that she could walk away without a second thought. "Sorry, sorry," he relented.

She studied the pendant he'd handed her. Its sparkling red stone glinted in the morning light. She glanced back at him. He did not try to hide his nervousness as he chewed his pink bottom lip. He blinked at her with wide eyes that spoke everything from desperation to hopefulness, a willingness to do anything to be forgiven. It showed weakness, she thought. She smiled and opened the door wide enough to let him in.

20

It was noon on a Saturday and Angelique shifted uncomfortably in the chair as she watched Dahlia buzzing around her kitchen. She didn't know why she had agreed to go over to Dahlia's place. Angelique was caught off guard when she and Dahlia crossed paths as Angelique was entering their apartment building. Dahlia had greeted her with a bubbly, "Hey gyal!" as if nothing had happened and months of silence had not divided their friendship.

Dahlia immediately invited her over for one of her favorite past times—eating. Angelique had opened her mouth to ask her if she'd gone mad, but her former friend had smiled at her so sweetly, it reminded her of the days when they first met and Dahlia had treated her like a sister. Angelique missed her friend and even though she had Dennis, she was still lonely, and so in a moment of weakness and nostalgia, she accepted her invitation. Dahlia still owed her an apology though.

Dahlia peered at the bottom of the dumpling she'd been frying. Satisfied with the golden brown color, she began transferring the batch from the pan onto a plate. She then scooped the ackee and saltfish from the other frying pan into a serving bowl and placed the steaming dish in the middle of the table in front of Angelique before sitting down herself. Angelique kept her hands folded in her lap.

"Eat, nuh!" Dahlia urged. "You act like a stranger." She laughed and pushed one of the plates towards Angelique.

"I've been treated like one."

Dahlia's smile faltered. She quickly grabbed a serving spoon and began heaping piles of food onto both plates, then reached for the dumplings. "I-I know, it was just..." her voice trailed off as she searched for words to explain her behavior. Instead, she offered, "I just want to leave that all in the past and move forward, you know what I mean?" Dahlia heaped some more food on Angelique's plate. "And I'm sorry, alright?" she added. She smiled again when Angelique finally picked up her fork and began eating. "It's good, eh?" she said as she shoveled a forkful into her own mouth.

"Modesty was never one of your strong traits."

"Move yourself!" Dahlia exclaimed as she threw a tea towel in Angelique's direction. They broke out into laughter, breaking the tension in the air.

"So, what have you been up to?" Angelique relaxed into her chair a bit, but was careful not to be too direct in her question. She had no intention of asking about Isaac. Not only because of how Dahlia had behaved the last time they spoke, but also because of the rumors she'd heard around the nursing home about Lisa. She was a nurse's aide with a slim figure, cat-like eyes, and skin the color of deep cocoa who worked the day shift and who had also been laying a claim on Isaac, bragging about her "intended." Which was exactly what Dahlia was doing now.

"Oh, I've been keeping very busy, you know. Trying to plan for our future and then with work and cooking, and I wash and iron Isaac's work clothes so when he leaves out of here at nights to go home, he'll be ready for the morning." Dahlia took a bite out of one of the fried dumplings. "He says he likes the way I make his shirts smell," she proudly added.

Angelique looked down at the naked left hand Dahlia was using to sop up the drippings on her plate. Dahlia caught Angelique staring and waved the hand as if she could dismiss Angelique's thoughts with it.

"Oh, he had to send the money he was saving for the ring back home for his mother so she can go to the doctor. I just need a wedding band. We're practically married already," she gushed.

Angelique nodded and tore off a piece of the dumpling and popped it in her mouth. "So when is this blessed event taking place?"

Dahlia got up to put the kettle on the stove. "No date as yet." She dug around in the cupboard and retrieved a box of Red Rose tea. "Soon though," she added. "So never mind me, what is going on with you? And who is that man I've been seeing picking you up everywhere?"

Angelique hesitated, not ready to trust Dahlia with all her business. "Oh, that's Dennis. He's just a friend."

"Friend? He looks like more than a friend to me, though he doesn't look like your type."

Well, you don't look like Isaac's type, but I'm not judging, Angelique thought. She shrugged. "He's nice."

"Well, we should all go out soon. Maybe a dance or something. Isaac hasn't taken me out in a long time. Now he'll have no excuse!" Dahlia wound her hips to an imaginary beat.

Visions of spending an evening with that sly dog eyeing her and Dahlia ready to chat up all of her business was more than Angelique could take. "I have to run," she said and stood up. "Schoolwork," she threw in.

"Alright," Dahlia said, looking startled. "Well, so we'll get together soon, okay?"

"Right, okay." Angelique flew out of the door before Dahlia could ask any more questions.

Dahlia watched the apartment door swing shut, wondering what she had said that made Angelique run off so quickly. She looked down at the plate of food Angelique had barely touched. *A waste of good ackee.* She reached over and scraped the contents of the plate onto her own.

21

The envelope had arrived a few days before, but Angelique had tossed it on the dresser where it lay until curiosity finally got the best of her. She slowly pulled the letter out of the envelope and unfolded it. The picture slid out and she instinctively reached out to grab it before it fluttered to the floor. She studied the image for a moment before turning her attention to the words on the page:

Dear Angelique,

Hope this letter finds you well and enjoying your studies. Things are good here for the most part. It seemed like your brother was going to marry that one girl from down the road, but now he's saying he wants to go to England. I don't understand that boy. Anyhow, your mother says she's not feeling too good, but you know how she is always complaining about every little thing. Not to worry yourself about it.

Carmen is doing fine, but she misses you. Here is a picture of her from when last we were in town and I took her to buy some shoes. She looks like you when you were a baby, na true? When are you coming home? Hope to see you soon. Make sure you write because we haven't heard from you in a long time.

All the best,
Dad

P.s. Your cousin Hazel asked if you can send her a linen table cloth with the lace trim on it. I don't know what she need with linen and lace, like she is expecting the Queen for tea or something. Anyhow, you know I don't ask no questions.

Angelique re-read the letter then studied the picture of her daughter. The girl looked so much older than the one she left nearly a year ago. Not just because she had grown taller. Her eyes looked as though they had seen or experienced more than most girls her age. Angelique folded the letter back up and slipped it inside its envelope before laying it inside her top drawer. She tapped the photo on the top of the dresser and looked around the room, before finally sliding it into the bottom corner of the dresser mirror behind the perfume and talcum powder.

"What do you mean I have to retake the class? I never failed any test."

"You did. You only got 63 percent on your last written test and you didn't do all that well on the practical either."

Angelique stared at the nursing instructor. Her blonde hair was curled tightly and sprayed stiffly into place. Her pale skin under the bright light of the office made her look even colder than the icy personality she already projected. Angelique knew the instructor never liked her ever since the first day Angelique walked into the classroom, convinced that Angelique had taken the spot of some better, more deserving Canadian. Sitting in that office reminded her of the last time she'd sat in the headmistress' office back in Jamaica.

Now, she sat facing this pinch-faced woman, half-expecting to be disciplined for failing the class, only there was no monetary reward for enduring the shame this time.

"If you want to pass, you're going to have to put in the work like everyone else. Laziness will not do—where are you going?" The instructor's words hit the floor in the empty space where Angelique had been standing before she walked out the door.

"You should start your own business."

They were in Dennis' tiny front yard. He was digging a hole for the tree he'd bought at the nursery, along with the dozen petunia plants Angelique had selected. He didn't really care to have a bunch of pretty flowers all over his yard, particularly pink ones, but Angelique had talked him into it. "Because that's the way your house is supposed to look," she had told him when he questioned why he couldn't just put down some sod and be done. He leaned on the shovel and wiped the sweat from his face with the back of his left gloved hand, leaving a streak of soil across his forehead.

"My own what? What are you going on about?" he asked her.

Angelique looked at the big streak of dirt across his face and covered her eyes so he couldn't see her rolling them. "Start your own business. Instead of you killing yourself to make money to put in other people's pockets, why don't you start your own business?" she asked.

"It's not that easy," Dennis said, dismissively.

"It's not that hard," she said, refusing to let the subject drop. "My father did it. My—" she caught herself before she added "father-in-law." She still hadn't told Dennis that she was still married. "I know lots of people who have started their own business," she said instead.

"In Jamaica? That's not the same thing as starting a business here."

It's not like he hadn't thought of this before, but in order to run an accounting business, you needed clients. Dennis had been grateful that his boss, Troy, had decided to give him a chance by hiring him. He'd had many doors closed in his face by many uncertain or unwilling potential employers. Troy had let Dennis work on some of his largest clients' accounts, but knew how some of them might react if they learned that a black man was handling their financial affairs before first seeing his work. Partly because he never liked to be told what to do and partly because he liked to see the looks on their faces, Troy would quietly let Dennis do the work on the accounts, and then introduce Dennis after the work was completed. Not all Canadians were as open-minded as they would like the rest of the world to believe and Troy enjoyed watching some of his clients choke and sputter as they wrote out their checks for payment with plastic smiles pasted on their faces. Most remained loyal customers and the few that took their business elsewhere he could care less about anyway. He'd made enough money in the 20 years since he started the business that he could afford to lose a few narrow-minded clients and the laugh at their expense was worth it.

Dennis knew trying to build a client base with the color strike against him would be hard. Besides, he liked his job.

"I could help. I could be your assistant. I was always good in math," Angelique lied. Half the time that she received discipline was at the hands of some teacher who believed she could beat an understanding into Angelique when she got her schoolwork wrong. "Laziness," they always concluded, was the reason why she never did well in math.

"So you are giving up on nursing altogether?" Dennis said, his eyebrow raised.

"Never mind! I was only trying to help you out. It really doesn't make a difference to me, one way or the other," Angelique shot back.

It did make a difference. Since leaving school more than a year ago, Angelique had been struggling mentally to find some status that she could proudly report back home. She'd ignored letters from her father asking her to come back to visit, and the few letters she sent in reply were short, containing the barest of details and avoiding altogether the question of what she was doing with herself or whether she'd finished her program yet.

Dennis decided to ignore the heated outburst from Angelique, placating her in his normal way. "Let me think about it."

Her face relaxed and Angelique seemed willing to let it go for the time being. Dennis breathed a sigh of relief.

"So when will you decide?" Angelique pressed.

Lawd God. Dennis dropped the seedling into the hole he'd finished digging before turning to her to say, "Just pass that bag of manure, please."

Dahlia excitedly waved them over to the table where she sat stirring a glass of rum punch with her straw. She wore a yellow shift dress that was the usual one size too small. Her large chest strained against the fabric and the drugstore perfume she wore threatened to overpower them as they sat down across from her.

"This is Dennis and that is Dahlia," Angelique said. "From my building," she added. She couldn't quite bring herself to introduce Dahlia as a "friend."

Dahlia examined Dennis, taking in his buttoned up shirt, tortoise shell eyeglasses, and low cropped hair. He smiled at her, revealing his small, even teeth hidden behind the lips that were dotted with freckles, and she happily concluded that he was not as nice looking as her Isaac, who had yet to arrive. Dennis didn't look like Angelique's type. He definitely looked like a bookkeeper, or whatever Angelique said he did. She wondered what Angelique saw in him, as she observed how uncomfortable he seemed, looking around the place, pushing his eyeglasses up his speckled nose. She thought about Isaac, his easy, relaxed manner, dark good looks, and his smile that made every woman's heart melt. Isaac hadn't proposed yet, but he never shut down the discussion whenever she brought it up, which she thought was a good sign.

Dennis got up to get them some drinks and see whether the food they were serving was as good as it smelled. Dahlia bobbed in her seat while stealing glances at her watch. Angelique finally decided to break the silence and ask where Isaac was.

"He's coming. Probably just running late, you know how men can lose track of time."

Angelique nodded.

"So did you hear what happened with Pauline?" Dahlia asked.

"Do I know her?"

"Yes, she was that mopey-looking one that used to live on the first floor across the street?"

Angelique searched her memory for a picture of the woman Dahlia was describing. "Didn't she used to look after those two bad children for that woman whose husband was some big politician or something?" Angelique remembered seeing Pauline trying to control those little hellions as they ran around terrorizing the other children at the playground by the bus stop. Their mother never disciplined her children, believing they should be "free spirits" or some foolishness like that. The older boy, about 10, took it upon himself to remind Angelique that she was "black," and giggle every time he crossed her path. He'd say "black" like it was a curse word and Angelique would have to resist the urge to box him down. Pauline would grab his shirt and the boy would try to struggle out of her grasp while the eight-year-old would laugh at the whole scene.

"Yes, that's the one. Poor thing had all she could take of them two little buggers and gave the oldest one a good backhand. When the mother came home she screamed to high heaven and called the police to have Pauline arrested. They didn't take her away, but that woman kicked up such a fuss until her husband had to make arrangements to have Pauline deported. All because these people refuse to control their children in this country." Dahlia shook her head. "What an injustice," she added.

Angelique nodded again. Life certainly wasn't easy here. At least she had Dennis to help her. He walked back just in time with drinks and Dahlia eagerly slurped on the rum punch he placed in front of her. She looked towards the door again, and then glanced at her watch before going back to sucking contentedly on a cube of ice. It was clear that Dennis hadn't developed as high a tolerance for the white rum as many of the men at the dance and he soon began feeling the effects of the rum over ice he'd half-finished. He closed his eyes, pressed his lips together, and began rotating his fists through the air to the music. Angelique and Dahlia exchanged amused looks. Dennis opened his eyes in time to see them suppressing giggles.

"What's so funny?" Dennis asked. "What, you didn't think I could move, did you?" he teased, and before Angelique could answer, he jumped up from his seat and pulled her up towards the dance floor. Angelique was caught off guard at first, but soon relaxed and began to move in time with Dennis to the reggae beat blasting from the speakers. Dahlia continued to bounce in her chair, looking occasionally at the door to see if Isaac had arrived.

Angelique and Dennis stayed on the dance floor for at least half an hour until the band took a break. They walked back to the table and collapsed in the chairs where an eager Dahlia waited, glad for company at the table again. Angelique fanned herself with both hands while Dennis tilted his head back to finish off the rest of his rum like it was water. In between songs, he had gotten himself two more glasses of rum and ice that had the effect of loosening him up to the point of making him a crowd favorite on the dance floor.

Dennis draped his arm casually around the back of Angelique's chair, and she in turn, leaned in closer to him as she surveyed the room. Dahlia watched them and felt a slight twinge of jealousy. Isaac had never been that affectionate with her in public. It took a whole lot of begging to convince him to come out to the restaurant tonight. He didn't really like to go out lately and only agreed when she told him Angelique and her date would be coming and she didn't want to be there with them alone. He'd told her he couldn't pick her up because he had to work late, so she should just go ahead with her friends and he would meet up with her later. It was nearly two hours past the time he said he would be there, and Dahlia was feeling anxious.

"So where is this man of yours?" Dennis asked, as if reading her mind.

Dahlia glanced back at the door before trying, ever so delicately, to slide the ice cube in her mouth back in the drink she had been nursing. Dahlia shrugged and quickly tried to change the subject.

"You two look happy," she said, not really caring about the response.

"The only thing that would make me happier is your friend agreeing to marry me," Dennis slurred, a sloppy grin spreading across his face.

Dahlia stiffened, but managed to keep a smile on her face. She looked over at Angelique, who seemed just as surprised as she was to hear the pronouncement, but seemed pleased, as she appeared to consider the proposition. Dahlia suddenly didn't feel like being there anymore. She was tired of waiting for Isaac to show and finally admitted to herself that he was standing her up again. Angelique's news should have been her news. Angelique had barely been with this man for however many months and already he was talking about marrying her. She had been faithfully waiting for Isaac for well over a year and he couldn't even be bothered to take her out or show up anywhere, much less to make a proposal. Until tonight, it didn't even look as though Angelique even liked Dennis in that way while Dahlia would've put her own mother out if it meant she would be getting married.

"Well, isn't that something?" she finally said.

Dahlia stayed long enough so that Angelique wouldn't think she was leaving because she was upset by their news before announcing that she was going home. Angelique asked if she needed a ride home, but Dahlia firmly declined without offering an explanation. Dennis didn't look like he was in any shape to drive anyway and the thought of spending another minute with these two was more than she could bear. "I have a lift," she lied.

Angelique looked at Dahlia doubtfully, but didn't ask any questions about this "lift" that had not made an appearance all night.

Dahlia called over her shoulder, "I'll come see you tomorrow, alright?"

Angelique watched Dahlia leave with a mix or perplexity and apprehension. She didn't have long to think about it as she watched Dennis swaying in his chair, that stupid grin still plastered across his face. She didn't like driving, but Dennis could barely sit up straight, which meant he would probably have to stay on her sofa for the night because she was not in the mood to drive across town to his place. How was she even going to get him into the car? Fool.

Dahlia finally reached home after walking for close to an hour. She had been so mad that Isaac had not shown up, but by the time she made it upstairs she had convinced herself that he probably had a good explanation. Perhaps he had fallen asleep or had to stay late at work and couldn't call her before she left to let her know he wouldn't be able to make it. She called him several times when she got home, but he did not answer. She finally fell asleep waiting for him to call back. In the morning when she woke and remembered she had not heard from him, she called again, worried and not really expecting a response, which was why she was surprised when he answered the phone on the first ring.

"Isaac?"

"Yeah."

"Where were you? I was waiting on you all evening," Dahlia said.

"Who is this?"

"What you mean, 'who is this?' You trying to tell me you don't know my voice?" Dahlia felt herself getting hot.

Isaac chuckled. "Wha'ppen? You don't like jokes anymore?"

"It's not funny, Isaac. Where were you yesterday? Why you never call me? And why you never pick up the phone when I called you last night?" She could hear the lazy slumber in his voice as he sighed.

"I told you I didn't want to go."

"But you didn't tell me you *weren't* coming. I waited over two and a half hours for you to show up and you had me sitting there like a fool with Angelique and her boyfriend looking at me."

"Angelique was there?" he asked. "How she look?"

"Why?" She tried to control the anger that was building in her.

He laughed again. "Why you let that bother you so? I'm just joking with you. Lawd, everything gets you worked up!"

"You didn't answer me. Where were you last night?"

"I was here, minding mi own business. Cha," Isaac said. "I just woke up and you're bothering me already."

She backed off. "Well I was hoping we could all go out and have a good time last night—"

"Another time. Look, I have things to do. You cooking tonight?"

"Well, I could make a little something—"

"Alright. I'll pass through," he cut her off. "Layta!" He hung up the phone abruptly.

"Hello? Hold on a minute."

The only response was silence. She replaced the receiver in the cradle. She was unsure what had her more upset—the fact that Isaac had stood her up without remorse, that he was inquiring about Angelique again, or that she was sure she heard another woman's voice in the background just before he'd hung up.

Angelique rolled over and strained to look at the little alarm clock beside the bed. It was almost twenty past 10. She rolled back over and placed her hand on her throbbing forehead. She couldn't understand why she had such a headache; she hadn't had that much to drink. She struggled to recall the events of the previous evening. She hadn't really eaten since lunchtime yesterday. She remembered not getting home until the early morning hours and having to half drag, half push Dennis up the stairs to her apartment and barely managing to dump him on the chesterfield before falling into bed herself.

She debated whether she should go check on him.

"Oh Lawdgawdamercy!" The pitiful groan from beyond the closed bedroom door filled her ears.

Serve him right, she thought. *Who told him to drink so much anyway? He better not mess up my good carpet.*

Satisfied that he at least didn't die in her living room, Angelique turned over and pulled the blanket up over her shoulder. She would get up later and feign concern while she cooked him a little breakfast. She needed to get him up and over to Eaton's department store today. They were having a sale and she wanted to pick up a pretty pink bedspread and matching curtain set for the bedroom she was fixing up for Carmen. Dennis had mentioned sending for her daughter several times and in light of last night's announcement, it made sense. Whether it was because he thought that might convince her to say yes to his proposal, or whether it was his silent acceptance of Angelique's family situation, she didn't know, but it didn't matter. That wasn't her biggest problem. Her letters to Clifton had gone unanswered. She couldn't get a divorce and she was not sure she wanted one. She had no clue how she was going to work this out.

Not sending for Carmen before now had bought her some time, but her excuse that she didn't have the money for the plane ticket and paperwork had been eliminated, since Dennis had offered to pay the fare. Now she was only left with the excuses that seemed out of her control—the immigration papers and school records had not yet been processed. The bedroom set was enough of a distraction to make Dennis believe that Angelique was preparing for her child to come soon.

Angelique decided against getting up and drifted off to sleep. The half-completed immigration application remained tucked away in between the pages of one of her nursing textbooks on the bookshelf in the corner.

Dahlia huffed out of breath as she lugged the two paper bags full of groceries to her third floor apartment. She dropped the bags on the kitchen table and massaged her lower back for a moment before she began to unpack. The grocery receipt floated down to the floor as she pulled the yams out of the bag. She stooped down to retrieve it and sighed heavily as she looked at the total. She would call the hydro company again on Monday and make arrangements to pay the bill out of her next check so they wouldn't cut off the electricity. She shoved the receipt into her handbag and began pulling pots and pans out of the cupboard. She didn't have time to worry about the bills right now. She only had a few hours to clean up and cook before Isaac arrived.

"Damn it," Dahlia exclaimed as she opened the fridge. She forgot to buy his Red Stripe beer. She grabbed her purse to run out to the store. Hopefully he would show up just a little late this time and everything would be alright.

Dennis lay on his back trying to decide whether to move to the floor. His head was spinning and his stomach felt weak. He smiled despite his discomfort. He'd enjoyed himself the night before, even if he'd had too much to drink. Angelique seemed to have had a good time too. Today, they would be going shopping for linens or something Angelique said she needed for Carmen. He didn't mind that she already had a daughter and already felt for the little girl whose father, Dennis understood, had abandoned her and her mother without any notice or means of support. As long as she was willing to have more children, he could accept one that wasn't his.

Dennis sat up quickly as a wave of nausea hit him. He rushed towards the bathroom hoping to make it in time before he emptied the contents of his stomach on the carpet.

Dahlia skipped over to answer the knock at the door. She had gotten over her anger with Isaac and was now just happy he showed up this time, even if he was an hour and a half late. She flung open the door and grinned at him, smoothing her hands over her hips hoping he would notice how she looked in the form-fitting dress she had finally decided on after changing twice while she waited for him.

"Bwoy, it smell good in here! What you cook?" He tossed his jacket on a chair and walked past her into the kitchen to see what was on the stove.

Dahlia followed behind. "You never said anything about my new dress?" She said it like a question, hoping it would prompt a response.

He turned from the pot slightly so that he could look at her from the side. His eyes travelled up and down her frame with as much enthusiasm as if he'd been looking at a brick wall. "Yeah, it looks fine." He turned his attention to the fridge and rummaged inside until he found the Red Stripe Dahlia had put in there to chill. "You going to share out the food or what?" he asked as he popped the cap off with a bottle opener.

Dahlia moved slowly, shoulders drooping, towards the cupboard and pulled two plates out. She set the food out on the table and Isaac dove in without waiting for her to sit down. They said little during the meal and after Isaac was done, he got up and fished another beer out of the fridge and headed for the living room, leaving Dahlia to clean up the kitchen.

After she finished, she walked into the living room and sat down beside Isaac who was leaned back into the sofa cushion watching a show on the little black-and-white television. When she leaned over to rest her head on his shoulder, he stood up to adjust the volume on the television. When he sat back down, he rested his elbows on his knees and cradled his chin in the palm of one hand, looking intently at the screen.

After a few minutes of waiting for him to acknowledge her, Dahlia finally spoke. "You know Angelique is getting married and she only met her boyfriend eight months ago."

Isaac said nothing.

"You think that's too soon?"

Isaac looked annoyed. "That is her business. What does that have to do with me?"

"Well, we've been together for well over a year now and you haven't proposed to me yet."

Isaac didn't respond.

Dahlia was getting frustrated. She could feel the anger bubbling up inside her and knew it would explode at any minute.

"Well?"

He turned to look at her, and something else was in his eyes. It was no longer annoyance. "Well what?" he asked. "Is what you want?" His voice was getting louder.

"What do you mean, 'what you want?'" she demanded. "I want to get married. Don't I cook for you? Clean for you? Let you lie in my bed like you are my husband? Eh?" She could not control the rage flowing through her. She knew she should stop before he got angry and left. Knew it, but she couldn't hold back. "I even wash your dirty stinkin' draws and all you can do is sit there and ask me 'is what you want?'" she mimicked and glared at him.

He glared back at her and stood up suddenly, nearly knocking over the beer he had placed on the coffee table. He looked at the bottle for a moment before picking it up and flinging it over her head and into the wall behind her. She cringed as she heard the bottle smash inches away from her, the amber colored fluid bubbled before seeping into the carpet.

"Look, I never asked you to do nothing for me. You are the one who keep pushing yourself up on me. I never tell you anything about marriage so I don't know where you get this idea from."

Hot tears streamed down Dahlia's face, streaking her makeup and staining the front of her dress. Isaac looked at her again, the same way he had looked at her earlier. This time Dahlia knew what the look was—scorn. Like she was some piece of trash that he had picked up and was trying to dispose of. She knew what that look meant, knew what he thought of her. Without another word, he walked out the door, slamming it behind him.

Dahlia sat on the sofa breathing short, stunted breaths like a little girl who had just been punished. She used the back of her hand to wipe her nose. She picked up the phone and dialed Angelique's number, but after several rings, she hung up. She went into the kitchen and returned a few moments later with a dustpan and a bucket of soapy water. She picked up the broken glass, then washed down the wall and floor before returning the supplies to the kitchen. On her way back into the living room she felt a sharp pain shoot through her foot. She hobbled to the bathroom to examine her toe. Carefully, she pulled at the shard of glass that had pierced her, and then cleaned and bandaged her wound. She made her way down the hall to the living room to sit down, when she caught a glimpse of something blue out of the corner of her eye resting on the chair. She walked over to the jacket that lay half on the floor where Isaac had tossed it when he first came in. She picked it up and held it for a moment before drawing it to her face and inhaling the scent. She smoothed out the wrinkles with her hands as she held it against her before walking to the closet and hanging it inside.

Angelique had stopped by Dahlia's apartment several times over the past week, but there was no response when she knocked at the door. She was concerned that Dahlia had not shown up for work, but she also wanted to talk with her about their plans. Dennis had bought Angelique's plane ticket to go back to Jamaica to see her daughter and Dahlia was supposed to be going back at the same time for her holiday break. Dennis had wanted to come and meet her family, but she argued with him until he was convinced it wasn't the right time, and that Dahlia had already planned to come with her. The flight was booked for Friday and it was already Wednesday. Angelique and Dahlia were supposed to go shopping to bring back some things for their families and there would be no time the next day, so today was their only option.

"Dahlia, are you in there? Open the door, nuh!" Angelique banged more insistently on the door. It finally swung open and Angelique looked at the figure standing before her. Dahlia was wearing a dressing robe that looked to have been white at one time, but now was dingy with stains dotting the front. Her hair was matted against her head and looked like it was in serious need of a hot comb. The air was stale and smelled of dirty laundry and body odor. Angelique frowned and breathed out audibly through her nose. "Gyal, why it smell so frowzy in here? When last you bathe?" Angelique walked over to the window to draw the curtain open and pushed the window up. She wiped her palms together as she surveyed the room. Dirty dishes sat out on the coffee table and a thin blanket was crumpled next to a pillow with no pillowcase on the sofa where Dahlia had obviously been camping.

"What's wrong with you? You sick or something? I've been trying to catch you all week. We're supposed to be leaving in two days." Angelique started picking up dishes and putting them in the kitchen sink. "I still have to buy a few shirts for my father and I also have to get something for that miserable woman he's married to." She grinned, hoping Dahlia would laugh at her little joke.

"I'm not going."

"What? What do you mean you're not going?"

"I mean exactly what I said. I'm not going anywhere." Dahlia looked at her with bloodshot eyes.

"I don't understand what's going on. Why did you change your mind all of a sudden?" Angelique asked.

"You want to know what's wrong with me? You want to know what happened? I'll tell you what happened. After all I did for that damn blasted man and 'im tell me say he not interested in marrying anyone, 'im turn 'round and marry that fast gyal from Spanish Town!" Dahlia's accent came out thick as her anger seethed. "What am I going to go home and tell my family? I'm a laughingstock."

Angelique heard about the marriage. She'd actually worked the same shift as Shelley, the woman Isaac had married, and had overheard Shelley talking to one of her coworkers about Isaac. Apparently the two of them were from the same town in Jamaica and Isaac had sent for her some months ago after going back home several times to see her. They had gotten married the last time he was in Jamaica and she had finally arrived after her papers had been processed. Angelique had hinted to Dahlia that Isaac may have had someone, asking why he went back to Jamaica so often, but Dahlia had either been defensive or dismissive, so Angelique just dropped it.

Angelique watched as Dahlia broke down into tears, her body heaving as she sobbed. She wondered why the girl was surprised. Angelique walked over and sat beside her friend. "I'm sorry to hear about it. It can't be easy." She patted Dahlia's shoulder reassuringly. "You should come anyway. Nothing you can do about it now, right?"

"You're not hearing me," Dahlia said, raising her voice. "I said I'm not going anywhere. I don't want to go anywhere. What is so hard to understand?" She glared at Angelique.

"You're supposed to go back and stay with me. You already paid for the ticket, so you might as well go. What are you going to do here?"

"Everything is always about you. You don't care about anybody but yourself," Dahlia hissed. "I wonder how excited you'd feel to take a trip if your whole world fell apart. You know what you can do? You can get your backside out of my house."

Angelique's mouth fell open and she stared at Dahlia. "That's not what I meant. I—"

"You nuh hear me? I said fi *come out*!"

Angelique opened her mouth to speak, but stopped herself. She walked out of the door before Dahlia could say another word.

Dennis dragged Angelique's two suitcases down to the sidewalk. "You know it's only you going, right? Feels like you packed enough things for the whole neighborhood to go back with you," Dennis teased. He tried to get Angelique to smile, but she acted as if she didn't hear him. She rummaged through her purse to make sure she had not forgotten her passport when she heard the door slam behind her.

Angelique turned towards the noise to see Dahlia watching her from the top of the stairs. She had traded the dirty robe for a tan-colored dress and her hair was neatly curled into a bob. She leaned against the handrail and folder her arms across her chest, but said nothing. Angelique sized her up and decided to ignore her since it appeared that Dahlia had no intention of apologizing. Angelique snapped her purse shut and pulled the strap over her shoulder with her left hand. Dahlia shifted her gaze from Angelique's face to the stone on Angelique's hand that glinted in the morning sunlight. Angelique caught her stare and slowly twisted her hand around her purse strap to hide her fingers.

"Angelique, is that an engagement ring I see? Congratulations," Dahlia said sweetly. "What you hiding it for? Let me see it." She walked quickly down the stairs and grabbed Angelique's hand. Angelique looked over at Dennis who was beaming proudly.

"Oh it's beautiful," Dahlia said.

"Thank you." Angelique turned towards the car. "I'm running late, so I'll see you when I get back, alright?"

"So, Clifton decided to give you that divorce after all?"

Angelique froze. She looked at Dennis who was staring at her with a look she couldn't quite read.

Dahlia gave them both a satisfied smirk before heading up the street. "Yes, see you later." She nodded at Dennis. "Second choice," she said and laughed.

Dennis opened his car door and climbed in without a word. Angelique remained rooted to the ground. Dennis called to her through the open window. "You coming or not?" Angelique got into the car, her eyes never leaving the floor. Dennis wrapped his fingers around the steering wheel, his jaw clenched tightly while Angelique stole nervous glances at him. Every once in a while Angelique would attempt to explain, but Dennis would cut her off instantly. "How could you not tell me you were still married after all this time? You must take me for somebody's fool," he growled.

"It wasn't like that. It's just—"

"I don't want to hear anything from you," he said, ending the discussion.

When they arrived at the airport, Dennis unloaded Angelique's bag on the ground beside her. "Are you going to pick me up when I get back?" Angelique asked.

Dennis looked at her with disdain. "Find your own blasted way home."

22

Carmen

Summer, 1980

"Aren't you going to give your mother a kiss?" Carmen's grandfather pressed his thin, bony fingers into her shoulder and firmly pushed her forward. She hesitantly walked toward her mother and laid a peck on the woman's cheek. Angelique quickly embraced her daughter's rigid body before letting her go.

"You're so pretty," Angelique said.

"Say thank you," her grandfather ordered.

"Thank you," Carmen said.

Angelique smiled nervously and rubbed her palms together as Carmen studied her. Carmen recognized the woman as her mother from all the pictures her grandparents had displayed around the house. Seeing her again dredged up the sad memory of the day she saw her mother walking down the road in the early morning hours with a suitcase in her hand years ago. Carmen had waited and waited for her mother to return to take her with her, but she never did. Carmen did remember her mother visiting once years ago, shortly after she had started school, but just as suddenly as Angelique appeared, she disappeared again and Carmen eventually stopped waiting for her to come home. Now 12 years old, Carmen didn't know how she felt seeing this woman again, whom she now resembled so strikingly.

Last month, Carmen's grandfather told her that her mother was coming to take her to live in Canada. She wasn't excited about the news—the woman standing in front of her was a stranger. One that left her without as much as a goodbye. Still, it was better than where she was. Her grandmother made no secret of the fact that she was not happy that Angelique had run off and left her to raise Carmen. If not for her grandfather, Ruby would have driven to Kingston, Carmen in tow, to curse out the little girl's other grandparents and the father she hadn't seen since she was three years old. Carmen was their family, too, but nobody seemed to act like it, Ruby used to say.

At some point her grandmother must have decided that it was useless to bother with the Chambers, but that didn't stop her from occasionally threatening to take Carmen back to her father's family whenever she thought the girl was acting too bright.

When Angelique came home, Carmen avoided spending time with her mother as much as possible, choosing to disappear down to the river or over to a friend's house whenever she could escape. The little time she was around her mother she spent mostly pretending to be engrossed in a book and saying little. Carmen thought her mother was beautiful and sophisticated. She did not dress like any of Carmen's friends mothers who preferred to wear conservative dresses that hung on their bodies without movement. Carmen noticed how people reacted to her mother, too; the men were friendly and overly helpful. The women were standoffish, their eyes roaming over Angelique's fitted expensive dresses with envy and judgment. Carmen did like the way that her mother pretended not to notice, smiling and handing out compliments to them while insulting them under her breath. Everybody was country to her and Carmen thought that was funny. Still, she was uncomfortable around the woman who had abandoned her nearly nine years ago. She resented being left with her grandmother, who was overprotective and irritable, but at least she knew her.

"Carr-mon!" her grandmother yelled for the second time from the verandah where she'd taken to spending her afternoons. Carmen bristled at the sound of her voice. She had been sitting under the shade of a large logwood tree waiting. She had polished all the furniture in the house, polished the verandah with red paste, and brought her grandmother's afternoon medication to her—tea with a shot of amber rum—earlier than usual so that she could have some time to herself. They had a maid to do all those chores, but Ruby insisted that her granddaughter work around the house so she didn't grow up "slack" or "worthless." To Carmen, it seemed that her grandmother didn't want her to have a moment for herself.

"Carr-mon!" Ruby yelled again. Carmen dragged herself up the yard and onto the verandah. "What are you doing? Why did it take you so long to answer me?"

Carmen shrugged and said nothing.

"I asked you a question."

"Nothing."

Ruby eyed her granddaughter. "Nothing? Idle hands are the devil's workshop. Look what happened to your mother."

Carmen turned her head to the side so her grandmother couldn't see her roll her eyes.

"I want you to go into town and pick up some things for me."

Carmen tried to hide her smile. Going to town meant she could get away for a while.

"Here." Ruby reached into her bosom and pulled out a small wad of bills. She unfolded a few and handed them to Carmen who gingerly closed her hand around the money. The bill that was on the outside was slightly damp. "Take this list and go down to the market." Ruby handed her a small piece of paper.

Carmen skipped off the verandah and started towards the gate. Ruby yelled after her, "And don't forget to bring back mi change!" Ruby began to reconsider whether she should have let Carmen go off by herself, but by the time she changed her mind, Carmen was long gone.

Carmen picked up the items on the list, shortchanging half a pound here and there, then shoving the leftover bills in one pocket and the coins in the other. When she returned, she carefully walked around to the backdoor to avoid her grandmother who was now snoring lightly from her seat on the verandah. Carmen dropped the sack of items on the kitchen table along with the loose change and walked around to the gate. She headed back towards town, turning up the last street towards the main road where she knew she would see him. She walked past Mr. Smith's roadside bar where he served passersby with a shot of white rum or a stout. As she approached, she saw him among the small group of boys playing football in the street. He wasn't wearing a shirt and his dark skin glistened in the sunlight. She picked him out easily from the crowd, with his short dreadlocks dancing as he bounced the ball on his knees before shooting it across the street off the top of his head. He was nearly 15, too old for her, but she wasn't deterred. At 5'5" tall and with slight curves already developing, she looked much older than her 12 years. They'd known each other for several months; he lived in a rural area on the opposite side of the town from where she lived. She'd stumbled across the boys playing football on this street on one of her trips back from town to run errands. That day she first saw him, Carmen stayed around for over an hour. When she finally returned home, her grandmother had interrogated her unceasingly. Carmen said she had almost made it home when she'd realized she'd forgotten the Dettol disinfectant and so had gone back to get it. Her grandmother had looked at her suspiciously, but saw the two bags Carmen was carrying and decided to drop it. She warned her though, as she noticed her granddaughter's figure, that she "better watch herself." After that, Carmen had started volunteering to run errands in town every chance she got. She would catch a lift whenever she could to allow her extra time to watch the football games, and Peter in particular. She liked the way he moved and liked him even more the first time she heard him playing his guitar while taking a break after one of the games. He told her he had started a reggae band with some of his friends.

After a few minutes of play, he finally noticed her and came over. "What's up?" Peter said.

Carmen smiled. "I need you."

Peter smiled mischievously." For what?"

She pushed him. "Not that. I want you to take me to Kingston."

Peter frowned. "What for?

"I need to see my father," she told him.

He shrugged and said he'd take her, but not today. They had practice.

"Well can we go tomorrow?"

"Yeah man, we can do that."

She smiled again and they made plans to meet the next morning before she hurried home.

That evening, Carmen went to her room early, claiming to be tired. She went through her dresser drawers, picking out what clothes she would take with her the next day. She didn't bother to pack a lot of things; she knew her father's side of the family was well off since they lived in the uptown part of Kingston. Her grandmother had told her several times how they should have sent for Carmen. But they didn't know her anymore, Carmen reasoned. If her father knew her, he would take care of her. He would buy her all the things she should've had if her own mother hadn't taken her away when she was younger and left her with the woman she ran to Canada to be away from. Carmen wanted to leave Somerset Grove, also, but she wasn't sure about going to Canada. She wouldn't know anyone there and she wasn't good at making friends. Boys were another matter though. She was beginning to learn that boys were willing to do a lot of things for her if she looked at them a certain way. This is how she got Peter to volunteer to take her across the island to see her father.

Shortly after dawn the next day, Carmen walked a half mile down the main road to where Peter was waiting at the bottom of Mr. Johnson's gate. Carmen had chosen this spot to meet because it was far enough away from her house so that her family wouldn't hear Peter's motorbike and Mr. Johnson was old and half-deaf, so he couldn't tell anyone that he'd heard Carmen sneaking off with some boy in the middle of the night.

She would have preferred to have worn a dress to meet the other side of her family, but the motorbike had made it impractical, so she settled for a pair of pink pants and a short-sleeved white blouse. She had pulled her long hair into a ponytail and pinned the curly ends around the base so they wouldn't dry out on the ride. She climbed onto the bike behind Peter, slipping her arms through the straps of the bag on her back so she could hold on to him.

Peter sped down the highway at top speed, weaving around minibuses and trucks taking produce to nearby markets. They arrived in Kingston shortly after noon, and Carmen was relieved to have arrived after the harrowing trip. They finally found the house after stopping several times for directions. When they reached the bottom of the gate, Carmen looked up at the estate in awe. The lawn was perfectly manicured and the verandah that wrapped around the house gleamed in the sunlight while the two lion statutes flanked either side of the stairs. They walked up the path to the house and Carmen knocked on the mahogany door. She suddenly felt nervous, smoothing her blouse and ponytail with her hands, and then she took a deep breath to relax herself as she heard footsteps approaching the door. She would be alright. This was her family. She glanced over her shoulder and smiled at Peter, who was leaning casually against one of the lions. He looked out of place in his knee-length cut off shorts and faded red t-shirt, but he didn't seem to care.

After a few moments, the door swung open and a tall woman stood before them. Her closely cropped hair was graying slightly, but her smooth face did not betray her age. Her eyes swept across Carmen and then Peter before she spoke.

"Yes?" she said, not so much as a question, but more of a demand to know what Carmen was doing there.

"Is Mrs. Chambers home?" Carmen asked.

"Who shall I say is calling?"

"I'm her granddaughter," she told her. "Carmen." She felt the need to add.

The woman considered them both a moment. "Wait here, please." She disappeared inside the house, shutting the door behind her.

It seemed like several minutes passed before the door opened again. The same woman was standing there. This time she told them—rather Carmen—to come in. Peter followed behind and stood off to the side of the doorway. The woman pointed to a room to the left of the entryway and said, "In there so."

Carmen peered into the room and saw an older woman wearing a yellow skirt and a white short-sleeved blouse sitting poised on the settee, her reading glasses perched on the end of her nose as she examined whatever she had just finished writing in a journal. The woman didn't acknowledge them initially, which didn't seem to bother Peter who sat down and made himself comfortable in a chair as if he belonged there. Carmen hesitated, and then sat in a chair next to Peter. She looked back at the woman who had opened the door, half-expecting her to tell Carmen what to do or announce her or something, but the woman had already turned her back on them and was heading down the hall.

Carmen chewed her bottom lip and looked around the room, taking in all the dark furniture and rich tapestries and waited patiently for the woman seated on the other side of the room to say something.

"You know when you come into somebody's home, you should always say 'good morning' or 'good evening' or something," Mrs. Chambers said when she finally looked up.

"I'm sorry, good afternoon, um..." she trailed off, not knowing how to address this woman who was her grandmother, but still a stranger to her. She looked over at Peter for help. He yawned audibly and rubbed his stomach as if he'd just finished a good meal. He had no interest in this exchange.

Carmen looked back to her grandmother who was cutting her eyes at Peter. She shook her head and turned her attention towards Carmen. "That's alright. It's not your fault. You probably weren't raised to know any better."

Carmen didn't know how to react. She wanted to be angry, but she couldn't; she still needed this woman. She sat in the chair looking flustered.

"Come over here and let me take a look at you," Mrs. Chambers finally said. Carmen walked over to her grandmother. They studied each other for a minute before Mrs. Chambers reached up and took Carmen's hand. "If I didn't see you with my own eyes, I wouldn't believe it was you," she continued. "I haven't seen you since your mother took you and left, I don't even know how many years now. Lawdamercy. So where is your mother anyway? And who is this you brought with you?" She nodded towards Peter. Carmen introduced Peter, who said hello and not much else. Mrs. Chambers considered him for a moment then decided she'd paid him enough attention. She didn't like his dreads or the clothes he wore that said to her that he was poor or just didn't care what anyone thought. Still, other than the ragged clothes and hair, she had to admit that he looked clean, though that didn't stop her from disliking him. He had that air, like he didn't think much of who she was or what she had, and that bothered her.

Mrs. Chambers spent the next half an hour telling Carmen why the estrangement from her family was everyone's fault but hers.

"You know your mother just picked up and left without saying a word, much less a thank you for all that I did for her." She took Carmen's silence as an invitation to continue with her version of the facts. "It's true. I didn't even know all of what went on. I thought everything was fine. Well, I mean she had some disagreements with your father, but nothing to leave over. I don't think so anyway. I guess some people are never satisfied. No matter what you give them, it's never enough." She shook her head and adjusted the glasses perched on her nose.

By the time Mrs. Chambers had finished her rambling, Carmen was wondering if she made a mistake in coming there. She had imagined her grandmother being excited to see her. Instead, all she wanted to do was complain.

"But I'm glad to see you again," her grandmother said, finally.

Carmen ignored her statement. "Where is my dad? Is he here?"

"Oh, you want to see your father? Of course. Yes, he's around town somewhere. I'll have someone go look for him." She walked over to the entrance of the room and called for Miss Marlene. A few moments later, the woman who had answered the door appeared. Mrs. Chambers asked her to send someone to look for Clifton. "Tell him I need to see him." The woman gave Mrs. Chambers a strange look before shaking her head on her way out of the room. Mrs. Chambers pretended she didn't notice and turned back to Carmen. "So where was I?"

The swell of the afternoon heat began to fade into the cool evening. Carmen peered out of the window for what must have been the tenth time that hour alone. Every time she heard the sound of a car's engine as it rumbled up the road or a man's voice carried over the wind she looked out to see if it was her father. She turned down Peter's invitation to go into town while they waited for fear she might miss her father while she was out. Peter told her she shouldn't worry about that; that he wouldn't just leave if he knew she was there after not seeing her for all these years, but she resisted. Peter shrugged and told her he'd be back later. That was hours ago and she had not seen either one of them. Her grandmother had gone to lie down shortly after Peter left, apparently comfortable enough to do so now that he was out of her house. Now Carmen wished she had gone with Peter. She was bored and the day seemed to drag with nothing to do but stare out of the window.

Carmen dozed off on the settee for what seemed like a few minutes but when she awoke it was already getting dark outside. A small table lamp cast a slight glow on the floor making the opulent room feel cozy. She felt hungry and a little disoriented. She heard footsteps approaching and Miss Marlene appeared in the doorway.

"You hungry?" she asked.

Carmen nodded.

"Come," she ordered. Carmen followed her out of the room and down a hallway to a brightly lit kitchen. She told Carmen to sit down at the table while she fixed her a plate. Carmen devoured the food, forgetting her manners. Miss Marlene smiled.

"You always loved my rice and peas."

Carmen looked up from her plate and studied the woman. "You know me?" she asked.

"Yes, you probably don't remember, you were too young. But I remember you. I used to help take care of you. You used to call me Miss Bailey back then."

"My mother didn't take care of me when I was here either?" Carmen frowned.

"Oh, she did. She tried, but she was so young and your father was..." she trailed off. "Well, he wasn't always around, so I helped her as much as I could. And you used to love my cooking."

"Why wasn't my father around?"

"Well—"

Loud laughter floated up through the window and Miss Marlene leaned over to look outside.

"Is that him?" Carmen asked, getting up from the table.

"No, my dear. That is my oldest son. Looks like he must've met up with your friend in town."

The two boys walked inside. Miss Marlene's son sported dreads that fell just below his shoulders. He stood a few inches taller than Peter and had a full goatee, which he stroked when he laughed. He looked to be about 18 years old. Peter stood behind him, his hands casually draped over a black guitar case.

"Where did you get that guitar from?" Carmen asked.

"It's Gregory's." He gestured toward Miss Marlene's son. "You should've come into town. I saw these guys outside of a little restaurant. We had a nice little jam session. They like how I play." Peter grinned.

Gregory nodded. "Yeah man, you can play a little." He smiled, showing his perfect white teeth.

"That's Carmen, the one who came here looking for her father," Peter explained to Gregory.

Gregory nodded. He looked over at his mother who busied herself fixing plates for the boys without asking whether either of them was hungry. They ate anyway, and after they were done she cleared away the dishes while Gregory entertained them with stories.

Jennifer Chambers entered the kitchen just then. Carmen noticed the mood changed immediately, the lightness of the moment disappearing along with the last hues of color left by the sun.

"Well," Jennifer Chambers exclaimed in a tone that seemed artificially light. "Looks like you're all enjoying yourselves, eh?" She tried to hide her disappointment at seeing Peter in her kitchen.

"We just had a little bite to eat, just waiting for your son to come," Miss Marlene said. "You haven't heard from him yet?" She said it more as a statement than a question. She looked at Mrs. Chambers pointedly.

Mrs. Chambers avoided her gaze. "You know I've been in my room all this time. I don't know how you think I would have gotten any news in there." The light, sing-songy tone of her voice did not disguise the irritation that lay underneath.

Mrs. Chambers told them it was late and they should go to bed. She told Marlene to set Carmen up in her mother's old room and reluctantly requested that she also prepare one of the other guest rooms for Peter to stay in—the one farthest from her own, before she left for the day.

Carmen piped up. "What about my father? I want to wait up for him."

"I don't know, I don't know!" The exasperation in her voice no longer hidden. "It seems like that boy I sent to find him must've gotten lost or something," Mrs. Chambers said. "We'll just figure it out in the morning. Too late to do anything now anyway."

Carmen reluctantly agreed. Miss Marlene made up their beds before she and Gregory left for the evening. Carmen fell into bed, still exhausted from the day's journey and hopeful of the promise of the next day.

Carmen was awakened by the early morning sun's gentle kiss of warmth on the side of her face as it illuminated the entire room. She got out of bed and quickly dressed before venturing out of her room to see if her father had finally made his way to see her. Despite being exhausted, she had struggled to stay awake long after the house had settled into stillness the night before, the only sound coming from the grandfather clock in the sitting room announcing the hour. Every time a vehicle passed, she raised her head from the pillow, straining to hear whether the car was making its way up to the house. She eventually stopped resisting and let slumber envelope her in its embrace.

The house itself was quiet, but Carmen could hear voices drifting in from outside. One of them sounded distinctly male and older, so she followed the sounds towards the back of the house, her excitement building as she neared with every step. When she arrived at the back door to the kitchen, she was disappointed to see that the male voice belonged to a much older man who looked to be about her grandmother's age. She could see they were arguing, but she was not close enough to make out the words. She stepped outside the door in time to hear the man tell her grandmother that he shouldn't be surprised she wasn't able to tell the child the truth since she couldn't even admit it to herself. The man had his back towards Carmen, but he turned to follow the direction of her grandmother's stare when she told him to be quiet. He looked down at Carmen and smiled sadly. The lines around his eyes and his mostly gray hair spoke more of fatigue than age. Carmen recognized him from the photo she had framed in her room. This was her other grandfather. He beckoned to her and she walked towards him. He lifted her chin and looked into her eyes, then used the same hand to smooth over the stray hairs that escaped from her ponytail.

"I can't believe you traveled all this way by yourself," Mr. Chambers said. "I wish I had known you were coming. I just found out this morning that you were here and I have to go out of the country tomorrow," he said. "Anyway, my dear, sorry you came all this way for nothing." He looked at his wife as he spoke. She looked up at him defiantly, her hands resting on her hips. "I'll be back later on to take you home. Your other grandparents must be worried about you." He walked away without another word, got into his car, and backed down the driveway.

Carmen looked at her grandmother, confused. "What does he mean 'for nothing?'"

Mrs. Chambers waved her hand in the air as if she were brushing away a bothersome fly. "I don't know what that old fool is talking about," she said, and walked inside the house.

"Where is my dad?" Carmen called after her but received no response. Carmen went in the backdoor and stood in the kitchen, her brow furrowed with frustration. Miss Marlene was in there, removing seeds from the freshly picked ackee. A pot of water bubbled on the stove cooking out the salt from the fish she would season and sauté with the ackee and scallions. She threw each seed into a bowl with such force that some of them bounced out and hit the counter.

"Do you know where my father is?" Carmen asked.

Miss Marlene didn't turn around. "He's not coming here and s*he* knows it," she said, pointing her lips in the direction of Mrs. Chambers' room. "She act like she don't see what is going on." Miss Marlene kissed her teeth with her tongue.

Carmen stared at her back, confused. The knife in Marlene's hand steadily coming down hard on the scallions was the only noise in the kitchen.

"All the opportunities that boy had and gone to waste. My son never had any of that." She threw the knife in the sink. Carmen fought the tears burning her eyes. She ran back to the room she stayed in and began putting her things in the little bag she'd brought with her.

Carmen didn't understand why her father would not come and why her grandmother avoided telling her the truth. She felt the heavy undercurrents running through the house that tugged at her, threatening to drag her down, but she didn't know what they were. Had she known that her grandfather no longer *lived* in that house and that he only maintained a residence there for appearances, she might have understood her grandmother's state of denial. Had she known that her grandfather's real home for the past two years was now about five miles away, that it was small, but modern and was rumored to be serviced by a woman who did more than just the cooking and laundry, she might have understood why her grandmother seemed so miserable. Had she known that Clifton had stopped coming around this house not long after his father moved out because, with his mother blaming him for the departure of his wife and daughter and now her own husband, Clifton had no reason to call this place home, Carmen might have understood why her father again ignored one of his mother's frequent requests to please stop by. And if she knew that her grandmother never told the boy she sent to look for Clifton to mention that Carmen was there because she wanted to see if her beloved son would come back just to visit her, she would have understood why he had not come to see her.

Carmen didn't know that although her grandmother had coveted her grandfather since that first day she had seen him in the town square in Kingston wearing his military uniform and that he had coveted her grandmother as she passed by in a fitted dress on her way to class, they had never really been attracted to one another. She didn't know that Jennifer Anderson was most impressed by her perception that Anthony Chambers was interested in a career in politics and he by her drive to become a writer. She didn't know that the reason they decided to marry was not so much for love as it was to please those around them who thought they would make an elite power couple. Carmen didn't know that her grandparents were months into their marriage before they discovered that they didn't really have much in common. Tony Chambers would have preferred to work as a photojournalist and Jennifer had only been interested in the status that marriage would bring her, a girl from a family of modest means.

As soon as they were married Jennifer Chambers put her typewriter up and announced her pregnancy. Tony Chambers reluctantly put away his true ambitions and became the stable professional that everyone expected him to be.

To the world, they were the envied perfect couple, but in private they merely tolerated each other, a fact not lost on their only child, Clifton, who chose rebellion over conformity, thumbing his nose at his parents' notion of success and happiness.

For his part, Tony Chambers set about to prove to his father that he was responsible, building a successful business for himself, and then a successful political career in the Prime Minister's Cabinet. And Jennifer Chambers, for her part, set about to prove that she could move in her husband's world. She learned to tip her head back while looking down her nose at others she now considered below her. She no longer found humor in anything, but developed the fake sounding laugh that hid her less-than-perfect smile. The more the gap between her and Tony grew, the more she tried to fit into his world, spending more time socializing with Kingston's elite, throwing parties, talking about how useless the help was, and cutting off communication with her family, even foregoing attending her own father's funeral after he battled a long illness. She did, however, dote on her prize, the one thing that ensured her entry into this life—Clifton.

Jennifer did herself more damage than good. The one redeeming quality her husband thought she had was that she, having grown up not having much, would be the type of person devoted to her family and family values. Instead, she showed herself to be self-centered, arrogant, and a worthless mother, letting her son grow up to be spoiled, wild, and one more thing for him to deal with.

Tony was the model husband in public, attentive as much as needed at social affairs and providing Jennifer with the financial means to do what she wanted or needed, but in private he kept away from her as much as he could get away with. He worked hard and stayed late at the office and volunteered for trips abroad when the opportunity presented itself. He slept in the guest bedroom whenever he could, claiming he did not want to wake her after coming in too late. And when he got tired of being lonely, he dealt the ultimate insult to her by keeping company with someone from downtown Kingston.

There was speculation in town that the dreadlocked aspiring musician and son of Miss Marlene bore a slight resemblance to the Cabinet member, but those rumors were brushed off as nonsense, no more fervently than by Jennifer Chambers. In private, she disliked Miss Marlene, who displayed more arrogance than she thought the woman would be able to get away with working for anyone else, coming from an area of town even worse than her own. But, her husband would not allow the woman be terminated, putting his foot down on the matter and ending the discussion on it. Besides that, no one else would tolerate working for the temperamental Jennifer Chambers and for whatever reason, Miss Marlene had always kept the family's sordid secrets to herself.

Letting Clifton grow unfettered by the rules of society and the expectations of his father became Jennifer's way of getting back at her husband for the rumors that floated behind her back. She was confident that when Clifton inherited all of his father's good fortune he would take care of the mother who had adored him all his life. That all changed when Angelique appeared on her doorstep that day. At first, she liked the strong-willed girl who had shown up out of the blue demanding her son take responsibility for his actions. Angelique reminded her of herself and with this young girl, came a daughter that would love and take care of her mother-in-law in her old age. The turmoil in the marriage between her beloved son and daughter-in-law changed all of that. Angelique's heated departure that summer so many years ago followed by the years of silence—no visits, no letters, no messages—put an end to any plans she had for the future of her second chance family. And as much as she loved Clifton, she knew that she raised him to be too selfish to give any thought to her or anyone else.

When the boy she had sent looking for Clifton came back to tell her that he had found Clifton at his latest girlfriend's house and that he had waved the boy off when he had relayed Mrs. Chambers' message, she had remained expressionless. She thanked the boy and told him she was sure Clifton would be by sometime later in the day and that he shouldn't say anything to anyone who asked. The boy had shrugged at the explanation and headed back to whatever he had been doing before being directed to run all over town looking for the son that never wanted to be found. Mrs. Chambers hadn't said a word to anyone else although it was clear that Miss Marlene knew what had happened without Jennifer saying a word, and she hated her for it.

Jennifer Chambers went to lie down as she always did when the pressure became too much for her. She had taken a cup of bush tea with her to help her sleep, one of the few customs she had from her past that she had not discarded. She would deal with the Clifton issue later. The tea took effect quickly, so she didn't hear Carmen's footsteps slapping down the tiled hallway as she went looking for Peter. She didn't hear Carmen tell Peter she was ready to leave now and didn't hear the roar of Peter's motorbike as they sped down the road. By the time she would awaken, Carmen would be halfway back to Somerset Grove and Jennifer would feel the emptiness of the house deep within her soul.

23

Carmen looked around the classroom and chose the seat closest to the window. She looked outside and watched her mother walking away up the street. She wondered if she would come back this time. She felt twenty pairs of eyes boring into her. Carmen hated it in Winnipeg. The kids looked at her like she was some sort of exotic pet. They ran their selfish fingers along her skin, trying to see if the color would come off. They tugged at her braids or the soft, wavy puffs from her pigtails, fascinated that it was not slippery or bone-straight like their own. It felt like cotton to them and they told her so and ignored her protests to stop touching her.

Carmen hated her teacher even more. Whenever Mrs. Hammond called on her, the woman always acted like she couldn't understand what Carmen was saying, even though Ruby had never let her granddaughter speak anything but the Queen's English and she spoke it better than anyone else in that class. After a while, Carmen would only look at her and shrug whenever she asked her the answer to a question. Eventually Mrs. Hammond stopped calling on Carmen and essentially ignored her, which suited Carmen just fine.

At lunch Carmen preferred to sit alone rather than answer all those questions about whether she could tan, what she ate, what she put in her hair, and why her father didn't come to Canada with them. They, with their perfect little families headed by fathers who worked in offices and came home for dinner every night at 5:30, and their mothers who made casseroles out of canned soup and tuna, but no seasoning, for dinner on the nights when they didn't have a PTA meeting. They furrowed their brows in confusion when she told them her mother worked at a hotel, but that she didn't know *exactly* what her mother did. It was not that she didn't know, but they had no business judging her or her mother. It wasn't any of their business that even though Carmen's mother was assigned to the front desk, she spent as much time checking in guests as she did collecting out-of-town boyfriends lounging in the hotel bar where she would spend her off-hours. On those nights, Carmen would let herself into the apartment, make her own dinner, and get herself off to school in the morning. She got used to it over the years. By the time she was 16, Carmen lived as much of an independent life as any adult.

Carmen arrived home from school to find her mother stretched out on the sofa, one jean-clad leg hanging over the side while her hand balanced a glass of wine on it. The other hand was draped across her forehead. The revealing tank top, bangles, and large hoop earrings were unchanged from the night before, signs that Angelique had recently returned home from a night out. She looked to be asleep and Carmen wondered whether she should extract the glass from her mother's fingers before it tumbled to the ground and she would have to clean it up. She pushed the front door close with her hip and dropped her backpack to the ground with a thud.

"Do you have to make up so much noise?" Angelique did not move.

Carmen walked past her mother toward the kitchen. "Sorry."

"What are you doing home already?"

"It's 4:00," Carmen replied.

"It is?" Angelique pushed herself up on her elbows and squinted at the clock that hung above the dining room table. "I'm supposed to be at work at 4:30." She swung her other leg onto the ground and ran her fingers through her long locks. "Pass me the phone," she ordered.

Carmen scanned the room looking for the cordless receiver. She sighed deeply as she kicked at the newspapers lying on the ground and pushed aside the pile of clothes laying on the loveseat. She had just cleaned up the house before she left for school that morning and Angelique had already started messing it up in the few hours she'd been home. Carmen located the phone underneath the jacket that Angelique must have dropped on the dining room table on her way to getting her wine from the kitchen. She handed it to her mother, and then began straightening up the living room—again. She heard Angelique on the phone expertly fabricating an excuse to her supervisor about coming down with some sort of stomach flu. She tossed the phone down and sighed with satisfaction.

"I didn't feel like going today anyway. That Cheryl is so jealous of me. Working with her is just miserable," Angelique said, referring to the 50-something white woman who apparently did not care for Angelique's flirtatious behavior or her casual attitude towards work.

Carmen ignored her mother's last comment. "Should I make something for dinner?" she asked as she looked at the bare stove. "I could make some pork chops."

"No, don't bother to cook anything. I'll take care of dinner," Angelique said.

Carmen didn't feel like cooking anyway, but the alternative, spending an evening with one of her mother's greasy "friends" as he mooned over her all night just so she wouldn't have to cook and her mother wouldn't have to spend her own money, was not palatable either. Particularly if it meant that Lexroy, the latest one, would be coming over. Lexroy was a tall, dark chocolate man who split his time equally between the gym and his "business." The self-described entrepreneur always made Carmen uneasy; he wore too much jewelry for a man and used way too much Drakkar Noir. He always made a big display of giving Angelique money or peeling off bills to pay the check at a restaurant instead of using a credit card. Angelique didn't seem to mind his flashy ways and didn't seem too interested in knowing exactly what Lexroy did in his business anyway.

Whenever Angelique wasn't working, she was out at lounges and bars peddling herself as a master's student, trying to set herself apart from the other women who had nothing to offer but their bodies and unyielding devotion in exchange for a better life. Angelique had learned that rich or poor alike, men were more impressed by women pursuing degrees and she used this bit of knowledge to her advantage, taking whatever these men would give, even if it meant that they couldn't pay their own bills. She accepted it all with a smile, not caring what hardship it left or what heartbreak resulted when she tired of them and moved on to the next. She almost never gave them anything, but allowed them to assume that an affectionate touch or flirtatious smile would lead to something more down the road. She usually juggled two at a time in the city, with a reliable third back home in Jamaica who always shuttled her around the island, happy for any attention she would give. Most of the wealthier ones cut their losses and moved on. A few of the others became angry when they found out that she was using them, but she usually managed to get away unscathed and with everything she had gained from them. The new BMW Lexroy allowed Angelique to drive was just the latest example of the items she'd collected.

Despite her distaste for her mother's manipulative ways, Carmen did not really complain about the money, clothes, and nice furnishings, even the three-bedroom rambler house that trickled down to her as a result of her mother's beguiling ways. She was, however, disappointed by Angelique's lack of motherly instinct. Even when Angelique was around, it was Carmen who was making sure that the house they lived in was clean and dinner was on the table every night.

"I have too much to do tonight. Can I just run up to the Chinese restaurant and get something?" Carmen asked.

"I thought you had too much to do? Don't worry about it."

Angelique picked up the phone and punched in a number. After a few moments, Carmen could hear the sound of a deep male voice on the other end. She hoped her mother wasn't talking to Lexroy, but that was wishful thinking.

Angelique hung up the phone. "Lexroy will be here in half an hour." She stood up from the sofa and stretched. "I'm going to get ready." She turned to head towards the bedroom. "Please clean this place up. Such a mess," she tossed over her shoulder and giggled.

Carmen let out a loud sigh and stomped around the room as she picked up the things that had been dropped.

"What are you sighing for?" Angelique turned back on Carmen.

"Nothing," Carmen replied.

"No, don't tell me 'nothing.' I heard you. What is wrong with you?"

Carmen could hear the tension in Angelique's voice, but she couldn't stop herself. "I already cleaned up this morning and it's messy again and you make it sound like it's my fault." Carmen picked up a dirty glass from the coffee table, rubbing at the water mark left behind while trying to avoid Angelique's gaze.

Angelique stepped in front of Carmen, forcing her to straighten up and make eye contact with her. "Look," she began, "it is I who makes sure the bills get paid around here, puts clothes on your back, and food in your belly. You putting any clothes on my back? You putting a roof over my head? Answer that," Angelique demanded.

Carmen looked at her mother in silence. As Angelique stood waiting, it seemed she suddenly realized that Carmen was now as tall as she was, and the girl could look her directly in the eye. Angelique backed away a few feet.

"That's what I thought," Angelique said. "You think you're a big woman? Go and get a job and start paying some bills." Angelique started walking towards her bedroom and stopped. "As a matter of fact," she continued, "if you think you can do better for yourself, you can leave anytime, but until then, this is my house and you will do as I say. Are you hearing me?"

Carmen drew her lips together tightly before finally speaking. "Yes, Mum," Carmen responded.

Angelique started back down the hall, mumbling to herself. Carmen finished straightening up the living room before tackling the mess in the kitchen. She had just finished wiping down the countertops when she heard the doorbell ring twice. From where Carmen was standing, she could see Lexroy's hulking frame through the frosted glass of the front door. She stayed in the kitchen until she saw Angelique appear around the corner, heading for the foyer. Angelique shot Carmen a warning look before she reached for the door handle. As soon as Angelique turned her head, Carmen slipped out of the kitchen and down the hallway. Inside her room, she flopped down on her bed and pressed her palms against her eyelids as she felt the tears threatening to spill from her wells.

From somewhere in the house she thought she heard Lexroy's voice say, "You're not bringing the gyal?" Carmen knew he was referring to her.

"She must be in her room," Carmen heard her mother respond. The voices became muffled as they talked over each other. Finally she heard her mother's voice more clearly as it grew closer. "I'll check," she hissed. Carmen heard her mother's footsteps coming down the hall. She quickly got off the bed and threw herself into the chair at her desk and pretended to read a book. Angelique opened the door without knocking. "We're going out instead. You want to come?" she asked Carmen in a way that suggested the answer.

"I can't," Carmen replied and gestured towards the textbook.

"We'll bring you something back," Angelique said, already closing the door.

There was some brief discussion before the front door closed and a car drove off. She got up from the desk and looked out her window which faced the front street. The road was quiet and empty, except for the shiny black BMW that sat in the driveway. Carmen rummaged through her closet, holding different tops up in front of her, and then discarding them on her twin bed. She swung the closet door closed and headed down the hallway to her mother's bedroom. Her eyes roamed all over the large closet taking in all the clothing before spying a brand new white silk tank top. Angelique had so many new clothes she never ended up wearing that Carmen was not concerned that her mother would notice one missing. She ripped the price tag off and slipped the tank top on over her head. It dipped low enough in the front to expose her cleavage. Carmen examined herself in the mirror, pleased with how the top looked on her. She glanced over at Angelique's dressing table on the other side of the large four-poster bed, her eyes drawn to the little jewelry box. She walked over, flipped the lid open, and selected a pair of 14-karat gold hoops and bangles to complete her look. As she was turning towards the door, she noticed the spare car key sitting on the other end of the dresser. She reached over and picked the key up, turning it over in her hand. She smiled, walked out of the room, and closed the door.

Carmen tooted the horn several times before Lori finally opened the front door and looked out at the BMW idling in the driveway. She hesitantly stepped outside to get a better look when Carmen popped her head out the driver's side window and waved excitedly. Lori let out a squeal and half-ran, half-skipped towards the car, her blonde, shoulder-length bobbed haircut bouncing around her face. She jumped in the passenger side and looked around the car interior.

"Holy crap, Carmen, your mom actually let you use her car?" Lori's green eyes flashed in amazement as she ran her hands along the dashboard, as if checking to see that the car was real.

"Not exactly," Carmen said.

"Ohmigod, Carmen, are you serious? You just *took* it?" Lori looked a little worried.

"She won't know that I ever drove it. She's out with one of her boyfriends and knowing her, she won't be back until late anyway." Carmen shrugged. "That's what she gets when she leaves me unattended. She didn't even leave me any food for dinner, so it's only reasonable that I take it. It'll be fine. Let's go get Aamani."

They drove for about 10 minutes before stopping, rather abruptly, in front of Aamani's house. Carmen only had her learner's permit and her lack of driving ability showed on the ride over. She'd turned the corners too widely or too narrowly, and she had trouble maneuvering the car down the residential streets whenever there was one car heading in the opposite direction and another parked on her side of the road. More than once she narrowly missed side-swiping a parked vehicle. By the time they arrived, Lori was feigning whiplash.

"Shut up, Lori," Carmen said as she watched Lori rubbing her neck.

"What?" Lori suppressed a giggle.

The front door of the house swung open and Aamani came out dressed in a loose-fitting red track suit, followed by her mother dressed in her traditional sari. Aamani's long black hair hung down the middle of her back in a large braid and on her shoulder she carried her school backpack. Aamani looked irritated as she walked towards the street where the car waited. Aamani's mother stood on the front steps. "I don't understand why you need to go out to study. Why can't you and your friends stay here? I can make you something to eat and you can study in the kitchen."

"No, Mother. It's too loud," Aamani said, barely hiding her annoyance. "Besides, I need to get something from the library."

Aamani's mother put her hands on her hips and peered inside the car. Carmen and Lori instinctively sunk lower in their seats so that the woman could not see what they were wearing. They waved and called out hello from the car. Aamani's mother half-heartedly waved back and finally gave in. "Don't stay out too late. Your father would have a fit if he knew you were leaving the house now."

"Yes, Mum." Aamani ran to the car and jumped in the backseat before her mother could change her mind.

Carmen drove away carefully as Aamani's mother looked on, and turned the first corner to get out of view. She nearly swiped another parked car by turning the corner too wide again, but quickly got the car under control.

"I don't know, Carmen. You could get in trouble for this," Lori said. "We could all get in trouble for this." Lori peered out the window to see how close they had gotten to the other car.

Carmen rolled her eyes. "You want me to bring it back?" she asked. "It's either this or the bus."

"No way," Aamani said. "I wouldn't risk getting caught by my crazy dad because I got home late from riding the *bus,*" she added. "Just relax, Lori. It'll be fine." Aamani slid down in her seat and pulled off the track suit. Underneath she wore a red fitted t-shirt and tight jeans. She unzipped her backpack and pulled out her purse and makeup kit. "Where are we going?" Aamani asked as she began to apply eyeliner.

"Dream," Carmen said. Dream was a lounge-style restaurant that the high school students were talking about. With the drinking age being only 18 and the lax security, many an underage student outfitted in pumps and makeup had flirted her way into the club.

"Yah?" Lori perked up from the scolding and started fluffing her hair.

"Yeah," Carmen said. "I think we could probably stay until around 10:00 or so and be back home before Aamani's dad gets off work or my mom gets back from her date."

"That's so early." Lori groaned.

"Your parents let you get away with everything. Mine don't," Aamani said.

"And my mom thinks I'm at home studying. If she knew I was out clubbing, I'd be dead," Carmen said.

"Next time you guys should sleep over," Lori said.

Carmen and Aamani both let out exaggerated laughs.

"You have your own bed. Why do you need to sleep out at anyone else's yard? You want people to think you don't have a home?" Carmen imitated her mother's Jamaican lilt.

"Exactly!" Aamani giggled. "Nice girls don't go around sleeping out at other people's houses. What for?" Aamani said in a perfect Indian accent.

"Okay, so that's out." Lori rolled her eyes and smiled. "Let's just go see what's going on."

They arrived at the tail-end of the happy hour when the deejay started to play. Carmen threw her hands up in the air and swirled her hips in time to the bass of the of the R&B rhythm.

"Ahhh, yes! This is my song," Carmen yelled. She quickly moved to the tiny dance floor centered between the restaurant and the lounge. Aamani followed behind, leaving Lori who decided to wait by one of the standing bars and watch her friends from the side. Carmen and Aamani bounced along to the rhythm and before long, two guys who appeared to be college-aged invited themselves to join them. The two girls danced for several songs enjoying the company so much they had not noticed that Lori had disappeared. Around 9:30 they began looking for Lori who was nowhere to be found. They circled through the dimly lit restaurant and bar a second time with no success.

"Where the heck did she go?" Aamani asked, looking through the bobbing crowd one more time.

"I don't know, but if she doesn't show up in the next few minutes, we're leaving," Carmen said, visibly annoyed.

"We can't just leave her, can we?" Aamani asked.

"Why not? She knows you and I can't get caught out late. If she gets home at midnight, her mother will probably fix her a cup of cocoa and ask her if she had fun. If we show up late, our mothers will be measuring us for coffins."

"They'd get you a coffin?" Aamani asked.

"Shut up!" Carmen laughed. "Come on, let's go check outside. Maybe she's out there cooling off."

"Or heating up," Aamani said. "Hang on a sec." Aamani ran over towards the guys they had met earlier and exchanged small pieces of paper with them.

"What was that all about?" Carmen asked.

"I was exchanging numbers with them," Aamani said matter-of-factly.

"Are you crazy? You can't have them calling your house."

"I know. That's why I gave them your number. They'll be calling us tomorrow. I'll come home after school with you."

"You should've asked me first. What if my mom doesn't go to work?" Carmen shook her head. "Whatever. We can worry about it tomorrow. We have to worry about *tonight*. Let's get out of here."

The girls circled the streets around the restaurant with no luck. After about twenty minutes, they got in the car to leave.

"Can't say she didn't know. It's already ten after ten. We gotta go," Aamani said.

They started to leave, driving by the front door of Dream one last time. Just as Carmen was ready to pull off, Aamani spotted Lori bounding towards the car.

"Stop," Aamani shouted. Carmen slammed on the brakes, jerking them both forward. Carmen turned to yell at Aamani when the back door flew open and Lori flung herself on the backseat, breathing hard.

"I can't believe you guys were gonna leave me!" Lori accused.

"Believe it," Carmen shot back. "Do you see what time it is? Are you trying to get us killed?"

"Oh please," Lori said. "It'll be fine. Your parents are not going to kill you."

"Watch," Carmen said.

"Where were you anyway?" Aamani asked. "We looked all over for you."

"I was in there," Lori mumbled, pretending to concentrate on something outside the window.

"Yeah, right," Aamani said. "We looked. You were definitely not in there." Aamani got on her knees and peered over the top of the seat at Lori who had sunken down in the back.

Carmen drove cautiously down the street as she tried to steal glances at Lori in the rearview mirror.

"What? Why are you guys looking at me?" Lori squirmed uncomfortably in the seat.

"If we're gonna risk getting in trouble for being late, the least you can do is tell us why. What were you *doing?*" Carmen demanded.

Aamani wrinkled her nose. "You smell weird."

"That was blunt." Lori grinned nervously.

Aamani just stared at her.

"Okay." Lori sighed. "You know that cute guy I was talking to?"

"No," Carmen and Aamani both said.

"Well, while you two were shaking it on the dance floor, I met this guy and we started talking," Lori said.

"And?" Carmen prompted.

"And, it was too loud in there, so we, um, went outside to talk."

"And?" Aamani raised an eyebrow.

"And so we were sitting in his car and after a while we um, sorta started kissing and then…" Lori's voice trailed off and she shrugged.

Even under the dimness of the passing streetlights, Aamani could tell that Lori was blushing.

"Wait a second. Did you do it with that guy in his car?" Aamani asked incredulously.

"Yes," Lori said in a barely audible voice.

"What?" Carmen said, looking over her shoulder.

"Watch out!" Lori shouted.

Carmen turned her head forward to see that she had let the car drift toward the right side of the road when she had turned her head to look at Lori. She jerked the wheel to the left, but not soon enough to avoid clipping the left front bumper of a parked car.

"Oh shit box! I'm dead!" Carmen cried.

She parked the car, and all three got out to examine the damage. "How bad does it look?" Carmen asked, showing concern for the first time that night.

"It doesn't look too bad, just a bit of a dent," Lori said as she ran her hand along the bumper. She looked at Carmen who was pacing back and forth muttering, "oh no, oh no" over and over. "It's actually more like a ding, right?" Lori made eye contact with Aamani and nodded in Carmen's direction.

Aamani watched Carmen who was standing under the streetlight with her hands on each side of her face. It looked like Carmen was trying to shade her eyes so no one could see her trying to blink back tears. "Yeah, more like a scratch."

"I'm dead," Carmen repeated.

"No, you're not," Lori said. "Hey, doesn't your mom always park to the left side of the driveway? If she asks, tell her you heard someone turning around in the driveway and they must've hit the car and then took off."

"You think she'll believe that?" Carmen looked hopefully at Lori.

"Sure. I have two older brothers who steal my parents' cars like it's their job. You think they haven't done something like this before? To this day, my mom thinks our driveway is the turnaround spot for lost, drunk drivers. It kills me how she never once thought how strange it was that these accidents never happen when she and my dad are home." Lori giggled and Aamani laughed too. Carmen finally joined in.

"Okay, I feel better," Carmen said. "We better get going, though. We're really pushing it."

The girls hopped back in the car and drove off. Carmen managed to drive everyone home and park the car without any further incident. The house was still dark when she went inside, except for the dim glow cast by the light above the kitchen stove that they always left on, which meant her mother was not yet home. She placed the car key back in the same spot on the dresser where she'd found it, and then quickly went to her room to change into her pajamas. She shoved the tank top in a tote bag and put it in the back of the closet to wash when her mother was at work, then crawled into bed and exhaled a sigh of relief as she sank into the pillows. She listened to the quiet of the house, only broken by the hum of the refrigerator which reminded her that she still hadn't eaten. Hunger soon consumed her and she wondered whether she should go into the kitchen and make something to eat. She started to get out of bed when the sound of a car pulling into the driveway drove her back under the covers. She heard the sound of two car doors slamming and waited to hear the front door unlock. When the door didn't immediately open, her stomach began to tighten as she pictured her mother and boyfriend catching sight of the dent in the BMW's side and examining it for further damage. She turned to the wall and pulled the covers up closer to her face as if the fabric would protect her from whatever consequence that would be dealt once Angelique got inside.

The front door finally opened and Carmen could hear her mother's voice, but could not make out what she was saying. Several minutes passed before she heard her bedroom door open and felt the presence of someone standing over her. She did not turn from the wall, but her body tensed in anticipation of the confrontation with her mother.

"What are you doing in here?"

Carmen heard her mother's voice, but it was coming from across the room. Carmen turned in time to see a large figure moving towards the door. The light from the hallway revealed her mother's silhouette in the doorway. The figure filled the doorway as it passed through silently. Carmen squinted at the light coming from the hallway as her mother stepped back to allow it to move by her. Carmen caught her mother's eye for a moment before she quickly looked away.

The confusion registered in her voice. "Mum?"

Angelique hesitated for a moment, but did not look up. Instead, she closed the door behind her. Carmen sat up and listened to the heated whispers that came from somewhere beyond her door. She waited for the sound of the front door opening and closing, but it didn't come for several hours. She stayed awake long after she heard her mother's boyfriend's car finally drive away. The house remained silent, leaving the darkness of the night to envelope her.

Angelique was gone by the time Carmen woke up the next morning. When Carmen returned home from school, Angelique was still not there. The only evidence that her mother had ever returned to the house was the bag of cold Chicken Delight left on the kitchen table. Carmen sat in front of the television watching the Cosby Show as she ate the chicken and French fry dinner she hadn't bothered to warm up. She stayed on the sofa for several hours, alternating between watching the television, the clock on the VCR, and the window that faced the driveway.

The sound of the phone ringing startled her awake. She picked it up on the second ring.

"Hello?"

"Hey!"

"Who is this?"

"It's Raymond."

Silence.

"We met yesterday," he offered.

"Oh. Hi." Carmen was distracted.

"Uh, is this a bad time?" Raymond asked.

"Sort of. I'm expecting my mom to call. I have to get off the phone."

"Uh, okay," Raymond said.

"Can you call me back later?"

"Not a prob. Bye." Raymond hung up and Carmen put the receiver down quickly.

A few minutes later, the phone rang again. Carmen reached over and grabbed it.

"Hello?"

"Hey, it's me."

"Hey, Aamani."

"Don't sound so disappointed."

"Sorry, I thought you were my mum."

"How'd that go? Did she say anything? You in trouble?" Aamani asked.

"She didn't say anything last night and I haven't seen her all day," Carmen said.

"Hmmm," Aamani wondered aloud. "I guess no news is good news, right? I got home before my dad and my mom had fallen asleep over her knitting. I know, she's a real wild woman. Anyway, I didn't want to push my luck by coming over there today. Did you hear from those guys?"

"Yeah, but I didn't stay on the phone too long. My mom might be calling and we don't have call-waiting yet," Carmen said.

"Funny. You keep looking for your mum to come home. Mine never leaves this house. Ever. Just one day, I'd like to come home and not have her hovering over me," Aamani said.

Carmen didn't respond. She was looking out the window at a car that had slowed up as it came up the street, but then turned into her neighbor's driveway.

"Okay. I seem to be the only one alive on this phone. Call me if you hear from those guys again," Aamani said before she hung up.

Carmen went to her bedroom and returned to the sofa with a blanket and pillow. She turned the light above the stove on before curling up on the sofa again. She flipped through the channels before settling on a movie. The VCR read 9:11 p.m.

The phone jarred her out of her sleep. She reached for it and mumbled a sleepy hello.

"Did you eat the chicken I left for you?"

Carmen bolted upright. "Mum!" she said. The excitement in her voice surprised her.

"Well?"

"Yes, thanks, Mum," Carmen said. There was silence on the other end of the phone. "Are you coming home soon?"

"Not for a while," Angelique said. "I took an extra shift tonight, and then I'm going out later. Why? You need something?"

Carmen pulled the blanket closer around her. "No, I was just wondering."

"I might see you tomorrow then." Her voice was flat.

"Okay."

"By the way, Carmen, do you know what happened to my car?"

Carmen tensed up. "No."

"There is a big dent on the back bumper and I know I didn't put it there. You sure you didn't take it or let one of your little friends drive it?"

"No."

"Humph. I don't like when people touch my things. Now I'm the one who must pay to fix it. If I find out who did it, there's going to be one hell to pay." She hung up without saying goodbye.

Days melted into weeks with Angelique hardly spending any time at home. Carmen would often come home from school to an empty house, always with some takeout or money left on the kitchen table and a note saying "make yourself something to eat, I'm at work." Carmen knew that wasn't always the truth. She had called the hotel several times and was told, always by the same woman, that her mother had already left for the day. She stopped calling when the woman finally asked, "Didn't your mother tell you? She no longer works nights, dear. Hasn't for at least a month."

The few times Angelique was there she was alone. Carmen hadn't seen her mother's boyfriend in weeks. She understood why when she came home one day and the BMW was gone. In its place was an older dark blue Toyota Tercel. It was midsummer and Angelique was sitting at the dining room table wearing a pair of shorts and a white t-shirt, her hair pulled back from her face and to the side in a low ponytail cascading over her left shoulder. She crossed her legs at the ankle and leaned her slim torso over the table, her brow furrowed as she studied what seemed to be a pile of bills. Carmen sat down across from her mother, dropping her purse to the floor. She crossed her legs at the ankles and ran her fingers through her short bobbed hair, tucking the stray pieces behind her ears. She wished she hadn't cut hers at the end of the school year. Maybe she would relax it to get more length.

"What are you doing?" Carmen asked.

"Trying to find a way to pay these bills," Angelique said without looking up. She shuffled through the papers and wrote some figures on a notepad.

Carmen watched her mother for a few moments, waiting for her to say something. Angelique continued with her paperwork in silence.

"Are you mad at me?" Carmen asked.

Angelique flicked her eyes up briefly from the bill she was holding. "Do I have a reason to be?"

"No," Carmen said cautiously. She knew her mother well enough to know that the question could be truth-seeking or rhetorical.

"Hmm. Then why did you ask?"

"I don't know. You haven't really talked to me since…" Carmen trailed off.

"Since when?"

Carmen hesitated. "Since that night when you came home late with Lexroy and he came in my room and—"

"You mean the night when you took my car and mashed up the side of it?" It was more of a statement, not a question. Angelique eyed Carmen steadily. "Well? So tell me what happened, Carmen. I'm really interested to know," she said, her voice thinly veiled with anger.

Carmen chewed on her bottom lip for a moment, feeling the weight of her mother's stare. "I'm sorry," she finally said.

"Sorry for what, Carmen?"

"We just took it for a few hours—" Carmen immediately stopped herself.

"And who is we?"

Carmen didn't say anything.

"*Who is we?*" Angelique repeated. She had pushed the bills aside and was glaring at Carmen.

"Aamani and Lori."

"You mean the one little fast girl that's pregnant now?"

Carmen stared at her mother, wondering how she'd heard about it. She and Lori had not really talked since the night they took the BMW out. Lori had become withdrawn, then started acting and dressing differently, wearing heavier makeup and dying her hair black. Lori's normally liberal mother had hung up the phone on Carmen the few times she'd tried to call. The last time she asked Carmen not to call back. Aamani had reported the same experience. Neither girl had seen their once bubbly blonde friend the last few weeks of school. Aamani had heard the rumor going around at school that Lori might be pregnant or that she had developed some type of eating disorder and that her mother had packed her off and shipped her to Calgary where her aunt lived, but Carmen didn't believe it.

"That's not true."

"It is. What? You thought I wouldn't find out? Her mother called here the other day going on about how she let her daughter hang around with you and that Indian girl and how you two got her daughter in trouble," Angelique said. "Talking to me like I never raised you."

Carmen looked away, but not before cutting her eyes at her mother. Angelique caught the look, but let it go.

"Anyway, I know it was you who damaged that car. And it was me who had to find money to pay the deductible to get it fixed. That whole thing caused me to get into a fight with Lexroy over you."

"The car? Is that what you argued about?"

Angelique eyed Carmen steadily. "Is there something *else* I should know about?"

"What are you talking about?"

Angelique examined Carmen, seeming to realize how much they looked alike. Carmen was now sitting eye-level with her. They had the same wasp-like figure, though Carmen was slightly thinner. Carmen's almond-shaped eyes looked back at her from her copper bronze complexion. Many people had commented how much they looked alike, including Lexroy. "A dead stamp of you," he had said one day as Carmen walked out of the house in a pair of tight whitewashed jeans and a cropped t-shirt on her the way to the mall. "You want a ride, Carmen? Come, make I drop you over there," he had offered with a broad smile.

"No thanks," Carmen had responded.

The next weekend he'd shown up unannounced at dinnertime and commented on how well Carmen's food tasted. "Almost better than yours, Angelique. What you think?" he had teased. Carmen, feeling the uncomfortable silence, had left the kitchen followed by Lexroy's eyes. That last exchange happened the week before she'd sensed Lexroy standing in her room late at night.

"Don't ask me what I'm talking about. You forget who you're talking to?"

Carmen opened her mouth to respond, but stopped.

"You know, you're getting too big. And now you have men calling my house. I had to tell one not to call back here the other day. Some Raymond-somebody-or-other. If you don't watch it, you're going to end up like your friend." Angelique hesitated a second before she'd said "your friend" and it did not go unnoticed. Carmen turned her head to the side and rolled her eyes.

Angelique gathered up the papers and tapped them into a neat pile. "We're going back to Jamaica," she announced.

Carmen sat up and looked toward her mother. "Really? For how long?"

"I don't know. For as long as I need to."

Carmen pressed her lips together trying to hide the smile that had been hidden away for so long.

24

The plane touched down in Montego Bay a week later. Carmen quickly unbuckled her seatbelt and stood with one leg on the ground while she kneeled on the seat with the other. She looked at her mother who was sitting in the aisle seat. Her buckle remained fastened and she hadn't bothered to reach for her purse that was tucked under the seat in front of her.

"Aren't you getting up?" Carmen finally said.

"Calm down, Carmen. The door hasn't even been opened yet." Angelique rubbed her temples. She was getting a headache and the three gin and tonics she'd had on the flight down weren't helping.

"By the time you get up and get our luggage out of the overhead compartment half the people will be off this plane."

"Will you just sit still for a minute? We haven't been on the ground two minutes and already you're making me regret bringing you down here. Cha!"

Carmen stopped talking, but stared at her mother, willing her to get up. The flight attendant swung the door open and a wave of moist heat rushed onto the plane. Angelique finally eased herself out of her seat and grabbed the luggage from overhead. Carmen stepped on the heels of Angelique's feet twice on the way down the aisle. She slowed her pace after Angelique turned around and glared at her.

By the time they retrieved their bags, Angelique was in a better mood. They breezed through customs as Angelique flirted her way through the processing. She sauntered through the airport with her head held high, drawing attention from passengers and airport workers alike. Carmen tried to match her mother's confident strides, but couldn't manage to look as self-assured as she struggled to push the luggage cart ahead of her. Her feet were already beginning to burn inside the new white leather flats she wore. She regretted not packing her sandals in her carry-on luggage. She'd worn the white flats because she thought they looked cute with her white mini skirt and because they would keep her feet warm on the air conditioned plane. She instantly regretted it when she was reintroduced to Jamaica's humid summer heat as they walked around by the waiting taxis. Angelique looked comfortable and poised in her open-toed sling backs, having kept warm on the plane with the help of an airline blanket wrapped around her feet. She glanced back at Carmen and shook her head.

Carmen searched the crowds looking for a familiar face. She had assumed her grandfather or uncle would be picking them up, but Angelique hadn't said anything. She stood beside her mother who leisurely scanned the crowds until her eyes settled on someone and she smiled, smoothing out the front of her skirt that hung just above her knees. Carmen followed her mother's gaze, but couldn't identify the man moving towards them. He was approximately six feet tall with a slim, athletic build. His head was shaved bald and he wore a neatly trimmed mustache and goatee. When he embraced Angelique, Carmen could smell his clean scent of aftershave mixed with Zest soap. He stepped back from Angelique and raised both her hands to the sides. Angelique turned her body, dropped her hip, and giggled as her friend admired her. "What a way but you look good, eh?"

Angelique smiled and said, "You're not looking too bad yourself."

He turned his attention to Carmen. "And who is this?" he said. His eyes growing wide with surprise.

"That's my daughter, Carmen," Angelique said, waving her hand.

"The two of you look like you could be sisters." He looked at Carmen and smiled.

"Say hello to Mr. Walker," Angelique said.

"Hi," Carmen said.

Mr. Andrew Walker, Carmen had learned on the car ride to Somerset Grove, was a few years older than Angelique and had grown up with her in the same parish. Back then, he was skinny and awkward. "Maga" was the word Angelique used to describe his lankiness when laughing with her cousin Hazel who had come over later that evening. Carmen didn't think he was so skinny. He was okay looking, but not good looking enough to make Angelique forget herself, the way Lexroy made her do. Carmen noticed the nervous way that he kept licking his lips and the way he looked at her mother with such a longing that she almost felt sorry for him. He wasn't her mother's type. Carmen didn't necessarily dislike him, but she thought he was weird and told her mother so after he'd dropped them off.

"Don't talk about people like that," Angelique had said. "It's not nice."

"You know he's doing well for himself," Hazel had said. "He has one of those jet ski rental businesses up in Negril."

"That's what he told me. He wrote me every so often when I was in Canada, and he said next time I was here he would come check me," Angelique said and shrugged. "At least I won't have to be stuck up in this house all the time." They were sitting around the dining room table in the family home after just finishing a huge dinner prepared by Carmen's grandmother. The reunion had been awkward; Angelique had given Ruby a cheek kiss when she came through the door, but Carmen fell into her grandmother's waiting arms.

"Hi Grandma!" Carmen had uttered excitedly.

"Look how big you've grown," Ruby had said. "She's pretty just like you, Angelique."

Angelique smiled with lips pressed together. "So they tell me," she said as she watched Ruby smooth Carmen's frizzy curls. A look of sadness flickered in her eyes, but quickly disappeared.

"You shouldn't have let her cut her hair," Ruby said as she stretched Carmen's curls trying to make them longer.

"She's a big woman now," Angelique said. "I can't tell her anything anymore."

"You have to show her who's the mother, right?" Ruby gave one of Carmen's curls a playful tug. "Anyway, it's always harder when both parents are not in the home." Angelique grimaced at the not-so-subtle dig. Carmen had chatted excitedly throughout dinner with her grandparents about school and living in Winnipeg.

"It's too cold. I miss it here," Carmen said.

"There's nothing for you here unless you have money," Angelique said, stabbing at a piece of yam with her fork.

"You have opportunities in Canada that most people will never have," Ruby added. She looked wistfully out the window. "And your Uncle Marlon has gone and left us for England. You know he's got a degree in economics now? I don't know when he will ever be back."

Carmen's grandfather spoke up. "No matter where you go in this world, my dear, this will always be your home. That goes for everybody," he said, looking at both Angelique and Carmen.

They'd just finished their dinner when Hazel had appeared on the verandah. The tension that had been building in the room dissipated once Angelique's cousin had walked in and greeted Angelique with "Gyal, yu nuh dead yet?" Hazel breezed through the front door laying kisses on everybody in the room, causing everyone to laugh with ease.

Ruby and Byron left the dining room in search of a cool breeze outside. Carmen stayed at the table listening to the two women catching up on town gossip when the conversation had eventually turned to Andrew Walker. Hazel told them how he had married a girl from Savannah La Mar and brought her back to live in the beautiful house he'd built not too far from town. The marriage had surprised most people who weren't even aware that he had been seeing this girl, but upon meeting her everyone thought the two of them were well matched with their seemingly mild temperaments. That was until one afternoon when Mrs. Jarvis had been passing by on her way back from the market and saw a commotion going on in front of the post office so she stood across the street trying to find out what was going on.

"You know she will never miss an opportunity to get into people's business," Hazel said. "She practically broke her neck trying to catch up to a group of us walking home from church so she could tell us the story."

Apparently there was a man from out of town and he'd stopped to ask Andrew's wife for directions. Andrew came out of the post office and accused his wife of smiling up too much or something. He got into an argument with the man and the two of them started scuffling in the street. The man pushed Andrew down to the ground, and then took off running. Andrew tried to catch him, but the man was too fast. Andrew had to satisfy himself with nicking the man on the shoulder with a rock he managed to fling at him. After he caught his breath, he turned back towards the post office where his wife had retreated. He pulled her outside by her forearm and they argued all the way back to their house.

Mrs. Jarvis had followed them back to their house. "She said she wasn't really following them, because she had to pass their house to get to hers, but you know that part wasn't true. She nosy, yuh see?" Hazel kissed her teeth and Angelique laughed. "Anyway, she said that once they were inside the yelling and screaming must've gone on for a good 15 or 20 minutes and it sounded like he turned over everything in that house." Hazel slapped the table for emphasis.

"So I asked her what she did. You know what she told me? She said, 'Me? Nothing. I'm not the type of person that interferes in other people's affairs. I just mind my own business.' Can you believe that?"

Angelique shook her head.

Hazel went on to tell them that the women from the church had noticed that Andrew and his wife had not attended service that day, an unusual occurrence, and Lorna Jones, one of the women who worked with Andrew's wife at the post office said the woman had not shown up for work all week. 'He must have run her out. She probably went back to Sav La Mar,' Mrs. Jarvis had concluded. "I can't believe that woman never said or did anything. Who knows what happened. That's why I can't stand her, yuh see? She would never help anybody." Hazel spat. "She was the first to try and friend the girl up when she moved to town and then didn't turn a blind eye to help. I would never do that to my good friend."

"Did anyone go to Savannah La Mar to see if she was okay?" Carmen asked.

"I don't know why you're trying to insert yourself into this conversation," Angelique said. "This doesn't concern you."

Carmen looked down at the table. Hazel smiled sympathetically at Carmen. "Angelique, why you so hard on the girl? She's just nosy like you," Hazel said and laughed.

Angelique frowned at her cousin, but eventually relaxed. "Well, did anyone find out what happened to his wife?"

"I never heard anything else about it and I didn't even know her maiden name before she came here. To tell you the truth, I haven't even seen Andrew that much since that time. I wouldn't have even thought about him until you mentioned that he was picking you up from the airport. I didn't know you two were still in contact."

"We're not really," Angelique said. "But we needed a ride. I knew he would come."

"Humph. You better be careful with that one," Hazel said. "I couldn't deal with any jealous man."

Carmen walked alongside her grandmother Ruby towards the entrance to Dunn's River Falls. They had arrived there just before noon after a nearly two-hour drive. Carmen looped her arm through her grandmother's and bubbled non-stop about how quickly she was going to climb to the top and how she wanted to have her picture taken posing under the cascading waterfalls.

Ruby smiled. "Slow down," she said. "Let's eat first and rest a bit. I haven't had anything since morning."

Carmen readily agreed and ran to a food stand while Ruby settled herself at a picnic table in the shade. Carmen quickly returned balancing two containers of jerk chicken, hard dough bread, and two soft drinks. "Pineapple or cola champagne?" She held the two bottles before her grandmother.

"Pineapple, please," Ruby said.

Carmen set the drink down in front of her grandmother and twisted the cap off her own bottle. She took a long swig before turning to the spicy chicken pieces that beckoned her. The day had quickly turned around for the better and she had her grandmother to thank for it. A few hours ago she had been standing in the front room of her grandparents' house clad in denim cutoffs and a white t-shirt, the yellow strings from her bikini top peeking out underneath. After sitting around the house complaining of boredom for two weeks, Angelique had agreed to take Carmen to Dunn's River Falls today. Carmen was hoping to run into Peter on this trip to Jamaica, but so far she was not having any success. She'd seen some of his friends in town and they said they'd stop by later, but they never showed up. When she saw them again a few days later, they brushed her off, telling her they would "soon come" but they still didn't come. Carmen wasn't sure if it was pity or being tired of seeing her mope around that motivated Angelique to promise to take her to Dunn's River Falls, but whatever the reason, Carmen was happy. That was, until Angelique had changed the plan at the last minute.

"Dunn's River is too far and I don't feel like driving up there today. Besides, Andrew said he would take us to Negril for the day. We can ride his jet skis all day for free, and he'll take us for lunch at one of the resorts. Wouldn't that be nicer?" Angelique had said.

Carmen did want to learn to jet ski, but not with Andrew Walker. The more time they spent around him, the more Carmen disliked him. He always seemed agitated, especially when he was waiting for Angelique. Two days ago he had come over early to pick her up and Angelique had not returned yet from visiting Hazel. Carmen had been sitting on the verandah wall while her grandmother sat in a chair plucking the seeds from the large bowl of ackee she planned to cook with saltfish for their lunch. Andrew had paced up and down in the yard, looking down the road to see if Angelique was coming.

"You're making me nervous with all that back and forth," Ruby had told him. "Sit down, nuh? Watching the street isn't going to make her come any faster."

A look of embarrassment had passed over Andrew's face as he sat down on the steps on the verandah. He had tried to make small talk with Ruby, glancing every so often at the street when he thought no one was looking. When Angelique had showed up a little later, he jumped up a little too quickly from the stairs and had almost slipped on the smoothly painted steps as he made his way down the path. Ruby had watched him try to usher Angelique quickly towards the car. Angelique playfully maneuvered her elbow out of his grasp. "I just want to freshen up a bit, I'll only be a minute," she had said.

He chose to stand by the car rather than approach the verandah and Ms. Ruby again. When Angelique came out of the house, he'd rushed to open the passenger door and hurried her inside the vehicle. Angelique waved at Carmen from the open window and said, "I'll be back soon."

The ackee seeds made a pinging sound as Ruby tossed them into the metal pail. She had shook her head and muttered that something "wasn't right with that one." Carmen had agreed with her grandmother.

From that day Carmen decided she'd rather do anything than spend time around Mr. Walker, even if it meant getting into a fight with her mother that morning over it.

"But I want to go to Dunn's River Falls today," Carmen protested. "I don't like jet skis," she lied when Angelique tried to change their plans.

"Carmen, you've never been on a jet ski, so how can you tell me you don't like it?" Angelique had said.

"You promised we'd go to the falls today, just the two of us."

"We can go another time. We're here all summer. Let's go to Negril today."

Carmen had crossed her arms and fought back tears. It was useless to argue; Angelique's mind was made up.

"You go on with your friend to Negril," Ruby had said. "I'll take Carmen to Dunn's River Falls." They had both looked at Ruby with surprise. "Go on, nuh! I haven't seen my granddaughter in years."

Angelique had looked between her mother and daughter and then shrugged. "I'll see you when you get back. I'll probably reach home before you," she'd said, before running off to change clothes.

The ride to Dunn's River Falls had been uneventful. Ruby had easily maneuvered the car down the narrow highways, expertly passing the smaller vehicles and yielding to the faster ones on the one lane roads. They had driven mostly in silence, transported away by the sounds of Bob Marley singing of revolution through the car stereo. Carmen's disappointment soon dissipated and by the time they reached the falls, she was in much better spirits.

When they'd arrived, Carmen stood mesmerized by the falls. She glanced up at the 600-foot wonder looming majestically beside them. The sheets of water shimmered as it cascaded over the large rocks and crashed into a white froth at each level. The early afternoon sun's rays peeked through the trees and bounced off the clear water, making it sparkle like crystal as it pooled at the bottom. Carmen closed her eyes and felt the gentle spray caught by a cool breeze and carried over.

Carmen absentmindedly licked the hot jerk spice from her fingers as she watched the family seated at the next table. The mother was busy wiping sauce from her daughter's face. The little girl twisted away, kicking her feet for balance as her mother gently held her back. She smacked her lips in satisfaction when she'd finally managed to escape her mother's cleaning assault. She looked at Carmen and smiled as she reached for her sippy cup with her two chubby hands.

"What's wrong, Carmen?" Ruby said.

"Nothing."

"Pardon me?"

"Nothing, Grandma," Carmen corrected herself.

"Don't tell me nothing."

Carmen shrugged.

"Life is not always easy, but someone always has it harder than you. We should always be grateful for what we have."

Carmen looked wistfully at the mother of the little girl at the next table.

"I remember the first time I saw you. You were so beautiful. You looked exactly like your mother when she was your age." Ruby smiled as if reminded of some secret memory. "You were so independent, even back then. You never wanted help with anything and you had no problem playing by yourself. I was never invited to any tea parties." Ruby laughed and Carmen eventually smiled. "I can see you are growing into a strong young lady and you can take care of yourself."

"I could never have imagined you taking me to Dunn's River back then. You were so strict," Carmen said.

"I was, but I was afraid for you," Ruby said. "And your mother. I never wanted either of you to get into any trouble or have your choices taken away from you like I did." Ruby looked out at the falls.

Carmen gave her grandmother a puzzled look. "What do you mean?"

Ruby shook her head and smiled. "Nothing, darling. Aren't we supposed be having fun today?"

Carmen nodded and smiled back.

"Yep. You will be just fine. Just don't forget about your grandmother, you hear?"

"Of course not. I'll always come back to you."

"Good. Now what are you still doing sitting here? I thought you came here to climb the falls," Ruby said.

"I am. Are you coming with me?" Carmen got up and extended her hand towards her grandmother. Ruby playfully pushed it away.

"No, my dear. You don't see how my hair stay nice?" Ruby patted her freshly curled hair pinned up and piled high on her head. "I said I would take you here. You never heard me saying anything about climbing up any falls."

Carmen laughed. "Okay, I'll go by myself. You'll be right here?"

Ruby smiled. "I'm not going anywhere."

25

It had rained for three straight days. A torrential downpour that beat on the roof in a relentless steady drumming that had gone from soothing to dulling by end of the second day. The scent of ripening fruit and flowers that normally hung in the air was replaced by the earthy smell of red mud as it snaked its way down the hills of Somerset Grove. Angelique stood on the verandah with the front door open, peeking up at the gray sky.

"Would you mind closing my door, please?" Ruby called out from the sitting room where she'd been applying a coat of red polish to her nails.

Angelique ignored the request. "I think it's letting up. The sky looks lighter. I bet the sun will come out today."

Carmen walked in the room dressed in shorts and a t-shirt and carrying a glass of lemonade. She settled into an armchair across from Ruby, tucking her feet up beside her. Ruby paused with the nail polish brush in mid-air and look pointedly at Carmen. Carmen folded in her lips as she slid her feet out from under her, resting them on the floor. Ruby nodded approvingly and went back to her polishing.

"Maybe we can go out today," Angelique said. "Maybe into town or something." Angelique closed the door behind her and sat down on the other end of the chesterfield from Ruby, tucking her legs beside her. Ruby looked at her out of the corner of her eye, kissing her teeth with her tongue.

"There's probably nothing open today, but maybe you need to get out of this house for a while," Ruby said, looking at Angelique's feet.

Carmen watched the exchange between her mother and grandmother. The strained relationship that existed between the two women was no secret, and Carmen knew her mother was trying to subtly annoy her grandmother. Carmen was torn between siding with her grandmother and wanting to get on Angelique's good side.

"I'm going out. You want to come with me?" Angelique looked at Carmen and smiled.

Carmen jumped from the chair, bouncing on her feet. "Okay," she said.

Ruby looked up at Carmen then went back to her polishing. Carmen thought she saw a look of sadness flash across Ruby's eyes, but it was gone as quickly as it came. She felt like a traitor.

"Just be careful, please," Ruby said to no one in particular.

They decided to walk instead of attempting to drive. Angelique's father had taken the Jeep earlier in the morning to check on some of his farmland, and they decided not to try taking Ruby's Honda onto the slick, mud-soaked roads. They walked slowly down the road, avoiding the puddles that pooled in the large potholes and the tree limbs that had not survived the stormy weather. They made mostly small talk, commenting on the weather and the road conditions.

"Are you happy to be back here?" Angelique said.

Carmen shrugged. "It's been okay. Sometimes it's boring."

"I'm surprised to say this, but I'm actually enjoying myself," Angelique said. "Except for these last few days we've been trapped in there." Angelique waved her hand in the direction of her parents' house.

"You don't seem like you like Grandma too much," Carmen said. She glanced sideways at her mother trying to gauge her reaction.

Angelique bristled. "It's complicated. That's my mother so of course I love her. I just felt like I never did anything right in her eyes. I don't really want to talk about it right now."

Carmen decided not to push it further. They walked in silence.

"Another time, okay?" Angelique said.

Carmen nodded.

They arrived in town a good 20 minutes later and discovered much of the town was indeed shut down, with the exception of the barbershop that never seemed to close and always seemed to be hosting a domino game in front.

"Ruby was right," Angelique said. "This place is a ghost town." Carmen giggled hearing Angelique referring to her mother by her first name.

They stepped in the shop to see who was inside. Carmen was hoping she might catch sight of Peter though she knew if he still had dreads, he'd have no reason to be hanging around a barbershop. No one was inside other than the barber and two older men who had managed to make their way out to their daytime hangout. The barber waved at them and Angelique flashed one of her trademark smiles. The two men sat inside competing to see who could best describe the ill effects of the rain.

"Every'ting washout, man," one of them said, making a sweeping motion with his hand, referring to his yard.

"Is that all?" the other man said. "Water come straight through and run down the back wall of my house. Once the rain stop, I have to pay somebody fi come fix up the roof again," he said. "All morning I was in there mopping up water myself. Cha! Too much aggravation!"

"Well, hello! My luck must be changing. You looking for me?" The first of the two men had turned towards Angelique and Carmen. He was wearing a tan-colored cap, white shirt, and black pants. His eyes crinkled as he smiled. His face was smooth, though his jawline was softening with age. He might have passed for someone in his 50s, but it was the pure white hair and stiff fingers that gave away his senior citizen status when he waved at them.

Angelique smiled back. "Maybe next time. Have you seen Andrew Walker?"

The elderly man leaned back in his chair, the smile faded quickly from his face. "I don't bother with that one. You better ask somebody else," he said.

"I don't know if I know that guy. Who is it you're talking about?" inquired the other man. He wore a white beard neatly trimmed, though his unruly low afro suggested he had not yet taken advantage of the barber's services.

"You know that one with the yellow house not too far from here. He says he has some type of business in Negril. He was the one outside there last week kicking up a fuss because some youth was leaning up against his car," the first man said. "The way he was carrying on you would think somebody did scratch it up or something," the first man said.

"Oh! Oh! I know which one you're talking about now," the second one said. He turned to Angelique and frowned. "What you want with that one?"

Carmen watched her mother who seemed caught off guard by the question and a moment passed before she reacted. "Nothing. I was just asking if you'd seen him. Have a good day." She ushered Carmen out of the shop and walked quickly down the road. Carmen had to run for a few seconds to catch up.

"What's wrong, Mum?" Carmen said.

"What? Nothing is wrong. Why do you think something is wrong?"

"Why were those men talking about Mr. Walker like that?"

Angelique brushed it off. "I don't know what those old fools were going on about. People love to exaggerate. That's one thing I don't like about coming back here." Angelique tucked a loose curl back behind her ear. She tugged at her tank top and put on a smile that said she wasn't bothered by anything. "Let's go. There's nothing happening here, but I know someplace fun."

They turned off the main street and walked up a narrow unpaved road. Carmen was glad she wore her running shoes, though by the time they got to the top of the first hill they were stained red from the earth. She looked down at her feet and frowned.

"You can get a new pair when you go back to Winnipeg," Angelique said. "Leave those here. Somebody will be happy to have them if you don't want them."

They trekked up a second hill before turning into a small driveway lined with white stones. They made their way up to the salmon-colored house with the white railing surrounding the verandah. Angelique opened up the door and called inside. "Hazel?"

Hazel stuck her head out from the back of the house wiping her hands on a dish towel. "Hey! Come in, come in!"

Angelique and Carmen walked inside and were immediately greeted with the aroma of fish frying.

"I'm making escovitch," Hazel said. She added garlic, scotch bonnet peppers, and thyme to the other pot simmering on the stove. "Some of my friends are going to pass through, so I thought I'd cook up a little something," she said, turning the golden brown fish in the pan. "Are you going to stay?"

"Try and put us out," Angelique said and laughed. She took a seat at the small kitchen table, pushing the onion away from in front of her.

"I don't suppose you're going to help," Hazel said as she watched Angelique brush her hands across each other. Angelique raised her eyebrow in response and both women laughed.

Carmen took the seat opposite her mother, enjoying the light-hearted banter between the two women. Her mother seemed so relaxed and at ease around her cousin. She felt a kind of sisterly love that existed between the two women that she never knew her mother was capable of. Despite the years apart, they seemed, to Carmen, to be closer than Angelique was with anyone else in their family, including herself.

The house started to fill up as people ventured outside after the rain battling their cabin fever and looking for something to do in the town shut down by the weather. Hazel's tiny house had always been the gathering spot for her friends in Somerset Grove, so she had already prepared for the small crowd when she learned of the rain storms headed their way, stocking her little refrigerator with the fish she'd thawed out and seasoned the day before and mixing the ingredients for the fried festival she would serve on the side.

Somebody turned on the old stereo system and Beres Hammond's voice crooned out a soulful song. Within 30 minutes the house was full of people enjoying food and filling up on rum punch. As usual, Angelique had two men competing for her attention, and she was enjoying every minute of it. Carmen watched her flirt effortlessly with each of them. She would toss her head back and laugh at one's jokes, or playfully slap the other one, letting her hand linger a moment longer than necessary. The men competed, but did not become aggressive with each other, and Carmen marveled at her mother's ability to make each of them feel special.

After a few minutes, Angelique noticed Carmen watching her. "Why don't you go in the kitchen and see if Hazel needs some help."

Carmen dutifully got up and headed into the kitchen. As she expected, Hazel did not want any assistance cooking, enjoying all of the praise that came from her guests about her food. Not wanting to be scolded by Angelique, Carmen busied herself tidying up, then retrieving the used dishes left in the front room or on the verandah to be washed. Even though it was not her idea of a good time to be cleaning up after people, she still enjoyed being able to eavesdrop on the mostly adult conversation that filled the air in between the dancehall beats flowing from the speakers.

Somebody put on *Ring the Alarm*, causing Hazel to run from the kitchen waving a towel above her head like a flag. She grabbed Angelique away from a group, pulling her into the middle of the room to dance. They both swayed their hips to the sound of the bass and sang along. Others soon joined them on the side, but left the two women in the center where they wound their bodies low to the ground, and then raised themselves back up in a suggestive manner. A few of the men stood around with drinks in their hand, watching the women with eyes that unabashedly betrayed their thoughts. Carmen tentatively walked over to her mother and was glad when Angelique grabbed her hand and pulled her into the circle.

"Come on, Carmen! I know you can wine," she said as she pushed her hips back and looked over her shoulder, turning her backside in a circle. Carmen laughed and followed her mother's lead, enjoying the attention she was getting from her and some of the men in the room. She became lost in the music, turning in circles and moving between her mother and Hazel.

Nobody noticed the dark figure that had slipped in the doorway, standing off in a corner watching the action. Halfway through the next dancehall track the figure moved from the corner and into the lighted area in the middle of the room. Carmen saw him first when she turned her back to her mother and threw her hands in the air. She lowered her arms and squinted into the dark room at the figure that was now standing by Angelique. She recognized Andrew Walker as the light from the hallway passed over his face and he moved a step closer. His brow was furrowed and his mouth was set in a thin line. When he noticed Carmen looking at him, he smiled quickly. Angelique turned around to see what had caught Carmen's attention.

"Andrew! How did you know I was here? You know we were looking for you earlier," Angelique said, gesturing towards Carmen who stood motionless beside her.

"I went by your house and you were not there," Andrew said. "I waited for a while, and when you didn't come back after sunset, I started driving around. Somebody told me your cousin lived up this way."

"We hadn't planned to come by, but we walked to town and nothing was going on, so we ended up over here. Hazel cooked some fish. You hungry?" Angelique said.

"I waited over half an hour at your house," Andrew said.

"So you found me, what's the problem?" Angelique sounded annoyed.

Andrew changed his tone. "Nothing, nothing." He pasted on a smile.

Angelique turned to Carmen who was planted on her mother's left side. "Oops! I nearly stepped on you. Why are you standing so close?" she asked. "Carmen, why don't you dish out some food for Mr. Walker," she said, and turned away without waiting for a response.

Carmen frowned at her mother, but walked toward the kitchen. The way Andrew looked at her mother like she had stood him up and he'd caught her with another man made her stomach feel unsettled. The lighthearted atmosphere that existed before he showed up had all but evaporated, though Angelique seemed to brush it off. Carmen walked into the kitchen and grabbed a plate. She didn't bother to check if it was clean. Hazel's friend, Nicole was tending to the stove while Hazel danced in the front room. Carmen looked at the platters on the table. Most of the fish and festival had been picked over. The pieces that remained were cold and starting to dry out.

"If you wait a minute, I'm cooking up some fresh fish now," Nicole said as she turned a few pieces in the frying pan.

"This is fine," Carmen said. She scraped the leftover pieces onto the plate and walked out of the kitchen. She searched through the crowd at the front of the house, but couldn't find her mother or Andrew. She looked outside on the verandah, but there was only a group of men engaged in a lively game of dominoes. Carmen approached one of the men she recognized as Hazel's older brother. "Uncle Robbie, have you seen my mother?"

Robbie slammed a domino down on the table in victory and looked up. "Who?"

"Angelique," Carmen repeated.

"I don't know, my dear," he said. "Look inside and see if you see her." He pointed towards the house before turning to the man beside him and instructing him to hurry up and play his cards.

Carmen sighed and went back in the house. She searched the small crowd carefully, then checked the bedrooms and was relieved to find that her mother was not in there. Her annoyance soon turned to concern and she asked Hazel if she knew where her mother was.

"She must be around here someplace. Why do you look so concerned?" Hazel said.

Carmen wanted to talk to Hazel about Andrew, but didn't think this was the proper time or place to have a discussion. "Nothing. She told me to make Mr. Andrew a plate and now they just disappeared."

Hazel didn't say anything for a moment, then waved her hand dismissively. "She'll be back. Don't worry."

Carmen decided to go outside again, this time walking out by the road. There she saw what looked like Andrew's jeep. As she approached it, she saw her mother leaning casually against the vehicle while Andrew stood in front of her with his arms folded. Carmen walked up to them and held the plate in front of Andrew's chest.

"Here," she said without looking directly at him. Andrew paused a moment before taking the plate. "I was looking for you," she said to her mother.

"I was here," Angelique said.

"I want to go home now. Can we leave?" Carmen said.

"I'm not ready to go yet. Why don't you go, you can find your way home."

"It's too dark. I don't want to go home by myself," Carmen said.

Angelique looked as if she just realized this. "Right," she said.

"We can drop you home and come back," Andrew offered. He bit down on a piece of fish and made a face.

Carmen crossed her arms. "No, that's okay. I'll get there on my own."

"Why are you being so stubborn? Come make we drop you. Or else let me ask if one of Hazel's friends will walk with you." Angelique started to move towards the house.

"I'll ask somebody. Don't worry about me."

"You sure?" Angelique asked. "Well, let me know who is going to take you so I know," she said quickly before Carmen could respond.

"Okay," Carmen said, and walked in the direction of the house. She waited a few minutes inside the doorway, and then walked back out towards her mother. "I found somebody."

"That was quick," Angelique said. "Who?"

"Uncle Robbie," Carmen lied. "He's on the verandah. He'll take me home as soon as he's done with his game."

"Alright," Angelique said, and turned back to Andrew. "We're going to stay here for a little while. I'll be home soon."

Carmen started back towards the house then detoured up the road once she was sure her mother wasn't looking. The night air was warm and the road was dimly lit by the lights coming from the houses that lined the path. The road was still muddy and the effort combined with the August heat made her sweaty and annoyed. Even though the district seemed friendly and benign during the daytime, under the night sky it took on a different air. The thick trees and bushes seemed to close in, and every rustle or crackle of leaves made her jump and her eyes widen as images of some lone gunman or obeah man snatching her into the bushes played in her mind. After 20 minutes, she finally reached the edge of town. She saw a small group of people hanging out by one of the bars set up on the roadside. She breathed a sigh of relief, glad to see the familiar sight of locals just liming. She looked for the turn off that would lead her to her grandparents' house. The road home was wider and the trees trimmed, allowing more of the moon's light to illuminate her path. She found the road by the bakery and started walking towards home.

After a few minutes had passed, Carmen felt as if she was being followed. At first she ignored it and continued up the road, but she couldn't dismiss the feeling. She stopped and looked back into the darkness, but seeing nothing, she forged on. She thought she heard a noise like a laugh and quickened her steps in response. She heard something fall with a thud in the dirt just behind her. She kept walking, choosing not to look back to see what it was. She heard another thump, followed by a third after something had nicked her right calf. She looked down and saw a single guinep lying on the ground by her foot. She started to run and this time heard footsteps behind her. She panicked, looking up and down the road for a light coming from a familiar house, but there was none that she recognized. As the footsteps closed in on her, she spotted a house and headed for the gate.

Suddenly she heard a deep voice call out "hey!" just behind her. She slipped in the mud and tumbled to the ground, landing in a heap just a few feet away from the gate. Before she could scream her pursuer was standing over her laughing. She squinted in the moonlight and saw a tall, slim man with dreadlocks falling just past his shoulders. He had even white teeth that shone even in the dim light. He sported a thin moustache and looked at her with eyes that danced with amusement.

"What are you running from? A duppy?" He laughed.

"Peter?" Carmen asked. She gingerly pulled herself up, brushing at the mud soaked spot on her pants and frowned. "A duppy is right. You could have been a ghost the way you scared me half to death. Why didn't you say something?" She held her chest and breathed hard.

"Now what would that look like? Me running down some gyal and balling down the place in the dark of night. You want to wake everybody?"

Carmen giggled and felt foolish. Peter was right. Half of this district was already asleep and if they were awakened by the sound of a rasta chasing down some girl in the middle of the night, that would have caused a whole lot of confusion. "How did you know it was me?"

Peter smiled. "You had foreigner written all over you," he said. "I saw you from the bar in town. Only a foreigner would walk through town looking so scared. And only a foreigner would wear white shoes in this red mud." Peter looked down at Carmen's stained runners.

"Don't forget I was born here. I've only been gone five years," Carmen said.

"Foreigner," Peter concluded and laughed.

Carmen feigned hurt, but eventually laughed along with Peter. He looked much like how she remembered him, though he was taller and more muscular. His dreads had grown longer, giving him a dark, mysterious look. Carmen's hand unconsciously fluttered up to her neck and moved upwards towards the tight curls tied back in the short puff of a ponytail. She wished she had let them hang loose.

Peter smiled. "So do you have to go home right now?"

"No." Carmen smiled back.

Peter led her back to town to the local bar where he had spotted her walking home. The two guys Peter introduced her to eyed her like ice water on a hot day. The two girls with them gave her a cool hello, checking out her clothes that clearly told them she was not a local. Peter slid his arm loosely around Carmen's waist to let everyone know she was with him and that she was okay. Carmen drank the rum that was offered to her and soon relaxed into an easy space among the group. The girls warmed up to her when they saw she was not interested in either of the other two guys and the guys resigned themselves to the fact that Peter had Carmen's full attention when she wasn't talking with the girls. Peter casually pulled Carmen close so her back was resting against him as she chatted with the other girls. She smiled and placed her hand over his, easing back into him. Her night had definitely taken a turn for the better.

They decided to see what was going on in the next town, so the girls jumped on the backs of the motorcycles and the guys easily navigated through the darkness of the trees. Carmen held on tight to Peter, inhaling his clean soapy scent. They found another bar and ran into a few more of Peter's friends. The new friends examined Carmen with curiosity while raising an eyebrow at Peter. Peter ignored the questioning glances and kept Carmen close by his side. A dark-skinned girl perched on a chair near the end of the bar watched them. She wore cut off denim jeans that Carmen thought looked more like underwear than shorts. The red top she wore was tied in a knot above her navel and her feet were pushed into pointy flat shoes with the heels pressed flat into the inner soles, as if they were bedroom slippers. Her formal-looking up 'do, held firmly in place with setting lotion and gel, looked odd paired with the casual sleazy outfit. Carmen thought she would be pretty if she didn't have such a hard look on her face. Peter caught her staring at them and turned his body so that he and Carmen were no longer facing her. The girl moved from the chair over to the counter and leaned onto it, resting her elbow on the weathered wood, her jaw cradled on top of her balled up fist. Carmen could feel her eyes on them and looked up at Peter who acted as though he didn't notice.

"Peter," the girl said.

He turned his head and looked over his shoulder at the girl.
"Have you talked to Karen?"
"No," Peter said.
"Well she was looking for you."

Peter turned away without answering. Carmen looked up at Peter, but he avoided making eye contact. Carmen could feel the girl staring at them, but she didn't say anything else. The mood at the bar had changed noticeably, and the conversation seemed stiff and forced. When one of Peter's friends suggested everyone go over to his house, they all quickly agreed. They got on their motorcycles and drove off, leaving the girl at the bar staring after them.

At the house, the couples listened to some music before pairing off to different areas of the house. Peter and Carmen stayed in the living room. Carmen sat on the other side of the sofa at first, but eventually moved closer to Peter. She hesitated when he began to stroke her cheek, thrilled by his touch, but the images of the girl from the bar dominated her mind. When she asked him who Karen was, he brushed it off and told her she was nobody. She didn't believe him, but gave in to her desires. She let him kiss her and she melted into him.

Carmen questioned her judgment later in the early morning hours when he told her he was ready to take her home. She picked her top off the floor as he zipped up his khaki pants. He didn't look at her as he rushed her along. Carmen played the last few hours over in her mind trying to figure out what caused him to pull back from her. It did not take long for her to get her answer. They sped down the road leading to the edge of town. Carmen pressed her body into Peter's back and held on tight, hoping to evoke some reaction from him. She closed her eyes and laid her cheek against his spine. She felt the motorcycle slow down abruptly. She opened her eyes in time to see what caused Peter to suddenly steer into a skid. Standing in the middle of the road was a woman dressed in cut off whitewashed jeans and a black t-shirt that hung off one shoulder where she'd obviously altered the collar. Her hair was corn rowed and wrapped into a knot at the top of her head. Carmen thought this girl would have also been pretty except for the hard scowl that she wore on her face. She stared directly at Peter then shifted her gaze to Carmen. She didn't say anything, but folded her arms across her chest and waited.

Peter looked at her before shifting the bike into gear and twisted the throttle a little more than necessary. The bike shot forward and Carmen had to hold on tight to avoid slipping off. She chanced a look back at the girl who had turned to watch them drive away, her arms still folded.

Peter managed to make it all the way to Somerset Grove without having to brake or slow down. When he had finally stopped a few houses away, Carmen slid off the back and waited for him to say something. Peter studied the handlebars and avoided her gaze. When she asked him who the girl was, he only kicked at the dirt below his toes and said he would explain it to her later. He promised he would come back that evening for her. She accepted this. He would be coming back. She waved at him as he rode off, and she made her way through the banana trees and around the back of the house. Whatever her mother yelled about would be worth it for Peter. Once her mother had a few days to cool down, she planned to ask her if she could stay here and finish school in Kingston. She almost changed course to head towards the front door, but thought better of it; the appearance of a little shame would go a long way to getting what she wanted.

"Where were you all night?" Angelique demanded while Ruby paced the floor muttering, "My God, my God," over and over. It was nearly six o'clock and Carmen had attempted to sneak in the back door holding her shoes in her hand so as not to make any noise walking across the tile floor. Angelique had positioned herself in the living room chair that gave her a view of the front door and the hallway. She had been there since 4 a.m. Ruby had kept watch in the kitchen after being woken up by Angelique asking where Carmen was all night. Byron had gone to Mandeville just before sunrise to take care of some business, but promised to call when he got there to see if Carmen had turned up.

Carmen knew she probably looked like a sight. The clothes she wore were disheveled and stained where she'd slipped in the mud. Her hair, which had been pulled neatly into a ponytail when she left, now danced wildly around her head. She slid her hand through it, pulling the curls to one side so they hung in her face as she cocked her head to one side and waited.

Angelique watched her daughter's movements—her nonchalant posture, her lack of concern at being caught walking in the house in the early morning hours. It was the way that she held Angelique's steady gaze that seemed to infuriate her the most, like she was challenging her mother to do something. Angelique's body tensed. She held her arms close to her body and curled her fingers into her palms. Her lips disappeared into an angry line as she searched for words.

Ruby looked between her daughter and granddaughter and stepped in. "We were worried sick about you, Carmen. Where were you all night?"

Carmen waited a second before shifting her eyes from her mother to Ruby. "I'm fine. I ran into some friends I knew from when I lived here. I didn't think it was that late. Sorry to worry *you*, Grandma," she said, not looking at her mother.

"Excuse me? What is that supposed to mean, 'sorry to worry you, Grandma?' Didn't you see me sitting here waiting on you, too? And who told you that you could stay out all night? And what were you doing? Wrapping up with some dirty boy?" Angelique fired one question after another at Carmen.

"I didn't think you'd notice."

"What you mean by that?"

"As soon as Andrew came, you didn't pay me any mind. That's the way it always is with you and men."

"What are you talking about?" Ruby asked.

Carmen knew her mother would be angry, but she didn't care. She had been excited to see Peter last night. Seeing his muscular body and watching the easy, confident way he moved stirred something inside her.

She was prepared for a good talking to if she got caught when she walked in the back door, but Carmen didn't expect the conversation to deteriorate the way it did. She took the wrong approach with her mother, confronting her about her men, especially in front of her grandmother, but the sight of Angelique also wearing the same clothes from the night before and acting as though she were concerned about Carmen when she probably just beat her home was too hypocritical for Carmen not to comment. Referring to Peter as 'some dirty boy' was the last straw. Carmen felt herself losing control as she told Ruby about how Lexroy came into her bedroom that night and her mother didn't even throw him out, how she hinted that it was somehow Carmen's fault because the man stopped talking to her and took away her car. She told Ruby how Angelique had virtually abandoned her last night when Andrew showed up, ready to let her walk the dark country roads home by herself.

"It was a good thing Peter showed up. He took care of me," Carmen said.

"You ungrateful wretch! After all I sacrificed for you? All I put up with from your worthless father so you would have a good home? I worked and brought you to Canada so you could have a good education. I put a roof over your head. You never one day went without food and this is how you thank me?" Angelique fumed.

"Wait, what is this business with this pervert you let in the house? What kind of mother puts her child at risk?" Ruby stepped in front of Angelique, blocking her path to Carmen.

"Who put her at risk? I never let anyone touch her. I even gave up my nice car to make sure of that. You, on the other hand, beat me when I was pregnant. You forget? It's a lucky thing I didn't lose her. I had to leave here to take care of us."

"That's not true," Ruby said.

"Yes, it is!"

Carmen held her head between her hands. Her mouth hung open as she stared at her grandmother.

Ruby's eyes pleaded with Carmen. "Don't believe her. It wasn't like that. I only slapped her."

Carmen felt the air in the room getting thick. It was hard to breathe. Her eyes burned as she fought back her tears—she was determined not to cry in front of them. She picked up her shoes and ran out the front door.

It seemed like she'd been walking for hours, lost in a fog. Eventually Carmen found herself walking towards the far end of the main road in town. She spotted Michael, one of Peter's friends from the night before in front of Mr. Chen's grocery store talking with another guy she did not know and the girl that was staring at them at the bar last night. She walked up and asked Michael if he knew where Peter was. Michael hesitated, avoiding making eye contact with Carmen, and said he really didn't know. The girl with the stiff hair and flattened shoes regarded Carmen with narrowed eyes for a moment and then spoke up.

"He's probably at work," the girl volunteered. "He works at one of the resorts in Negril. Duval knows the place," she said, gesturing at the other guy standing with them. "He can take you there if you want."

Michael frowned at the girl. "I don't think he's really supposed to have people come to his work, you know. They don't like it," he said.

"It won't be a problem. She looks like a foreigner. They'll probably think she's a guest," the girl said, eyeing Carmen. "Why you don't want her to go, Michael? You don't think Peter would be happy to see her?" She smiled and turned to Carmen. "Duval is my brother, you'll be fine," she said. When she noticed Carmen hesitate she said, "I'll go with you. Come, let's go." She tugged at Carmen's sleeve directing her towards a rusted out car. Carmen let herself be led to the vehicle and sat in the backseat as Duval sped down the highway. The hot wind blew Carmen's hair around her face and she squinted to keep her eyes from drying out. The girl looked back at Carmen periodically, but only directed her conversation towards her brother. Carmen pretended not to listen and marveled at how the girl's up 'do had still not moved in the car's wind tunnel.

They arrived at the resort a while later. Duval parked further down from the entrance and nodded at the security guard as the three of them walked up to the gate. The security guard gave the two girls a questioning look, but let them through when Duval told the guard they were all together. They walked through the tiled lobby of the resort with fans spinning overhead. Carmen was temporarily distracted from her sour mood by the beauty of the resort. Outside, guests lazed around a large swimming pool with a bar that people could swim up to and perch on underwater stools while they enjoyed their beverages. Carmen walked around the pool's edge, taking in the tropical paradise designed with the ocean as the backdrop. She almost forgot why she was there until she spotted Peter. He was a ways from the resort, working at a bar set up on the beach serving the guests who preferred to relax on lounge chairs placed closer to the ocean and those just returning from taking a turn on jet skis. Peter was behind the bar wearing a crisp white shirt, popping tops off beer bottles.

Carmen ran across the sand to the bar and breathlessly called out, "Peter!" He looked up when he heard his name, but did not smile when he recognized her. She reached the bar and said his name again. She started pouring out the details of the morning's confrontation to Peter, barely pausing to take a breath. She was so intent on telling him about her horrible morning that she didn't notice the way he was looking at her, and then beyond her, as if he were looking for something. Carmen rambled on and finally said, "I don't want to go back there." She waited for him to say something.

He frowned at her. "I told you I was coming by to see you later. How did you know where I work? How did you get here?" he demanded.

Confused, Carmen turned around and pointed at Duval and his sister who were now just a few yards away. "With them," she said. It was then that she realized they were not alone. The girl from last night, the one they almost ran over when Peter skidded to a stop was also with them, wearing the same white uniform shirt that Peter was wearing. Carmen squinted in the sunlight, studying the girl's face when she noticed that the girl shared similar features to Duval's sister. Both girls wore satisfied smirks on their faces. Duval looked down at the ground, his hands shoved in his pockets. The girl who looked like Duval's sister was carrying a plate of food. She stepped in the bar area and walked around Peter, placing the plate in front of him and rubbing his shoulder with her free hand. She kept her eyes on Carmen and seemed to take great pleasure in seeing the surprise slowly spread across Carmen's face.

Carmen looked at Peter who avoided making eye contact with her, focusing his attention on an imaginary stain he was trying to rub out of the counter.

"Peter?" she said.

Peter looked up at Carmen for a second, and then quickly looked across to the other side of the bar where two deeply tanned couples had seated themselves. "What can I get you?" Peter said as he quickly made his way over to them. He took his time getting their drink orders, engaging them in banter while he blended cocktails. He occasionally glanced over his shoulder to see if Carmen and the others were still there. He raised his eyebrows at Duval as if to say, *do something*. Duval shrugged as though to say there was nothing he could do. When Peter had finally prepared all of the drinks and the guests appeared to be done interacting with him, he slowly made his way back to the group. "We're out of daiquiri mix. I'm going to get some," he said to no one in particular. He started towards the hotel and Carmen turned to watch him, shading her forehead with her hand. "I told you, I would come by later to explain," he mumbled in a low voice as he passed her.

"Don't bother," she said and jogged past him to the hotel.

26

Carmen tossed her toiletry bag into her suitcase, and then looked around the room to see if she had forgotten anything. She had awakened earlier than necessary to finish packing, now realizing they had a little more than two hours before they had to leave for the airport. It had been over two weeks since the argument with her mother and the scene with Peter. Since then, she had kept to herself, spending most of her time at the house on the verandah, following the paths down to the fruit tree groves a few miles away from the house, or going down to the beach whenever she could get a ride. Ruby tried to get her to go with her on errands to town or other parts of the parish, but Carmen would usually politely decline, except on the few occasions when she couldn't get a ride on her own. On those days, Carmen would agree to go along, but would then wander off once they arrived at their destination, returning a few hours later when she thought

Ruby would be ready to leave. The only time she stayed with her grandmother was when they went to Montego Bay because she was not familiar with the city.

Angelique hadn't spent much time at the house since the argument, sometimes not returning for days. When she did return, it was only for a brief time, usually to change clothes and pick up her clean laundry, dropped off by the woman Ruby paid to do the washing. Angelique told her mother that she was staying with Hazel most of the time, but Ruby didn't believe her. She suspected her daughter was spending most of her time with Andrew, but felt it wasn't worth the argument. The only thing she was concerned about now was whether Angelique would show up in time to catch the plane back to Canada with Carmen. Ruby didn't know what she would do if she had to send Carmen alone, even though she was 17 years old and it would be a non-stop flight.

One hour before they were supposed to leave, Ruby fussed in the kitchen while her husband stood in the doorway, leaning against the wall.

"Cancel it, Byron. Just cancel the ticket. See if you can get the money back and we'll buy another ticket when Angelique comes to her senses," Ruby said. She was taking things out of cupboards and putting them back in again, not sure whether to make Carmen a quick snack or start cooking dinner. Miss Mavis didn't come over to cook since Ruby told her they would be gone most of the day traveling back and forth to the airport. Now Ruby regretted not asking the woman to come by the house. She couldn't focus on anything except the sound of the ticking coming from the grandfather clock in the hallway.

"I'm sure she will be here any minute. She's just trying to worry you," Byron said. He pulled the brim of his fedora down and ran his hand across his grisly salt-and-peppered whiskers. Normally his moustache and beard were neatly trimmed, but he had let his facial hair grow over the last week, bothered by the heightened strain that permeated his household of late.

He spent more and more time at his workshop, a reluctant compromise with his doctor who agreed that the stress at the shop was probably less than that at home, and thus less likely to elevate his blood pressure.

"Ruby, make me a cup of tea, please." He thought the task would at least give Ruby something to focus on and help him relieve his stress.

As soon as Ruby placed the steaming cup down in front of her husband, the front door opened and Angelique breezed into the house.

"Good morning, everybody!" Angelique sang as she bent down to give her dad a kiss on the cheek.

Ruby stared at her daughter like she had escaped from the mental ward at Bellevue. She glanced in her husband's direction with a look that said, *has this girl gone mad?* Byron answered his wife by resting his forehead in his left hand and stirred his tea with his right.

"Where have you been? You know your flight is leaving to go back home today, right? Everybody in here waiting on you and you walk in here like it's nothing," Ruby said.

"We're fine, we have plenty of time. I can be packed in half an hour. Where's Carmen?" Angelique replied as she walked towards the bedrooms. She opened Carmen's door without knocking. "There you are," she said, smiling. "You ready? I won't be long. Just need to put a few things in my bag."

Carmen had been laying on the bed, but bolted upright when her mother walked in, caught off guard by both her sudden entry and sunny disposition. "I'm ready," she mumbled.

"Good. Ask your grandfather to help you put your bags in the trunk."

Carmen rolled her bags into the living room and her grandfather took them out to the car. Ruby had given up trying to figure out what to make Carmen to eat, finally shoving some patties in the oven to heat up. All three of them sat waiting on the verandah expecting Angelique to take the full hour to finish packing, so they were surprised when she appeared in the doorway thirty minutes later wearing a new outfit and clutching the handle of the smaller of the two suitcases she had brought with her.

"I'm ready," she said brightly.

Byron eased himself out of his chair. "I'll go and get your other bag," he said.

"This is all I'm bringing."

Her father stared at the little suitcase, and then looked at Angelique quizzically.

"It's mostly just summer clothes I'm leaving. I'll be back here before I'll need those in Winnipeg," Angelique explained, beaming.

Byron shook his head in confusion, taking the suitcase from Angelique. "Alright. Well, if you're ready then let's go, I guess."

"I'm ready," Angelique said.

27

Carmen sat at the kitchen table of their apartment pouring over the course catalogue trying to decide what classes to register for at university. It was unusually hot and sticky for June in Winnipeg, and Carmen had the air conditioning turned up high in the little apartment. Angelique had put their house up for sale shortly after they returned from Jamaica the summer before and moved them into the apartment six months ago when the house had sold.

"I don't want to be tied to a house," she told Carmen when she asked why they had to move. "This gives us flexibility to pick up and go when we need to."

Angelique had made enough off the sale of the house to travel back and forth to Jamaica twice since they moved and now was planning a third trip right before Carmen started university.

"I thought you didn't like it there—too slow for you," Carmen said when Angelique started searching for airline tickets.

"I never said that."

"You always told me how you couldn't wait to leave there and come here," Carmen said.

"Well, it's different now. I don't know if I'd live there, but I like to go home and visit. I have a good time."

Carmen knew her mother was referring to Andrew, who spent all of his money on Angelique whenever she went down there, buying her clothes, gifts, and taking her all over the island to stay at different resorts. The first time Angelique went back last fall he told her he would build her a house if she would move home. She brushed his offer off initially, but her frequent trips and sudden sale of the house that they'd lived in for so long made Carmen believe that her mother was at least considering the possibility. Angelique had long given up on getting her nursing degree and was not content working as a practical nurse. "I didn't come here for that," Angelique told Carmen one time.

Angelique and Carmen had existed in polite unease over the past year. Angelique made no mention of the argument at Ruby's house, pretending like everything was fine, but it was obvious that there was a riff between the two of them that Carmen felt would not heal. Angelique treated Carmen more like a roommate, rather than her daughter. They made benign conversation about things like school, the people at Angelique's job, and what would happen on *A Different World* now that Denise Huxtable's character was no longer on the show. Once in a while, Angelique would take Carmen to the salon and then to the mall for a new outfit, or cook dinner at home. On these occasions, Angelique would let her guard down and become almost nurturing.

One Saturday after treating Carmen to a manicure and pedicure, Angelique took her to Baked Expectations where they shared a large slice of the fruit trifle piled high with kiwi and strawberries. Carmen had hers with a hot cocoa while Angelique drank a glass of wine. They laughed at the size of the dessert, which was large enough to serve at least four people. Angelique had swirled her glass and took a sip of her wine. "Take advantage of your schooling so you don't have to depend on anybody for what you want."

Carmen felt the unspoken "like me" hanging in the air between them. She licked the whipped cream from her lips and nodded in response. They talked about what Carmen wanted to study at university and ended the discussion with Angelique assuring her that she could do anything she wanted, that she would be proud of her no matter what she chose to do.

Other times Carmen would feel the weight of Angelique's resentment at being a young mother, particularly when she was going to or coming home from work. "I sacrifice so much," she would mumble. Carmen would feel her mother's eyes traveling over her lithe frame, making her uncomfortable until she understood why. A few weeks before she went back to Jamaica for her second trip that year, she came home to find Carmen curled up in the corner of the living room sofa, giggling into the receiver and twirling the telephone cord around her fingers. Angelique dropped the bag of groceries on the dining room table that had weighed her down along with her small lunch bag and the stack of bills that had been tucked underneath her arm. She sighed heavily as she collapsed into one of the dining room chairs and looked at Carmen.

"Every time I come in here, you are sitting on that phone," she'd said to Carmen.

"I gotta go," Carmen had said into the receiver and hung up. She waited for her mother to say something else, but Angelique just rested her elbow on the table and stroked her temple with her index finger, her brow raised causing worry lines across her forehead. "What's wrong, Mum?" Carmen said.

"I don't know," Angelique told her. "I just need a change, I feel restless."

That conversation had been two weeks before Angelique left for Jamaica without her. Carmen didn't mind; she spent most of her time at Aamani's house. Over the past year, Aamani's family had welcomed Carmen into their home, after deciding that she was a "good girl" because she and Aamani seemed to spend all their time studying. "You're going to be a doctor like my Aamani?" Aamani's mother had asked Carmen one day. Aamani had rolled her eyes when her mother wasn't watching. Carmen suppressed a laugh and simply smiled, saying, "maybe" in response. That was good enough for Aamani's mother, who always had two steaming cups of creamy chai waiting for the girls whenever Carmen came over after school to study. When she eventually found out that Carmen's mother was in Jamaica, Aamani's mother insisted that Carmen stay for dinner, too. She would have let Carmen stay over in Aamani's room, but Carmen insisted that her mother was only going to be gone for a few more days. She did not want people to know her mother had been gone for nearly a month. She was almost eighteen anyway, and enjoyed the extra freedom most of the time.

When Angelique returned after the second visit, she seemed renewed. She started a new job working in a doctor's office, which she enjoyed because of the day shift hours and because she got along well with the other staff. She bought herself new clothes in anticipation of summer and spent more time fixing up the apartment, though she invested nothing in items that were not easily portable; she covered the worn sofa with chenille throws and replaced the plain dishes with a trendy black set.

It didn't last. After Carmen's graduation, Angelique became restless and withdrawn as Carmen prepared for university. "I'm going back to Jamaica in a few weeks. This time I think I might stay for a while," Angelique announced when she came in the door of their apartment.

Carmen looked puzzled. "You just came back from there. And what about your job? You just started. How can you get vacation already?"

"You don't need to worry about that. I can get the time off," Angelique snapped.

Carmen shut her mouth and went back to her course catalogues.

"What are you doing anyway?" Angelique asked.

"Picking out classes."

"That reminds me. What would it cost for you to live on campus?" Angelique said.

Carmen looked up. "I don't know. Why?"

"I'm just asking," Angelique said. "You don't have to ask me a question every time I ask you one."

"Why don't you just put me out now?" Carmen mumbled.

"What did you say?"

"Nothing."

Angelique got up from the table and headed to her room. "Let me know when you find out about the on-campus living," she said and closed the door behind her.

Carmen waited for most of the crowd to disperse before she made her way over to the wall where the first semester grades were posted. She traced her finger down the sheets of paper until she found her student number, then holding her breath, slid it across to the column with the grades. Her eyes grew wide. She checked the student number again, and then slowly slid her finger across the paper again to make sure it was correct.

"What'd you get?"

Carmen turned to see a tall girl with skin the color of smooth, dark cocoa. She wore her hair in long, skinny braids that hung midway down her back. She was holding the economics class textbook to her chest and she had a slight accent—a mix of British and something else that Carmen couldn't quite discern. Carmen recognized her as the girl that sat on the other side of the auditorium.

"A+," Carmen said and smiled.

"Me too," she said.

"I'm Carmen."

"Nice to meet you. I'm Isabel," she said. "I recognized you from class."

"Hard to miss me. There are only three of us out of three hundred in there."

"That's true. I am not used to being in the minority," Isabel said. "Where are you from?"

Carmen smiled at the question. In her years in Canada, she learned that it was the second most common question people asked each other, right after 'what's your name?' She no longer took offense to it, realizing that everybody asked that question, regardless of what they looked like. Her address book looked like a directory for a mini United Nations.

"Jamaica," Carmen said proudly. "What about you?"

"Ghana," Isabel said with just as much pride.

Carmen nodded her head. "Nice."

Isabel buttoned her wool coat and pulled a pair of red mitts out of her pocket. "Well, I'm going home for dinner," she said as she walked towards the exit. Isabel pushed open the door and a cold wind whipped inside bringing with it a trail of crystal-hardened snow that swept across the floor and settled against the walls. She turned back to Carmen who was now checking to see how many A's had been awarded. Carmen pulled her dark gray pea coat tightly around herself.

"You want to come over?" Isabel said.

Carmen looked over her shoulder at Isabel, her eyebrows raised quizzically. "Me?"

Isabel laughed. "Do you see anyone else in here?"

Carmen smiled. "Oh! Okay, yeah, thanks." She grabbed her backpack off the floor and rushed out the door into the fading light of the afternoon.

28

"Your mother called you again last night. I told her you were at work," Isabel said. She was sitting at the small dining room table highlighting a paragraph in her political science textbook.

"Thanks," Carmen said. She stretched her arms above her head and bent to one side before heading into the kitchen to grab a bowl out of the cupboard. She filled it with Frosted Flakes and milk. Her fuzzy purple slippers slapped against her heels as she shuffled over to the dining room table with her breakfast.

"Are you going to call her back?" Isabel asked.

"Maybe later," Carmen said between mouthfuls. She reached for one of Isabel's pens and began to spin it in circles on the table, avoiding Isabel's eyes.

"You can't stay mad at her forever. That's your mother. And I can tell she loves you. Why else would she keep calling?"

"Whatever."

Carmen hadn't spoken to Angelique in two months. Before that, they had only spoken twice since last January. It was now August and Carmen still couldn't bring herself to forgive her mother. When Carmen had gone home and told Angelique about her economics grade, Angelique had said it was good news. She even took Carmen out for dinner to celebrate. The next day as Angelique was getting ready to go out to run some errands, she told Carmen it was time for her to look for a place.

"You're growing up, and I'm going to be going back home more often now," Angelique said after coming in from warming up the car. "You don't really need me anymore."

Carmen had stared at her mother in disbelief. Angelique didn't seem to notice as she stood in the entryway of the apartment, dusting the snow off her coat and checking her reflection in the mirrored hall closet door.

"I'll help you look," Angelique said as she gathered up her purse and gloves. "I'm going up the road for a bit. Soon come," she tossed over her shoulder as she walked out the door.

"My roommate is moving out. You can move in with me," Isabel had told Carmen when she came over in tears that day.

Carmen moved into Isabel's apartment in mid-January, lugging the few boxes of her belongings in from Angelique's car. Angelique had offered to help, but Carmen refused, letting her pride overrule her common sense. Isabel had gone home to visit her father for the winter break, so she wasn't there when Carmen moved in. Carmen had refused to wait for Isabel to get back, determined to move out before Angelique could ask her when exactly she was leaving again because she needed to give notice on the apartment so she could move her things into a coworker's basement. Angelique's plan was to pay a small amount to store her belongings, and then rent a bedroom from her friend whenever she came back to town. It was -20 degrees Celsius the day that Carmen moved and after her third trip to the car, her fingers started to go numb and her ears hurt from the cold, but at least she had a home now.

Angelique had gone back to Jamaica for the rest of the winter after Carmen moved out, returning only for a couple of months in late spring before heading back to Jamaica again. Carmen had managed to avoid seeing Angelique when she returned, telling her mother she was busy, but would stop by Angelique's temporary place later. She never did.

Angelique called several times, but Carmen would not answer the phone if she knew her mother was calling. Isabel had taken to answering the phone and telling Angelique that Carmen was at work or studying, but she was getting tired of making up excuses and didn't like lying to Carmen's mother.

"She seems nice, Carmen," Isabel told her when she gave her the message. "You only get one mother. You should talk to her. I wish I could talk to mine again," she said, wistfully. "Besides, you need her help."

Carmen felt a twinge of guilt. She knew that Isabel had lost her mother to cancer when Isabel was only 13. She had been raised by her older sisters, her father too heartbroken to look after Isabel like he should. Sending Isabel to Canada to attend university had been his way of taking care of her, while at the same time easing the pain he felt each time he looked at the daughter that looked so much like the wife he lost.

"Maybe I'll call her tomorrow," Carmen said.

Isabel shook her head and said nothing. She'd heard that one before. Tomorrow never seemed to come for Carmen. Carmen had stayed in a funk for the first two months after she moved in with Isabel, but eventually got out of it with the arrival of spring and upcoming final exams.

"If you don't focus, you're grades will slip," Isabel had told her.

Carmen had pulled herself together in the nick of time, pulling out mostly B's and two A's. She'd contemplated taken a summer course to raise her GPA, but with the uncertainty of whether Angelique would be sending money to take care of her tuition, Carmen decided to take a full-time job working at the hydro company as a billing clerk. By the end of July, she'd made enough to cover the first semester's tuition payment and estimated she could cover the rest of the year by the end of October, but would need to take out a student loan to cover living expenses if Angelique didn't send any money. She'd put off calling her mother as long as possible, but knew that she would have to call her and soon if she was going to get her to sign the student loan papers in time for the fall semester. But every time Carmen picked up the phone, her throat would grow thick with the lump that seemed to appear out of nowhere and wouldn't go down until she replaced the receiver. "Tomorrow," she would tell herself each time she hung up the phone.

Carmen finished up her cereal and got dressed. It was Saturday and some of the Caribbean students were planning a barbecue that afternoon. Carmen had agreed to make a fruit platter so she'd plan to run to the Safeway and pick up summer fruit to cut up. On the way out the door, she stopped by the mailbox. Their slot was packed with the mail that had been building up for close to a week. She shuffled through the pile absentmindedly, throwing out the flyers on her way out the door. She sighed when she saw mail for Angelique. Even though her mother had moved her things over to a friend's house, she decided to have her mail sent to Carmen to hold for her.

One envelope caught Carmen's eye. It was addressed to Angelique from Immigration Canada. Carmen turned it over in her hand, and then squeezed the top and bottom together, trying to peek through the clear plastic address window to see if she could read the letter. She couldn't see anything. She gave up and shoved the envelope in her purse along with the rest of the mail. Now she had reason to call her mother.

Someone answered after the third ring. "Hello?" the sing-songy voice said into the phone.

"Hi, Grandma," Carmen said.

"Oh, my goodness! Is this my lovely granddaughter?" Ruby twittered on the other end.

Carmen smiled. "Yes. How are you, Grandma?"

"Oh, much better now that I hear your voice," Ruby said. "And how is my superstar? Your grandfather and I are so proud of you. I heard you're getting all A's in school," she said.

"Not all A's." Carmen blushed. "But almost," she added quickly.

"Of course, dear. You'll get there. I'm just so happy to hear from you. I have to get your grandfather on the phone," Ruby rambled on.

"Is my mum there?" Carmen asked.

"Oh! Yes, she's here someplace," Ruby said, as if it just occurred to her that Carmen would be calling to speak with her mother. She told Carmen to hold on while she went to look for her. Carmen could hear Ruby calling Angelique's name several times before it seemed like she got a response. "Hurry up, nuh! Your daughter is calling long distance, you know," Ruby said.

After what seemed like an eternity had passed, Angelique finally picked up the phone. "Hello?" she said, as if she didn't know who was calling.

"Hi, Mum," Carmen said. She had to force herself to make her voice sound light.

"Carmen," I've been calling and calling and can never reach you. You're just returning my call now?"

Carmen cleared her throat. "Sorry, I meant to call. I've just been working so much when I'm out of school and sometimes I get home too late to call," she lied.

There was silence on the other end of the phone.

"How are you, Mum?" Carmen asked.

"I'm doing well. How are you?"

"I'm good," Carmen said. She could tell her mother was distracted by something in the background, but she couldn't tell what or who it was. "Did I catch you at a bad time? I can call back."

"No, I—" Angelique's voice became muffled and Carmen could tell she was holding her hand over the receiver. "Carmen, can I call you later today? I'm running late. I have to go."

"Well, I just have to ask you something quick. I need to get a student loan and they say I need for you to sign some papers. If I send them to you, will you send them back right away? I also need a copy of your tax return," Carmen said quickly.

"Yes, yes, we can talk about it some more later. Just send the papers. I have to get off the phone. I'll call you back." *Click*.

Carmen looked at the receiver in her hand in disbelief. After not speaking for months, her mother had stayed on the phone for less than a minute. Carmen hung up the phone and got ready to leave, tossing the immigration envelope on the stack of Angelique's mail piled on her desk on the way out the door.

It was now early October and Carmen hadn't heard back from Angelique. She'd left messages for her mother, but never received a return phone call. Ruby began to sound exasperated whenever Carmen called. "I'm sorry, dear. I don't know what to do. She's never here and when I tell her to mail back the papers to you, she just tells me she will take care of it."

Carmen had mailed the loan papers to her mother a few days after they spoke. At the last minute, she had slipped the letter from immigration into the same envelope; she didn't know why she had hesitated to send it. She was annoyed that her mother had not returned her urgent calls, but decided to send the letter along with the rest of her mail anyway. Carmen was already behind in her classes, not being able to afford the textbooks to keep up with the reading assignments. Today she'd gone home to check the mailbox and had returned to campus empty-handed. Now she waited in line at the financial aid office to see what she could do. After almost thirty minutes she finally reached the front of the line. The clerk looked over the reading glasses that sat at the tip of her nose at Carmen. Her hair, almost bleached white, tumbled loosely from the clip that pinned up the ends in the back. Her bangs were long and swept to the side, held their mostly by the quarter bottle of hairspray she probably used that morning after applying the *Oil of Olay* she hoped would keep her from looking all of her 50 years of age. She wore an expression that told of her exhaustion from hearing students' stories of financial hardship or irresponsibility that left them unable to pay their tuition and expenses. She waited for Carmen to tell her which category she fell in.

"I don't have enough money for school," Carmen said.

The clerk gave Carmen a look that said, 'obviously,' but instead asked, "Have you already applied for a student loan?"

Carmen told her how she'd tried to save money over the summer, but with rent and the increase in tuition, she just didn't have enough. "My mom is sick. I couldn't get all the paperwork together in time," she heard herself lie.

"It's probably too late for you to reapply as an independent student. By the time it would get processed, the semester will almost be over and you only have about a week and a half left to pay." She licked her middle finger and started pulling various forms together to pass to Carmen. "Here," she said. "You can try applying for a bursary from the university. It will process faster, and you wouldn't have to pay that back. The only problem is that it's not a lot of money."

Carmen looked down at the forms, and then shoved them into her backpack. "Thank you," she said and turned from the counter.

"Good luck," the woman called out, pushing away the mass of hair that had fallen in her face as she patted the rest of it in place.

Carmen gave her a slight smile before she headed out the door to catch the bus home. As the bus wound its way through the campus she pulled the papers out of her bag and read them more carefully. Her eyes welled up with tears and she frowned in frustration. At most, she could get 700 dollars. That wasn't enough, and what would she do next semester? She definitely could not afford tuition, books, and living expenses. She balled up the papers and shoved them back in the bag. She wrapped her arms around herself and fought back the tears as she watched the university campus fading away before her eyes.

29

"You're late."

"I know, sorry. I missed the first bus and the next one didn't come for half an hour." Carmen dabbed at her forehead with the back of her hand as she hurried between the pool tables to the storage room in the back to drop off her bag. "I'm just going to run to the bathroom and then I'll be right out," she called back.

"Hurry up."

Prick, Carmen thought as she intentionally slowed her pace. She'd been working part-time at Shark's Café for four months now, coming in for the 6-10 p.m. shift every night after her day job at the hydro company. It was guaranteed that at least once during the shift she would be tempted to pick up one of the pool cues and crack Danny the assistant manager over the head with it. Danny acted like he was running some upscale nightclub in New York City instead of the local spot that students came to hang out and shoot pool. He was known for trying to demean staff in front of customers to make himself look important, especially if there was a cute girl in the group he was trying to impress. He was still ticked at Carmen from last week when he tried to make her bring him the food he'd ordered from the kitchen.

"Slavery is over and it's not my job to serve you. Get it yourself," she had told him in front of the brunette wearing boy cut shorts and ankle boots he was trying to hit on. The girl had almost spit out the rye and coke she was drinking as she laughed and pointed at Danny. He glared at Carmen as she tossed her ponytail and walked away. Mark, the bartender, told Carmen that Danny had tried to have Kevin, the owner, fire her, but the man had refused, telling Danny that Carmen was right. Everyone knew the owner had a crush on Carmen anyway and all Danny managed to do was get on his bad side. Mark and Carmen had been like best friends almost since the day she started working at the café when she told him he looked like Johnny Depp. Mark had beamed and ever since then he always covered for Carmen or let her leave early when Danny wasn't around so that she could catch the bus that came at 9:45. Mark couldn't stand Danny either, so whenever he was in trouble, it made Mark's day.

"The dragon is not in a good mood," Mark said, referring to Danny.

"What's his problem?" Carmen tied the black apron around her waist.

"You missed the show. Kevin went off on him earlier," Mark said. "Not sure what he did, but he's feeling pretty foul now, I guess. Watch out," Mark warned and laughed.

Carmen rolled her eyes. "I'm in no mood for him tonight, so he better watch out for me."

The long work days were wearing on Carmen, especially since it seemed she never got to see the sun. Ever since she had to drop out of school, she had been working as much as possible to save up enough to resume classes the next school year. She didn't want to have to rely on anyone else again and if anyone got in the way of that, she would handle them.

Danny avoided the rest of the staff for most of the night, choosing to hide out in the back office to do "paperwork." Towards the end of the evening, he finally emerged and surveyed the room. Mark had gone to the back for supplies to restock the bar and the cook was busy making a platter of loaded nachos for everyone to share after they shut down. The only two people on the floor were Carmen and Theresa the new girl, who'd spent most of the evening correcting the food and drink orders she'd messed up. Carmen tidied up the pool equipment while Theresa hovered around the bar, waiting for everyone to get back so they could divide up the tip jar.

"Carmen," Danny barked. "I need you to clean the bathrooms."

"I did them yesterday and on Tuesday," she reminded him. "It's someone else's turn," she said and looked towards Theresa.

"But I assigned it to you," Danny replied.

"And I'm not doing them again this week is what I'm telling you," Carmen said as she slammed pool balls into a tray.

"You don't run this shift. I do, and cleaning the bathrooms *is* part of your job duties, so get to it," Danny sneered.

"It's part of everyone's job description, not just mine," she retorted.

Theresa walked over. "I'll do it, I don't mind," she volunteered.

"No, I told Carmen to clean the bathrooms, so she'll do it."

"No, she won't," Carmen said and folded her arms across her chest.

"You will if you want to keep your job," Danny shot back. By this time, Mark had returned from the storage room carrying a case of beer. He put the box on the bar and moved towards the area where Carmen, Danny, and Theresa were now standing.

Carmen held her hand up towards Mark who stopped in his tracks. She still gripped one of the pool balls in her other hand as she spoke. "I can handle him," she said, and then moved her arm through space so that it was now pointing at Danny. "You," she began, "with your little dead-end job, you think you're running things?" she asked and put her hand on her hip. "Let me tell you something because you seemed to have been confused for a long time now." Carmen could feel the heat rising up her neck, warming her ears. Little beads of perspiration started to form on her forehead, despite the cool air that rushed in as some remaining customers walked out. She could feel herself losing control, her Jamaican accent, hardly noticeable at all nowadays, carried her words along like a strong Caribbean breeze with the sole purpose of knocking down its target. "You do not run this place and you certainly don't run me."

"You're fired," Danny screamed. "Get out!"

Carmen looked at him coolly. "You can't fire anybody," she said and tossed the pool ball up and down in her hand.

"I'm firing you," Danny said and stepped menacingly towards Carmen.

Carmen stepped her right foot back and braced herself. She stopped tossing the ball and held it steadily in her right hand. "What are you going to do, big man?" she mocked him.

Danny took in Carmen's posture and looked at the pool ball she clutched in her hand. Theresa had backed away to the other side of the pool table, nervously pulling her hair to one side and raking through it with her fingers. Mark stood by, fascinated, but poised to move. Danny narrowed his eyes and started to head towards the door. "You get your little friend out of here before I get back or both of you will be out," Danny said to Mark as he brushed passed him and headed out the front door.

"What the heck did I just miss? I was gone for like two minutes." Mark looked first at Carmen, then Theresa who by now was heading towards the back room.

Carmen shrugged. "He's crazy. Look, I'm going to get out of here before he gets back," she said.

"Wait, he can't make you leave," Mark spat out in disgust.

"No, but it's better that I go. I don't know what I might do if I see him again tonight," Carmen said and smiled.

"Okay," Mark said. "I'll call you tomorrow and let you know what happens."

The next morning Carmen sat on the living room sofa with her legs curled under her watching videos on MuchMusic when the phone rang. She looked over at the call display and saw the number for Shark's Café. She answered the phone casually, expecting to hear Mark's voice on the other end since he said he would call. "Hello?" she answered the phone distractedly.

"Carmen? It's Kevin."

Carmen sat up at the sound of the owner's voice. "Hi, Kevin."

"Carmen, we have a problem. Danny said you and he got into it last night. He said you were insubordinate and that you threatened him." Kevin sighed. "Carmen, I'm going to have to suspend you while we figure this out."

"What?" Carmen almost shouted. "That's a lie. I never threatened him. What do you mean *I* threatened him? How about he was threatening me? How about he is always trying to make me do the most demeaning work? He doesn't do it to anyone else, only the black girl," Carmen said and instantly regretted it. She didn't want Kevin to think she was the type to throw race into every work problem, but she was angry. Both at the accusation and that she was going to lose money while suspended. "Is he suspended?" Carmen asked.

"No," Kevin replied quietly.

"I see where this is going," Carmen said.

"That's not fair, Carmen," Kevin said.

"Fair? Are you kidding me? Fair for who?" Carmen demanded. Kevin was silent.

"This is ridiculous." Carmen gripped the receiver so tightly her knuckles began to ache.

"I'm looking into it. We'll be in touch," Kevin said and hung up the phone.

Carmen threw the cordless phone down so hard on the sofa it bounced off the cushions and landed with a thud on the coffee table, chipping the wood. "Damn it!" she said.

The phone rang again. She snatched it off the coffee table and pressed the "talk" button. "Yes?" she said, her voice filled with irritation.

"Hello, Carmen, it's me."

Carmen froze at the sound of her mother's voice. She had managed to avoid her all of these months, but now there she was on the other end of the phone because Carmen had forgotten to check the Caller ID before answering the call. "Hello," she said flatly.

"It's your mother," Angelique said.

"I know."

"I haven't talked to you in months. I would think you'd be happier to hear my voice. What's wrong with you?"

Carmen didn't know what possessed her to contemplate telling her mother what had happened. Maybe it was that she just needed someone to talk to and at the moment, Angelique was the only one there. Isabel had tried to convince Carmen that she shouldn't waste her energy trying to hold onto her anger at her mother for not sending the student loan papers and just accept that she would be taking the year off from school.

"You should know by now not to be surprised by anything your mother does. She is who she is," Isabel had said. Carmen finally agreed with Isabel and blamed herself for not being more prepared for her mother falling through on her promises.

Whatever the reason, Carmen now found herself pouring out all of the details of the incident at work, including the suspension.

"I'm sorry to hear that, Carmen," Angelique said. "That isn't right, but don't worry. It will work out. Nothing you can do about it right now, but when they do sort it out, you make sure they pay you back for all the money you're missing."

Carmen pouted, but let some of the tension release from her body. "Okay," she said.

"Anyway, the reason I called was to tell you I'm coming back to Winnipeg," Angelique said.

"Really?" Despite the lingering disappointment that Carmen had pushed down somewhere deep inside her, she found herself excited about her mother's return. "When? For how long?" The questions bubbled out before Carmen could even think about them.

Angelique laughed. "Goodness, I wasn't expecting that kind of reception to the idea."

Carmen smiled in spite of herself. She was glad her mother couldn't see her blushing through the phone.

"I was thinking in about a month. I have to take care of some things here first," Angelique said. "I'm going to stay at Dahlia's eventually, but if it's not too much trouble, I wanted to stay with you for the first couple of weeks. Dahlia is going to be in New York visiting relatives when I get there, so I won't be able to get into her house until she gets back."

Carmen smiled at the mention of her mother's old friend. She remembered the first time she met Aunt Dahlia several months after she first moved to Winnipeg. Her mother and Aunt Dahlia used to argue all the time, but they always managed to make up. Carmen was happy to hear they were on good terms again.

"Of course," Carmen said. "You can have my room. I'll stay on the pull-out couch in the living room."

"Oh, you don't have to do that. I don't want to put you out. I'll stay in the living room. You keep your room," Angelique protested.

"You're not putting me out," Carmen said. "You're my mother."

"Alright. Thank you, dear. I'll give you a call in a couple of weeks to let you know my flight arrangements."

"Okay," Carmen said. "Love you," she added quickly.

There was a brief silence on the phone. "Love you, too," Angelique replied and hung up.

Carmen sat on her bedroom floor, refolding the clothes that were in her dresser so she could store them neatly in the bins underneath her bed. She had spent the last three weeks getting the apartment in order for her mother's arrival, spending money on accessories and linen so the place didn't look like the student housing that it was. Isabel had helped out, vacuuming in the places normally hidden by furniture, dusting on top of the refrigerator, tidying the linen closet, and straightening up the cupboard under the sink that once overflowed with hair products, body scrubs, and scented lotions. Carmen hummed along to the mixed CD playing on her stereo. A gift for herself she had splurged on after she returned to work at Shark's Café. Mark and Theresa had backed up Carmen's story and Danny was eventually fired and replaced by Mark. The owner had agreed to pay Carmen for the time she lost from work. Profits increased when the owner realized that Danny had been skimming off the deposits. He was so happy with the improved morale and profitability that he gave everyone who had suffered through Danny's tirades a $300 bonus. Carmen took her bonus straight to the electronics store and bought the stereo.

Isabel stuck her head in Carmen's door. "So when exactly is your mother arriving?"

"On Saturday at four," Carmen said. "I'm going to make dinner first, and then go pick her up at the airport. Are you going to stay for dinner?"

"If you make that curry chicken I will." Isabel grinned.

"For sure," Carmen said.

Over the next week, Carmen made her final preparations. She managed to get someone to cover her shifts at Shark's Café and took a week of vacation from the hydro company so she could spend time with her mother after she arrived. On Friday she went to the grocery store, picking up all the things Angelique liked to eat and getting the ingredients for the dinner she was cooking. She decided to invite some other friends over for dinner as well, so she picked up extra chicken before stopping off at the liquor store to get some wine.

It was nearly nine o'clock at night when Carmen finally got back and managed to lug all of the groceries from the car up to the second floor apartment. She put away everything before she started to season the chicken. She planned to let it marinade until morning, then cook it and clean up so that the apartment could air out before Angelique got home. She'd just finished rubbing all the ingredients into the chicken when the phone rang. By the time she washed her hands and ran to the phone, it had stopped ringing. She checked the Caller ID and guessed it was Angelique calling. She quickly dialed back, but the phone rang several times before she finally hung up. *She'll call back,* Carmen told herself and went back to cooking, not noticing that the answering machine was blinking.

The next morning, Carmen got up early to start cooking. While the chicken browned in the pan, she began cutting up potatoes to add to the pot later. Isabel emerged from her bedroom and commented on the aroma.

"Smells nice in here. Let me know if you need a taste tester."

"You stay out of my pots," Carmen warned her with a mock frown. "If you start eating, all that will be left will be bones and a few grains of rice."

"That's not true," Isabel said. "I'd make sure all the rice was gone, too." Isabel grinned at Carmen as she plugged the kettle in to make some tea. She wandered into the living room and opened the blinds, letting in a flood of warm June sunshine that bathed the room in light. "Hey, there's a message for you," Isabel called from the living room.

Carmen walked out of the kitchen wiping her hands on a dish towel. "Who is it?" she asked.

"Your mother," Isabel said.

Carmen walked over to the phone. "I wonder if her flight's delayed," she said aloud and played back the message.

Isabel watched as the slight smile faded from Carmen's face. Her eyes darkened and her mouth pulled into a tight line. Isabel could see Carmen's jaw working as she chewed the inside of her bottom lip. She put the phone down and without a word, walked into the kitchen, pulled the steaming pan of chicken off the stove, and dumped its entire contents in the trash, splattering curry gravy all over the floor and the wall.

Isabel's eyes grew wide. "What's the matter?"

Carmen ignored her, walking into the bathroom and dumping the jasmine-scented body lotions and gels that she bought for Angelique into the garbage. She then walked into the bedroom and surveyed the space before grabbing the stack of mail addressed to Angelique that she had neatly tied with red ribbon. She marched back to the kitchen and threw the pile on top of the yellow curry before retreating again to her bedroom and collapsing face down on the bed, staining the white bedspread with the curry that had spattered on her clothes and burned her feet.

Isabel ran quickly to the bathroom and soaked a towel with cold water. She went to Carmen's room, rolled her over, and gently removed her curry-stained clothes. She examined Carmen's legs, then wrapped the cold towel around her feet. She ran to the linen closet and pulled out a foot bath and filled it with cold water, then forced Carmen to sit up and put her feet in the bath. "Good thing you were wearing socks," Isabel said. After she was satisfied that her skin was cooled off enough, Isabel gently dried Carmen's feet and applied aloe vera gel before wrapping them loosely in a gauze. Carmen let herself be nursed in silence. When Isabel was done, Carmen lay back down and closed her eyes, letting the tears slide down the sides of her temple, slicking her curls.

She awoke sometime later and eased herself gingerly out of bed. Her feet stung a little, but the pain was bearable. It was still bright out though the sun had moved across to the west side of the room casting long shadows on her bedroom floor. Carmen wandered out of her room into the kitchen to examine the damage, though she did not want to be reminded of all the work she had put in for nothing. There was nothing on the stove and the pots sat gleaming in the dish drainer. The only evidence of any cooking that day was the slightly yellow tinged wall where Isabel had unsuccessfully tried to scrub it clean.

Carmen smiled sadly at the marks. Isabel had taken care of everything and never questioned why.

"Are you hungry?"

Carmen jumped and turned around to see Isabel standing in the doorway. Darn carpet. Isabel could move like a ninja when she wanted to.

Carmen's feet burned with the sudden movement, but the discomfort quickly gave way to the pang in her stomach. She hadn't eaten all day, consumed with getting everything ready before her mother's arrival, then consumed by anger and disappointment when she heard her mother's message.

"Yes."

"Good," Isabel said and held up two bags from McDonald's. "I didn't want to eat this all by myself, but you know I would."

They sat at the dining room table munching on fries and cheeseburgers. Isabel asked Carmen how her feet were.

"Fine. It wasn't serious," Carmen said.

"You should go get it checked out, just in case."

"Maybe I'll go later. It's not really bothering me." Carmen reached for another fry.

"I'll take you. You don't want to wait too long," Isabel urged.

"Alright, alright. I feel sorry for your kids when you have them."

Isabel smiled. "Just concerned about my best friend…and the rent money. If you need to get some sort of disability, we need to fill out the paperwork now. We don't have time for delays."

Carmen laughed for the first time all day. "Gee, thanks," she said, and then chewed in silence. "Did you listen to the message?" she finally asked.

Isabel concentrated on pulling the pickles off her burger. She nodded.

"Can you believe she blew me off to go on a cruise with that man?" Carmen blurted out. "This was no surprise trip. She had to have known before today. And couldn't she just tell him no? She sees him all the time. I haven't seen her in over a year." The words kept tumbling out and Carmen couldn't stop them.

Isabel listened quietly and nodded. "I know your mother is kind of what they call a free spirit, but I must admit that was even surprising to me."

"Well, that's it for me. I'm done," Carmen said. She rubbed the back of her fist across her eyes to catch the tear that threatened to fall down her cheek.

"You'll get past this, and you'll forgive her," Isabel said.

"No," Carmen said and folded her arms across her chest like a defiant little girl.

Isabel let it drop, believing Carmen needed more time to cool off.

Angelique called a week later and Isabel answered the phone. "Hold on, Mrs. Chambers. I'll get her." When Isabel called her, Carmen walked over to the phone. She held Isabel's gaze as she calmly placed the receiver on the hook. "I'm done," she said, and walked out of the apartment. The phone rang again. This time, Isabel did not answer it.

30

Spring, 1991

The dawn arrived, angry and distressed. The thunder clapped and lightning pierced through the dark morning, slicing the sky into jagged pieces. Rain pummeled against the window announcing its presence and demanding attention from all who dared sleep through its arrival. The storm continued for hours, threatening to wash away the day and wreak havoc on the plans of worn out Winnipeggers who had waited patiently for the first warm weekend in May to finally be able to shed their winter wears and dawn their spring wardrobes.

By 9 a.m., the rain had stopped and a rainbow adorned the sky as the sun lay in the background. By 11 a.m. the sun had taken its place at center stage, bathing the city in warmth and the promise of a beautiful day.

Carmen stood toward the front of the line with the rest of the "C's". She looked out into the crowd of people sitting in front of the stage. Her eyes roamed until they found their target. She waved at the elderly gentleman, his hair more gray than not, his hands resting comfortably below his paunch. He put on reading glasses that didn't seem to help as he held the brown and gold glossy folder at arm's length so that he could study it. He looked up and lowered his glasses before spotting Carmen and waving back. He sat beside a woman who was much younger. She wore her braids pulled into a low ponytail. On her lap sat a baby dressed in a bright pink ruffled dress with that familiar mocha complexion who contentedly stuck her chubby fingers into her mouth as she kicked her tiny feet in excitement.

Carmen searched the line of people behind her before she finally spotted Isabel adjusting the mortarboard that rested on the micro braids cascading down her back. She jumped up and down excitedly and gave Carmen a thumbs up signal before waving to her father and sister in the audience who by now had spotted her as well.

Carmen could hardly contain her excitement when it was her turn to cross the stage and shake hands with the Dean of the Faculty of Arts. Her feet seemed to glide across the floor and she held her chin so far up that the mortarboard almost slid off the back of her head. When she was finally handed her degree, she could barely stand still long enough to get her picture taken before she skipped off the stage to be sure she would not miss Isabel being handed her degree, too.

Over the past three years the two young women had become closer than sisters, and Isabel's family had treated Carmen like a daughter. They were just as happy to see Carmen claim her degree as they were to see Isabel.

As soon as Isabel had her photo taken, she bounded off the stage. The two of them broke away from the alphabetical order so they could exchange a quick hug before being shooed back in line by the chubby registrar who tried to hide the smile that tugged at the corners of her mouth and threatened to take away from the stern demeanor she always tried to project to keep order during convocation.

It had taken five long years for Carmen to get to this place. She'd financed most of her education by working at Shark's Cafe on nights and weekends along with the money she earned in the summer working at the hydro company during the day, but it had been worth it to get to this point. Luckily, Isabel had switched majors after her second year, deciding she wanted to be an English professor rather than an economist, so the two friends ended up graduating at the same time. Now Carmen had a degree and a job waiting for her in Toronto when she got back from her trip of a lifetime. Isabel's family had invited her to come spend part of the summer with them in Ghana.

"From now on, it's work, work, work for you young women. Who knows when you will be able to take off a summer again and Carmen, you've never had an experience like this. Trust me, you will love it," Isabel's sister had told her over the phone when they were making plans to fly in for the girls' graduation.

When Carmen hesitated Isabel's family insisted on paying the cost of the airline ticket. "You're family and you'll both have enough expenses to take care of when you move to Toronto." Carmen had tried to refuse, but Isabel's family would not hear of it, especially since Isabel was adamant that Carmen had to come.

"You're coming and that's the end of the discussion," Isabel told her when Carmen tried to protest after they'd hung up the phone. Carmen's eyes had welled up with tears.

"Thank you. I can't believe this," Carmen said.

Isabel waved her hand dismissively. "It's really nothing, Carmen. Besides, next summer we are going to Jamaica and it will be your treat." Isabel grinned. "Start saving."

Carmen smiled, but didn't respond. Isabel had been pushing her for years to make peace with her mother, but Carmen refused after Angelique had cancelled her visit at the last minute. Angelique tried to call several times over the following weeks, but Carmen would not come to the phone. Eventually, the phone calls dwindled, and then stopped altogether. Carmen wasn't sure how she felt about her mother's withdrawal from her life. She was sure though that she was not ready to confront her and Isabel eventually let it go. Isabel's family eventually filled the void and the longing she had for her own family.

Carmen had heard nothing from Angelique for years until one day four months before graduation. She'd come home from class during a snowstorm. It had taken her nearly 45 minutes to walk home from where the bus had dropped her off. The road conditions wouldn't allow the bus to travel down its normal route, so Carmen had gotten off on Pembina Highway and trudged through a foot of snow on unplowed streets and climbed over snow banks to get to her apartment almost half a mile away.

By the time she reached home, her fingers were numb and her feet were soaked from the snow that had seeped in from the tops of her boots. When she got inside, her neck and back were stiff from hunching them up against the dampening cold that chilled her through to her bones. All she wanted to do was get into a steaming hot shower and allow her body to thaw.

Carmen kicked off her boots and shook herself out of her wool coat and scarf, letting them fall into a pile at the front door. She vigorously rubbed her arms as she half-ran on the balls of her feet towards the bathroom to start running the shower. She was rummaging through her dresser drawers for a pair of flannel pajamas when she noticed the light blinking on the cordless phone. She punched in the voicemail code and tucked the phone between her ear and shoulder as she searched for the bottoms to match the pajama top she located.

"Hello, it's me, Carmen. Um, hope all is well with you. Um, I need you to call me back as soon as possible, please. It's very important. Thank you."

Angelique's voice penetrated her and filled her with a chill deeper than the January cold had managed to do. Carmen held the receiver frozen for a moment, unsure of how to react. She missed her mother's voice, but the sound of it also brought back memories of abandonment and betrayal. Her thoughts ran back to that summer nearly four years ago when Angelique had chosen her boyfriend and a cruise over her. The disappointment from that day had faded, but the hurt was reawakened the moment Carmen heard the message. She felt a knot in her stomach and a headache forming in the space on her forehead where her brow began to furrow. Carmen sat down on the bed and mindlessly stroked her middle and third finger back and forth across her forehead. The other hand mimicked this movement, stroking her knee up and down as she rocked herself backwards and forwards. She hesitated for a moment, then picked up the phone and dialed the number Angelique left. Before it could ring, she clicked the "end" button and put the phone back on the dresser. She gathered up her belongings and headed towards the shower. Her mother could wait.

The next morning was bitterly cold as the temperature plummeted to -25 degrees Celsius. Carmen sat on the sofa watching the wind whip around the crystals of snowflakes that had hardened and now tortured the unfortunate souls who had to brave the cold to go outside. The university had mercifully cancelled classes that day, so Carmen managed to escape the fate of some of the other people who battled the snowdrifts trying to dig out their cars to get to work.

She turned back to the movie that was on the television. The characters droned on and on, and Carmen eventually gave up trying to figure out what was going on. The movie had been on for well over an hour, but she had been too distracted to follow the plot. She drew her knees up and rested her chin on top and looked down at the piece of paper with the number she had written down the day before. The paper was soft and wrinkled from her gripping it in her hand all morning. The moisture from her hands had smudged the numbers, but she could still make them out. She leaned over and grabbed the phone off the coffee table and was about to make a phone call when there was a rapid knock at the door. Carmen walked over and looked through the peep hole, then opened the door when she recognized the person standing on the other side.

"Hi, Mrs. Briansky," Carmen said to the elderly woman standing in front of her who had on ski pants underneath her long down-filled coat. A knitted pink beret rested on her head matching her pink wind burned cheeks.

"Oh thank goodness you're here," Mrs. Briansky said. "Can you help me? I didn't get out in time to do my grocery shopping yesterday and now my car is just covered in snow." She slapped her thighs for emphasis, loosening the flakes that had managed to cling on to her coat. "I tried to get it out myself, but it's just too much for me. I wouldn't bother you, but all the other people trying to get out of the lot are rushing to get to work, so I didn't want to impose on them. Wait, don't you have class?" The words spilled out of Mrs. Briansky in a flood.

"My classes were cancelled, Mrs. Briansky."

"Oh, that's good. Well, not good, but…could you help me shovel? I was waiting for my son to come by in his truck, but I called him hours ago. I can't wait any longer. Jasper is hungry and he can be intolerable when you're late with his food," Mrs. Briansky said, referring to the tabby cat that occupied the window ledge of her tiny apartment most days. "I knew I should have gone yesterday, but I didn't think it would be this bad this morning, and I thought that worthless son of mine would be here by now. Knowing him, he's probably out four-by-fouring in that truck. He's doing this on purpose. Jealous of Jasper."

Carmen laughed at the poor woman whose distress caused her to ramble incessantly. "I can help you. Let me get ready."

"Oh thank you, thank you," Mrs. Briansky gushed. "Jasper thanks you, too," she added.

"You're both welcome," Carmen said. "I'll be right out."

"And this is no time to be cute. Do you have a nice warm parka and a hat for your head?"

"Yes, Mrs. Briansky." Carmen reached passed her red pea coat and grabbed the ski parka she rarely wore from the back of the closet along with a ski mask. She had shoved the piece of paper in the pocket, slipped on her boots, and followed Mrs. Briansky out the door, putting all thoughts of her mother out of her mind.

Today, Carmen was getting ready to pack her suitcase. She carefully laid out the clothes she had pulled from her closet and tried to match outfits. "Isabel! Come help me. I don't know what's appropriate," Carmen yelled.

Isabel walked into Carmen's room with several summer dresses draped over her arm. "Wear whatever you want. No one's going to care. You're a foreigner!"

"I know, but I want to be respectful," Carmen said. "And I don't want to fry in that African sun either!"

"Same sun that shines on Jamaica, so be quiet," Isabel said and laughed.

Carmen threw a pillow at Isabel who ducked out of the doorway just in time to avoid getting hit. "Never mind. I'll figure it out myself," Carmen said in mock anger.

"You better think quickly," Isabel called from the hallway. "Our flight leaves at 5:30 and we don't want to be held up in security."

Carmen could hear Isabel struggling as she lugged the first of three heavy suitcases into the living room.

"If we get held up it's because they want to know whether you're just going on vacation or if you're planning to move back. Who needs three big suitcases for two weeks? They don't have washing machines in Ghana or something?" Carmen said, tucking her sandals in the sides of her suitcase. "Anyway, if there is any delay it will be on the way back into Canada when they're asking us if we got married while we were out of the country and are we planning to send for our new husbands." Carmen zipped up her suitcase and turned to her carry-on bag. "Treat me well or I'll tell them how much I enjoyed your wedding."

"You are so mean," Isabel yelled and laughed. "Hey, did you tell the post office to hold your mail?"

"Yep. It should start next week."

"Good. I'm just going to run down and check the box to make sure nothing is sitting in there now," Isabel said and walked out of the apartment.

Carmen did a final check to make sure she'd put her documents in her purse before dragging her bags into the living room. She had just dropped her carry-on on the floor when Isabel came back in.

"Here. Just one letter for you," Isabel said as she handed the envelope to Carmen. "Looks like they inverted the numbers by accident. It went to apartment 202 instead of 220. Someone must've stuck it in the corner at the top of the mailboxes so you'd find it."

Carmen took the envelope from Isabel and examined the shaky handwriting she recognized as belonging to her grandmother. They had fallen out of contact since Carmen's first year of university, mainly exchanging letters and cards at Christmas and on her birthday. Ruby was careful not to mention Angelique other than to say "everybody is fine," and Carmen never asked. Carmen shrugged and slid her index finger along the seal of the back of the envelope. "My grandmother," Carmen said as an explanation.

Isabel nodded and went about closing the blinds in anticipation of the taxi arriving.

Carmen pulled the letter from the envelope and shook it out behind her back. A habit she had picked up from her mother when she was younger. "In case someone is sending you something bad, like poison." Angelique would smile sheepishly as she did it, as if she knew it was silly, but she did it anyway, and Carmen started doing it whenever she got a letter from back home.

She brought the letter from behind her back and started to read its contents. Her mouth fell open slightly and her hands started to tremble as her eyes, now glassy with tears, read the lines over and over until they swirled. She looked up stunned and the letter slipped from her fingers, floating to the ground.

Isabel came back from the kitchen and gently touched Carmen's hand. "What is it?" Isabel tried to look into Carmen's face, but Carmen hung her head down, a stream of tears falling from her face and soaking the carpet at her feet. Her arms hung straight down at her sides and her shoulders began to shake uncontrollably. Isabel knelt down and picked up the letter.

Dear Carmen,

I'm sorry to have to tell you this, but your mother passed away this past Saturday. We couldn't find your new telephone number to tell you in person, so I hope this letter reaches you before too long. Please come home as soon as you can.

Love,

Your Grandmother

"Oh my God in heaven," Isabel said. Her hand fluttered up to her mouth. She reached for Carmen and pulled her into her embrace. "I'm so, so sorry, Carmen."

Carmen kept her arms at her sides but let herself be held as the tears continued to pour down her cheeks, soaking Isabel's new blouse and leaving a dark spot on her shoulder.

"Here, sit down," Isabel said and led Carmen to the sofa. Carmen obeyed, sitting stiffly on the edge of the cushion. "I'll take care of everything."

Isabel went to the phone and dialed her father's number and explained what happened. He expressed his sympathy and agreed that Carmen could not go back to Jamaica by herself. "I'll come home later, but I need to go with Carmen now," Isabel told her father. He offered his prayers.

"Yes, you must tend to your friend now. Worry about Ghana later," he said before hanging up.

Isabel called the university's travel agency and explained the situation. The agent listened sympathetically then put Isabel on hold while she tried to make alternate arrangements. Isabel sat beside Carmen and held her hand while she waited for the agent to return. Minutes later the agent was back on the phone giving Isabel instructions for picking up the reissued tickets once they got to the airport.

"I got you on the 6:30 p.m. flight going through Toronto. You'll get there at 1:45 in the morning," the agent said. "No extra fees. I called in a favor and you have some credits, too."

"Thank you so much," Isabel told the agent and hung up the phone. She turned to Carmen and pulled her from the sofa. "Come. Let's get you home."

The flight from Toronto was delayed for an hour, but it gave Isabel time to change currency and to call Carmen's grandparents to be sure someone would be picking them up. By the time they made it through customs in Jamaica, it was nearly 4:30 a.m. Carmen and Isabel were both exhausted, Carmen unable to sleep and Isabel unwilling to close her eyes and leave Carmen awake by herself.

Few people were at the airport at that time of night. Isabel spotted a couple that appeared to be in their late 50s studying the small crowd of travelers as they passed by. Isabel thought they were too young to be Carmen's grandparents, but they seemed to be the only ones who hadn't found their visitors.

The man wore a buttoned up white polo shirt and leather cap. The woman beside him barely reached his shoulder. She had wavy hair secured in a bun. It was jet black except for a few streaks of silver that highlighted her bang area.

Carmen looked up and spotted the couple and moved towards them in a trance-like state. When they saw her, the woman's legs buckled and the man gripped her tightly around her shoulder and pressed her into his side to hold her up. They reached for Carmen at the same time and folded her into their embrace. They stood that way for a long time, not speaking, but holding on to each other as if their lives depended on it. Isabel stayed off to the side, her hands clasped in front of her and heels closed together, as if she was trying to make herself as small as possible so as not to intrude.

Eventually Carmen pulled back and pointed at her friend. "This is Isabel," she said.

"Hello," Isabel said quietly.

"I'm Ruby, Carmen's grandmother," she said. "This is my husband, Byron."

Isabel nodded. "I'm so sorry for your loss," she said quietly. Ruby waved Isabel over and pulled her into the family circle. They held on tightly for several minutes before they finally released each other.

"It's late, or early, whichever way you want to look at it," Byron said solemnly. "We have a long drive. We should get moving."

They walked out of the airport towards the curb where a van was waiting. A man stood talking with a police officer and pointed towards their small, sad group. The officer peered at them below the brim of his hat, then nodded at the other man before walking towards the next waiting vehicle. The other man helped Carmen's grandfather load the luggage into the back while Carmen, Ruby, and Isabel all slid into the second row seats in the back. Byron climbed into the front passenger seat and raised his cap off to scratch his forehead before pulling the hat and brim down lower. The other man got in on the driver's side. He was young and looked to be in his late 30s. Carmen barely looked at him at first, but then noticed the dark, curly hair cut short, but it was the profile that made her draw in her breath. It was so familiar, and yet not. When he turned around to look at her she knew instantly who it was.

"Uncle Marlon?"

He smiled sadly at her. "Yes, baby girl. You remember me? I thought you would've forgotten me by now," he said. The slight accent laced overtop the Jamaican one gave away where he'd been living for the last 15 years.

"I haven't seen you since before you moved to England," Carmen said.

"Yes, well, we're all home now. That's good," he said as he pulled the van away from the curb.

By the time they reached Somerset Grove, the sun had begun to rise, painting the sky in warm hues of gold and yellow. Carmen slept on and off during the two-hour drive to her grandparents' home, occasionally waking up whenever the van rolled over a dip in the road. Isabel dozed with her head resting against the window, finally succumbing to exhaustion once she was comfortable that Carmen's family would be there if needed.

They pulled up to the yellow house with white trim. The house looked like it had been recently painted and the verandah freshly polished with red stain. The house stood out among the others on the road and Carmen knew that her grandmother would not have it any other way, particularly when they would be expecting so many visitors.

They went inside and Carmen immediately inhaled the strong scent of disinfectant and polish. Ruby had clearly attacked every solid surface with cleaning products and Carmen began to wonder if it was because she prided herself on keeping a spotless house or if she did it to distract herself from the reality facing her.

"Since your uncle is staying in his old bedroom, I fixed up your mother's room for you and Isabel," Ruby said. She studied Carmen for a reaction.

Carmen stood quietly by the front door, her hands clasped in front of her and her head hanging to the side as if pondering the situation.

"No, no. Don't put her in there. She and her friend can stay in my room. I'll go up the road to Johnny's parent's house," Marlon said, referring to his former schoolmate. "They offered for me to come stay there if we needed the extra room."

"I'm sorry, you know I didn't even think..." Ruby said, looking flustered. Byron seemed to appear out of nowhere and wrapped his arm around his wife again.

"No." Carmen spoke up. "I, I want to stay in her room."

Ruby tried to read Carmen's face. "Are you sure?"

"Yes, I'm sure."

Isabel stood quietly by looking between the strained faces.

"Alright," Ruby said. "You'll let me know if you need anything," Ruby said directly to Isabel who nodded knowingly. She was responsible for watching over Carmen while they stayed in that room.

Even though it was morning, both girls were still exhausted when they went to bed. Isabel quickly fell asleep, but Carmen could not will her eyes to close. She rolled over and put her face in the pillow, half-expecting to be able to inhale the scent of her mother. The pillowcase smelled of laundry detergent and fresh air. Telltale signs that Ruby had had everything in the room washed and hung out in the hot sun to bleach. It was as if Angelique had been intentionally cleansed from the room.

No one had told Carmen what happened to Angelique and she had not allowed herself to ask as though not talking about it would not make it real. She didn't even know the date that it happened; she'd barely grasped the words in the letter before she and Isabel had jumped on the plane to come home.

Carmen slowly eased out of bed, careful not to wake Isabel. She walked over to where Uncle Marlon had dropped their luggage near the door and fished the letter out of her carry-on bag. She crept over to the window and drew the yellow curtain open just wide enough to read the words again without casting too much light in the room. The date on the letter said Monday, May 15th. Carmen felt a lump form in her throat. The Saturday before the letter was mailed was the day of her graduation. Carmen recalled the storm that preceded convocation and the uneasy feeling she'd had that morning. She folded the letter back up and stuffed it in the pocket of her robe. She wanted to know what happened.

Her footsteps barely made a sound as Carmen crept down the hallway.

"Is that you, Carmen?" Ruby called from the kitchen.

Carmen stepped over the kitchen threshold. "How did you know it was me?"

Ruby sat at the kitchen table stirring a cup of tea. "I just knew," she said. "You want me to make you some tea or Milo? Something warm to help you sleep?"

Carmen shook her head. "I don't want to sleep anymore right now."

Ruby got up anyway and put the kettle on to boil again. She scooped two teaspoons of the chocolate crystals from the Milo can into a cup, and then added a spoonful of condensed milk after pouring in the boiling water. "I remember you used to like it very sweet," she said, and set the steaming cup in front of Carmen. They sat in silence for a while, each lost in thought.

"So…" Carmen began. "I just got the letter yesterday. Is, umm…" her voice trailed off.

"We did the burial on Monday. It was very nice. Very tasteful. You know, only the best." Ruby smiled sadly. "I know you would've wanted to be there, but we had to bury her right away, because…" Her voice trailed off as she searched for words. "Anyway, we are still having nine-night, even though we had to do things a little out of order. People will be coming by today and tomorrow still to bring food and say a final goodbye. They've been here all week."

Carmen remembered attending a nine-night gathering with her grandparents when she was a little girl after a friend of her grandfather had died in a work accident. It was a bittersweet celebration of the deceased's life that went on for eight days until the funeral. Carmen remembered being confused over the festivities. There had been lots of good food, like fried fish, dumplings, hard dough bread, and coffee. The women had sung hymns while the men drank rum and played dominoes. She remembered that Ruby looked uncomfortable and slightly disgusted by the mix of spirituality and rum. She'd sat in a chair at the far end of the room and refused to let Carmen play with the other children there, and then refused to go back the next night. "It's just disrespectful and country. All that carrying on," she'd said. Carmen was confused as to why Ruby was now allowing a nine-night gathering for Angelique.

Ruby answered as if she knew what Carmen was thinking. "Things change and people change," she said. "Funerals are so depressing and I've learned that nine-night is really a nice way of celebrating someone's time on this earth."

Carmen gripped the cup in her hands, feeling the heat gently warming then burning her palms. She let it go. "What happened to her? How did my mother die?"

Ruby drew in her breath. She grabbed the dish towel that lay next to her tea cup and began twisting it in her hand. "I told her. I told her that man wasn't any good. She wouldn't listen." Ruby pounded her hand on the table for emphasis. "Not at first anyway. By the time she came to her senses it was too late." Ruby got up from the table and went to the stove to wipe it down again.

Carmen waited for Ruby to continue. When it was clear that she wasn't going to say anything else, Carmen pushed again. "What happened?"

Ruby sighed and threw her head back. "He was a very jealous man, that Andrew Walker. He didn't want her to talk to nobody, not your uncle, not her cousin Hazel, not even me and your grandfather," she said. "And especially not your father."

"My father?" Carmen said. Confusion spread over her face. "She was talking to my father?"

"Yes," Ruby said. "About you."

"What did she say? He asked about me? Why did she go to see him?" The questions flooded out of Carmen as she tried to piece together what was going on.

Ruby sat back down. "I don't know, she never said anything to me, but, if I were to guess, I think she wanted to make sure you weren't alone. In case something happened to her. I think she finally realized something wasn't right with that man." Ruby shook her head. "I just wish she would have done things different. Maybe I should have done things differently."

Carmen could see her grandmother tearing up. Ruby abruptly pushed her chair back and wiped at her eyes.

"I'm going to lie down for a bit," Ruby said. "I'm not feeling so good." She hurried out of the kitchen and headed for her bedroom.

Carmen sat alone in the kitchen listening to the silent house for what seemed like hours before she finally decided to get up. She walked down the hall and noticed her uncle's bedroom door slightly ajar. She knocked softly and called his name. When she didn't get an answer, she peaked in the door and saw that the bed was neatly made. She surmised that he had already left the house with her grandfather, who had always been an early riser. The two had likely gone off to tend to the final arrangements for tomorrow. Byron Wright had always been the one to bring lightness to any conflict or darkness that surrounded the family, but this was too much for him to bear. When he couldn't make anyone laugh, he worked.

Carmen crept further down the hall and peeked in on Isabel who was still asleep. She was sure Ruby was asleep and was about to walk back towards the kitchen when she heard soft whimpering noises. She hesitated. She hadn't been close with her grandmother since the last time she was in Jamaica when she, Angelique, and Ruby had gotten into the argument the morning she came home late after the hurricane. There was still awkwardness between them that hadn't gone away. Carmen walked towards her grandmother's door and listened, then knocked softy. Ruby didn't answer, but Carmen could tell she was still crying, so she opened the door. Ruby lay on the bed curled up in a ball clutching a piece of fabric. When Carmen moved closer to the bed, she saw that the fabric was actually a white and yellow child's blanket. Carmen guessed that it used to belong to her mother. She felt a lump forming in her throat. She climbed into the bed and curled up facing her grandmother. Ruby reached over and grabbed Carmen's hand and held it until they both finally fell asleep.

The people started coming by in the late afternoon. They came in groups of two and three, bringing with them bowls of food covered in tin foil. By the early evening, the kitchen and dining room tables were overflowing with platters of rice and peas, escovitch, bammy, jerk chicken and pork, hard dough bread, oxtails, roasted breadfruit, and fried plantains. Some of the men brought their bottles of overproof white rum and Ruby looked at them harshly, but Byron took her to the side, gently rubbing her shoulders, and convincing her that they meant no harm and only wanted to celebrate Angelique's life in the traditional custom. Ruby acquiesced and personally brought the men glasses as a way of apologizing for the dirty looks she'd given them earlier.

Carmen pulled a folding chair into the back corner of the living room and sat watching the steady stream of visitors. Some stayed only a few minutes. Others came early and stayed until well after midnight. All commented on Angelique's beauty and what a shame it was what had happened to her whenever they stopped to talk with Ruby and Byron. A few who noticed and recognized Carmen would immediately drop their eyes and move away quickly when they saw the questioning look on her face.

Carmen got up to look for Uncle Marlon, but he had not come back all day. When she asked her grandfather why her uncle wasn't there, Byron only responded that he had gone off to take care of something and refused to elaborate any further.

Carmen grew restless and began wandering through the thinning crowd of people. It was late in the night when she spotted Isabel in the kitchen busying herself with checking on cakes she had put in the oven. Hazel was washing dishes in the sink.

"You hungry, Carmen? Sit down. I'll share out some dinner for you," Hazel said.

"I'm not really hungry," Carmen said.

Hazel ignored her, spooning some food onto a plate then pushing it towards Carmen. "You must eat. Look how your clothes stay. You're losing weight."

Carmen obeyed and began nibbling on the food. Arguing with Hazel had always been a lost cause.

Isabel and Hazel cleared some of the platters off the kitchen table so they could all sit down. Ruby came in a few minutes later and joined the group. "I'm glad to see you're eating. I was worried about you."

"I know," Hazel said. "If she keeps this up, she won't be able to wear shorts anymore. Someone will see her skinny legs and mistake her for a bird and shoot her." Hazel immediately covered her mouth and Ruby gave her a harsh look.

"Sorry, sorry. Bad joke," Hazel said and lowered her head.

Carmen looked between her grandmother and Ruby for an explanation. The only sound in the room was the low chatter that floated in from the living room and the verandah. Byron came in at that moment carrying an empty glass. He observed the silence that gripped the room and moved to stand beside Ruby's chair.

"Everything alright?" Byron asked.

"No," Carmen said. She drew in her breath and exhaled. "I want to know what happened. What happened to my mother?" Carmen searched the faces around her. Everyone exchanged glances, but the room remained silent. Finally, Hazel spoke up.

"Your mom," Hazel began, "was a very beautiful woman. Everyone loved her. When she came back here a few years ago, she was like a celebrity. She had all the latest fashion, she told everyone about the BMW she had and the house she lived in, and that she was a big time nurse in Canada."

Carmen frowned at the nurse comment, but didn't say anything.

"Everyone was so impressed with her, especially the men," she continued. "And that Andrew Walker, he latched on and didn't want her talking to nobody, no man, not her school friends, or even her family. He told everyone he was going to marry her."

"I would never have allowed that," Ruby hissed. Byron walked to the counter and filled his glass with white rum. He returned back to Ruby's side and took a long sip, screwing up his face. Carmen couldn't tell whether her grandfather's frown was caused by the burn of the rum or the thought of Andrew marrying his daughter.

"Your mother went along with it at first because Andrew would spend a whole heap of money on her trying to keep her attention," Hazel said.

"I know," Carmen said. "The last time she was supposed to come back to visit me in Winnipeg she cancelled at the last minute because he was taking her on a cruise."

Hazel let out a sarcastic laugh. "He didn't take her on no cruise, my dear," she said. "Is jealous, him jealous. Didn't want her to leave. Afraid she might meet up with some man once she went to Canada and then wouldn't come back."

"Why didn't she just come?" Carmen asked.

"Because he took away her passport and ticket. She came over to my house frantic and crying the day before she was supposed to leave. She didn't know what to do. It was me who told her to call you and say she was going on a cruise so you wouldn't be worried. I thought that would give her time to find her papers and then come in a few weeks. I'm sorry. I didn't know you would get so mad with her."

Carmen hung her head. She remembered how angry she had been and how she had hung up on her mother when she did call back a few weeks later.

Ruby reached over and grabbed Carmen's hand. "Don't blame yourself. You didn't know what was going on. None of us knew how bad it was." Ruby turned to Hazel. "Maybe we should continue this later. It's getting late anyway."

"No, I've been waiting so long. I want to know what happened," Carmen said.

Hazel studied the faces around her for a moment before she continued. "Anyway, last Christmas or early January, I can't remember when, but your mother said she was going to move back to Canada, but she didn't have her landed immigrant papers anymore because she'd been out of the country too long or something like that." Hazel fanned the air in front of her with her hands as if doing so would make the details clearer. "Anyway, she was going to call you to see if you could find a lawyer in Canada to help her."

"Yes, I remember she called during the snowstorm," Carmen said. "I forgot to call her back. I meant to though," she added quickly.

Hazel looked at Carmen and then kissed her teeth. "Stop blaming yourself. What were you going to do from Winnipeg besides worry? I told her to go down to the High Commission of Canada in Kingston and get it straightened out. That is how you're supposed to get your papers," Hazel said. "Anyway, so she went down to Kingston one day while that man was at work and started getting her papers processed. She saw your other grandfather down in Kingston. I think he still work for one of those government ministry offices, and he put her in contact with your father."

Carmen sat up and leaned forward in her chair at the mention of her father. Hazel took a sip from her glass of juice and continued.

"From what your mother told me, your father was glad to see her. It seem like he finally get mature and wanted to do the right thing. He still worked in the government somewhere so he offered to help get Angelique's papers processed and also wanted to come and look for you, too. She went back and forth to Kingston a few times over the next couple of weeks whenever she could get away."

Ruby twisted uncomfortably in her seat. By now, Byron was finishing his second glass of rum and getting ready to pour a third. Ruby eyed her husband, and then got up to warm up some food for him to go with the alcohol. Outside the room, they could hear a lively game of dominoes starting up as someone slammed a card on the table set up on the verandah.

Hazel took in a deep breath and sighed. "Andrew found out your mother had been going to Kingston in March. He demanded to know why and of course she didn't tell him she was going to get her papers to leave so she just told him that she had gone to see if your father would send you money to finish your schooling and for your graduation present. Unfortunately, your mother found out she was pregnant and was starting to show. Andrew accused her of cheating on him with your father."

"Imagine that," Ruby spat. "Cheating with her own husband. You ever hear of anything so stupid? She never divorced your father. That piece of trash had no standing. None at all. Clifton may have been immature, but at least his family was high class."

"He wouldn't let her out of the house. I had to go and get the papers for her when they were ready. Can you believe that?" Hazel slammed her hand on the table. "I told her she had to leave now because that man seemed crazy to me. I didn't trust him at all. So when the papers come two weeks ago, it was me who went and got her ticket to go back to Canada. We sneaked and packed up her clothes and everything. She was going to fly back on Saturday." Hazel was standing by now, waving her hands in the air as she described what happened next.

"The day she was supposed to leave, she was supposed to come by the house and pick up her papers I had hidden, and then my friend Darren was going to drive us to the airport to drop her off. She was supposed to come by at five in the morning because her flight was supposed to leave at 11. Five o'clock come and no Angelique. Six o'clock come and no Angelique. By seven o'clock I start to get worry, so Darren and I decided to drive down to her house and see what was taking so long. When we get down the hill, Lawd Jesus." Hazel's voice started to crack. She placed one hand on her hip and the other covered her eyes. Carmen could see the tears spilling below Hazel's hand and her lip trembled. Byron walked over to his niece and tried to get her to sit down.

"That's enough for now," Byron said. "You need to take a break."

"No," Hazel protested. She brought her hand down from her eyes and slapped her thigh. "If I stop now, I won't be able to finish later."

Byron poured her a glass of rum. Hazel took the glass gratefully and took a huge gulp. She coughed several times and slapped at her chest. Ruby got up to walk towards her, but Hazel held up her hand. "I'm okay, I'm okay," she said. She wiped fiercely at her tears with her free hand, and then took another sip of the rum, slowly this time.

Carmen sat rigid in her chair. She placed one hand on her stomach trying to ease the knot that was building. She folded the other hand into a fist and waited for Hazel to continue.

Hazel took a deep breath. "When we got down to the bottom of the hill, I saw the car." Hazel told them how she had seen the left back tire first. When they'd gotten further down the hill, she saw the car was in the ditch on the side of the road, the front end crushed by the large palm tree that blocked its progression. Angelique was in the driver's seat slumped over the wheel. They'd pulled her from the car and someone in a passing jeep went to get help. Angelique had been barely conscious when they laid her on the ground on the side of the road. By the time they reached the hospital there was nothing that could be done. Angelique had slipped into a coma. Ruby and Byron barely made it in time before Angelique passed.

They knew Andrew had been responsible. Before she slipped from consciousness, Angelique murmured his name and something about "ran me off." Hazel guessed that Andrew had found out Angelique was leaving and ran her off the road when she was driving to Hazel's house. Andrew was nowhere to be found, but the police were out hunting for him. Marlon flew in from England that day and went looking for Andrew with some of his school friends. By the time the police caught up with them, Marlon and his friends had already found Andrew hiding out in Black River. They'd beaten him so badly that the police had to take him to the hospital first before they could take him to jail.

"That's why we had to bury her so quickly. The accident was so bad," Ruby said and covered her eyes.

Suddenly the room was stifling. Carmen reached for her throat and gasped, trying to take in air. She got up from the chair, nearly knocking it over and ran outside.

"I'll go," Isabel said and ran after Carmen. Isabel found her leaning against a tree, her hands resting on her knees. Carmen was heaving. She looked at Isabel with the wide and wild eyes of an animal trapped, searching for an escape. A raspy sound escaped from her throat as she looked around desperately.

"You have to calm down, Carmen. You're going to make yourself sick."

No sooner had Isabel said those words than Carmen wretched on the ground in front of herself. Vomit splattered on the ground and on her legs. Her knees gave way and she sank lower against the tree.

"I didn't know, I didn't know," Carmen cried over and over again.

Isabel stepped to Carmen's side, carefully avoiding the pool of sick, and grabbed Carmen's hand, pulling her away from the mess. She held her hand tightly and squeezed as Carmen tried to catch her breath. "It's not your fault, you hear?"

Carmen nodded and allowed herself to be led back in the house where Ruby and Byron stood in the doorway, lines of worry creasing their faces. Ruby took Carmen into the bathroom and cleaned her off, and then she and Isabel put Carmen to bed.

The few remaining guests took the excitement as their cue to leave. They said their goodnights, promising to return the next day for the ninth-night. Ruby, Byron, Isabel, and Hazel started cleaning up the house after the last guest left. They went about the work quietly, each lost in their own thoughts. After they had finished, they gathered in the kitchen, not ready to retire for the night, but not sure what there was left to say. Byron was the first to speak up.

"I should've gone with Marlon to look for that boy. If I did catch him up, you see? There wouldn't have been anything left for the police to lock up." Byron pounded his fist on the kitchen counter for emphasis.

Ruby turned around in her chair to look at Byron. "What? So the both of you could be locked up and leave me here alone to deal with all of this? No, suh," Ruby replied. "I need you here with me." She reached out and took Byron's hand. He took the seat next to Ruby and held onto her hand, the slightest smile tugging at the corners of his lips.

"Is that where Marlon gone? Lawdamercy, I didn't know," Hazel said.

"Yes," Ruby said. "The police locked him up for beating that piece of rubbish. He turned himself in after we came back from the airport."

"I'm going to get him tomorrow. Once they knew what happened, they said he can be released. Him and his two friends," Byron said.

"So where is Andrew now?" Hazel asked.

"If not for my son ending up in jail, I would hope he was dead. I think he's still alive though. Once he get out of that hospital, they better lock him up for good," Ruby said. She let go of Byron's hand and folded her arms across her chest and twisted her mouth to one side.

"So what happens now?" Isabel asked.

"Tomorrow is the last night," Hazel said. "We say goodbye then for the last time."

The sky was a brilliant shade of blue, laying a serene background for the sun which rose over the mountains to the east and crept its way over the district, warming the earth as it stretched its rays, gently waking the residents of Somerset Grove. Carmen arose in a somber mood, the revelations of how her mother died still fresh in her mind. Ruby suggested they walk over to the grave so that Carmen could see it and say goodbye, but Carmen refused. Her emotions were in turmoil; there were so many unanswered questions and she felt abandoned by her mother again, yet she was horrified at how Angelique was taken.

Byron returned with Uncle Marlon later in the afternoon. Carmen noticed that he was wearing the same clothes he had on two days ago. He looked tired, but that was it. Byron later told them that the police had treated Marlon fairly well, but they'd had to take him to jail to figure out what had happened.

A steady stream of neighbors started coming by in the early morning, asking if there was anything they could do. Except for a few of the men that helped Byron and Marlon set up a tent and chairs in the front yard, the rest were thanked and asked to please return late in the evening. Ruby, Hazel, Miss Mavis, and Miss Brown from down the road would be responsible for providing the food for this last night. "Just come ready to celebrate," Hazel told them as she sent them on their way.

Carmen couldn't stand being around the house anymore so decided to take the long walk into town. Isabel decided to go along, too, so the two set off in the early afternoon. They reached town about 30 minutes later and stopped at a roadside bar. They each picked up a Ting, and then made their way down the main street. The town seemed unusually quiet for a Monday and Carmen wondered if people were preparing to come to nine-night at her grandparents' house.

They stopped in front of the bakery and sat at one of the tables sipping the cool grapefruit sodas. Carmen pointed down the street at a small peach-colored building with a large picture window. "That's my grandfather's shop. Everybody comes there for their furniture," Carmen said.

Isabel nodded.

"I don't know what to feel," Carmen said suddenly. "I'm mad. She owed me some answers. They all did—my mum, my grandmother, my father—and now my mum is gone. I'm mad at that stinking Andrew. He took her away and I never really had a father. I feel so alone and I just don't understand a lot of things. I feel robbed." Carmen wrapped her arms around herself in frustration.

"I know how it feels to lose your mum," Isabel said. "Remember, I lost mine when I was 13. I don't know what happened in your family, but it seems to me if you want answers, you need to talk to your grandmother."

"We're not so close, I was mad at her when I left here the last time, too."

"Well, you have to start letting some of that anger go and start talking. You should know now that you can't wait until tomorrow, and you can't let history keep you from your family and from moving forward. You'll always be alone if you do."

Carmen kicked at the dirt under the table. She examined the familiar red stain it left on the toe of her sneakers. She knew Isabel was right, but couldn't let go of the bitter ball of hurt that seemed to have made itself a permanent home in her chest. She took a deep breath and let it out slowly. "Okay. I'm ready."

They returned to the house in the late afternoon. The house had been scrubbed clean again and now the aroma of spices and scotch bonnet peppers began to fill the air. Carmen looked for Ruby, but Hazel told her she had gone to lay down for a while. "She is worn out."

Carmen and Isabel went to the bedroom to drop off their things and found the mattress turned up against the wall. "You'll stay in your uncle's room tonight. She has to know she doesn't sleep here anymore," Hazel told them, referring to Angelique.

Later when Hazel shooed them out of the kitchen, Carmen decided to get ready for the evening. She put on a red tank dress and black sandals. Angelique loved to wear red whenever she went out, so Carmen thought it was appropriate. When she came out of the bedroom, Ruby looked at her admirably. Ruby had put on a black dress and tied a red scarf around her neck. "You remind me so much of your mother," she said with a sad smile.

Carmen looked at her for a moment. "Tell me," she said.

They went out on the verandah and sat down. "You look so much like her. And very strong willed," Ruby said. She gave a little laugh. "Whatever I told her, she did the opposite. She used to make me so mad, but in truth, I sometimes wished I had the fire she had."

"You two never seemed to get along too well. What happened?" Carmen prodded.

Ruby sighed. "I wanted so much for Angelique. She did, too. We just disagreed on how she should get it, though. I wanted her to get a good education. Be her own person so she didn't have to rely on any man to pull her up like I did."

Carmen looked confused and Ruby smiled. "Of course,

you're confused. I suppose your mother was confused, too. I never told her or her brother how I came to be here." Ruby told Carmen how she had planned to marry someone else and move to England and how she was heartbroken when the man ran off with another woman. "A fair-skinned woman with long, silky hair. I was devastated and depressed. Your grandfather knew he wasn't my first choice, but I said yes to him anyway. In those days women couldn't stay single for long or they would stay single for life. I didn't want to stay here, but I felt I had no other choice. And when the children came, I knew I was stuck here. I resented your grandfather a little, and I guess I resented being pregnant. I thought I was better than this place."

Ruby stopped as some neighbors walked up on the verandah to give their condolences. Ruby thanked them, and then gestured for Carmen to get up so their visitors could have their seats. Ruby and Carmen walked toward the gate for more privacy. They leaned against a low sturdy branch from the logwood tree that stood at the end of the yard.

"When your mother and uncle were born, I felt blessed. I wanted so much for them. I especially wanted my daughter to grow up and make something of herself and get out of Somerset. She wanted it, too, but when she came home pregnant, oh gosh, I was so angry with her. I was ashamed, but disappointed too. I lost my temper and I shouldn't have," Ruby said, referring to the night before Angelique left. "I thought she would be stuck here too. But, she showed me." Ruby gave a little laugh and shook her head. "She packed up and marched down to Kingston and demanded your father marry her. You know the rest."

"Sometimes I feel like she didn't love me, or at least, she resented me, too," Carmen said.

"Not true. She loved you, but she was never happy with where she was. She always wanted the best for you and for herself. Seeing you do so well made her happy, but also made her feel like she wasn't who she could be. She tried to rely on men to get what she wanted and then when she realized she could only do it for herself, well, it was too late," Ruby said.

"How do you know all of this? I thought you didn't get along with her, either," Carmen said.

"Trust me, my dear. It took a long time. But one day we did talk. She came here and we talked." Ruby looked wistfully down the road. "We were making progress, and we made peace. I just wished I could have saved her. But she did tell me how much she loved you and how she was going to make a fresh start with you in the new year," she said. "Carmen, you are strong willed. All the woman in this family are. Just don't let your will keep you away from your family, okay?"

Carmen nodded. "Okay."

They headed back to the house as more people started to arrive. The mood wasn't as lively as the night before, but more people appeared. Shortly before midnight, the pastor said a prayer and a few words. Other people began to exchange stories about Angelique and the mood lifted. At midnight they took a moment of silence. Carmen and the family stood at the front of the tent holding hands. A slight breeze picked up and blew warm air across Carmen's body. She shivered slightly, but felt the ball of turmoil that nestled in her chest loosen up. When she opened her eyes again, she felt an air of lightness around her. She looked around at her family to see if they had felt it, too.

Ruby laid a hand across Carmen's shoulder and rubbed it gently. "She's gone."

The next day was sunny like the one before it. Carmen had stayed up late listening to stories about her mother and finally fell asleep around 3:00 a.m. when the last visitors left. Ruby let her sleep late and by the time she woke up in the morning, the house had been returned to its usual state, as though nothing had happened the day before.

Carmen entered the kitchen and was greeted by the rest of the family eating a late breakfast. She walked over and gave each of them a hug and kiss on the cheek. Byron got up and let Carmen have his seat.

"Sleep okay?" Ruby asked.

"Yes, thanks. What happens today?" Carmen asked.

"We move forward," Ruby said.

Carmen nodded in understanding.

"So what do you want to do today?" Ruby said.

Carmen's forehead furrowed as she contemplated her grandmother's question. After a moment she let the tension drain from her face. She inhaled, and then exhaled slowly as she looked around the room. "Take me to Kingston, please," Carmen said. "I want to see my father."

about the author

DIONNE L. PEART, a Jamaican descendant, was born in England and raised in Winnipeg, Manitoba, Canada. She currently resides in Washington, DC where she practices law and is working on her second novel, Blackheart Man. She enjoys writing and reading works that explore another time, place and culture. Her blog can be found at www.dionnepeart.blogspot.com.